Graynelore

Stephen Moore lives in the North East of England. He is an author of fantasy fiction for both adults and older children/young adults. Before he discovered the magic of storytelling, he was an exhibition designer, and he has fond memories of working in the weird world of museums. Sometimes he can still be found in auction houses pawing over old relics. His interests include art, rock music, movies, theatre and RPG video games. But most of all he loves to write, where he gets to create and explore his own worlds. He can be found on Twitter @SMoore_Author

Graynelore

STEPHEN MOORE

Harper*Voyager*
An imprint of HarperCollins*Publishers* Ltd
1 London Bridge Street
London SE1 9GF

www.harpervoyagerbooks.co.uk

This Paperback Original 2016

First published in Great Britain in ebook format by Harper*Voyager* 2015

A catalogue record for this book
is available from the British Library

ISBN: 978-0-00-812047-4

Set in Sabon by Born Group using Atomik ePublisher from Easypress

Printed and bound in Great Britain

For Carol

'Whenever you think I'm lost, and you cannot find me, look here. I am always here.'

If every man's life has the makings of a story, the comings and the goings and the things in-between, where does my story truly begin?

For want of a narrator, for want of a name and the soul it belongs to, I fear, it must begin here . . .

[From: *A Beggar Bard's Tale*. Anon.]

Prologue

I am Rogrig, Rogrig Wishard by grayne. Though, I was always Rogrig Stone Heart by desire. This is my memoir and my testimony. What can I tell you about myself that will be believed? Not much, I fear. I am a poor fell-stockman and a worse farmer (that much is true). I am a fighting-man. I am a killer, a soldier-thief, and a blood-soaked reiver. I am a sometime liar and a coward. I have a cruel tongue, a foul temper, not to be crossed. And, I am – reliably informed – a pitiful dagger's arse when blathering drunk.

You can see, my friend, I am not well blessed.

For all that, I am just an ordinary man of Graynelore. No different to any other man of my breed. (Ah, now we come to the nub of it. I must temper my words.)

Rogrig is mostly *an ordinary man. The emphasis is important. For if a tale really can hang, then it is from this single thread mine is suspended.*

Even now I hesitate, and fear my words will forever run in rings around the truth. Why? Put simply, I would have preferred it otherwise.

Let me explain. I have told you that I am a Wishard. It is my family name . . . it is also something rather more. I say it again, Wish-*ard, and* not *wizard. I do not craft spells. I do not brew potions or anything of the like. No. My talent, such as it is, is more obscure. You see, a Wishard's skill is inherent, it belongs to the man. You either possess it or you do not. (Most men, most Wishards do not.) It cannot be taught. As best as can be described, I have a knack. Rather, I influence things. I make wishes, of a kind.*

Aye, wishes . . . (There, at last, it is said.)

Forgive me, my friend. I will admit, I find it difficult, if not tortuous, to speak of such fanciful whimsy. Make what you will of my reticence; measure Rogrig by it, if you must. I will say only this much more (it is a caution): by necessity, my testimony must begin with my childhood. But be warned: if I tell you that this is a faerie tale – and it is a faerie tale – it is not a children's story.

Please, humour me. Suffer Rogrig Wishard to lead you down the winding path and see where it takes you. There is purpose to it. Else I would not trouble you.

Part One

The Beggar Bard's Tale

Chapter One

Graynelore

Children remember in childish ways. So, through a child's eyes, I will look again upon Graynelore. I can see a frozen wasteland. Deep winter's ice lying broken and sharp upon a horse-trodden path. The riders are long departed. My breath is a broken kiss upon the air. The land before me is a magical silence.

I can pass a child's hand across the ruts and crevasses of a cold, wet stone wall. It is the wall of a house, and built so thickly *this* Rogrig can stand at his full height and yet hide safely within the depth of its wind-eyes.

I can find a child's delight in the crackle and spark of burning logs, the heat of an open fire.

I can lift a child's finger to my tongue and taste the iron of an abandoned broken war sword. I can feel the dead weight of it again, as I struggle to drag it across a stone floor for the lack of body strength to lift it.

I can sting my nose with the smell of the piss and the shit of fell beasts – animals sheltered indoors against the rumour of coming raiders – and yet still know the comfort of it.

I can raise the beat of my heart and laugh at a tangle of drunken men, falling through an open doorway, playing at the Old Game. And I can wince at the foul cry a young woman gives them in chastisement.

'Ah! Be-having-you! Do you have to come kicking that fucking head about in here? You're spilling blood across my freshly strewn floors!'

I can ache to my soul for the death of my father; only slaughtered, it seems, for his surname. I can hear words, murmured together in a single breath: murder, blood feud, Elfwych, and understand them, with a child's innocence, only as the unbearable pain of my father's absence . . . and a mother's tears.

I can huddle with a grieving family, grimly gathered at our fireside, making the cursed talk of revenge.

Sick with fear, I can taste stomach bile at my throat on seeing the sudden stillness of my first human killing. He was a Bogart by grayne; though a Bogart out of an Elfwych. Upon a holyday, I once played childish sport with the lad. Yet I dropped a great stone upon his head – broke it apart – as he lay face down upon the ground. His body was already sliced open, that the work of another's sword, but it was I who killed him. *To possess all that is life, then, in a breath, in less than a breath, to take it all away . . .*

Before the raider's trail, I can sit piss-scared upon my own dead father's hobby-horse. And I can heed the old wives' warnings that came ringing to my ears.

'Mind how you go there, child! Keep off the bloody bog-moss. It swallows grown men whole! It sucks down full-laden fell-horses, carts and all! It will leave us no sign to remember you by . . .'

And, of a bright summer's day, without a care, I can run again through the long dry grasses with Old Emma's Notyet, chasing after the cat's tail. Mind, that is no man's business but my own, and I will thank you for it and keep it to myself.

Do you follow me, my friend?

Old Emma, my elder-cousin, was a long time dead. Notyet, her daughter, was my playfellow. She was a weedling child, plain-faced, stoical, yet not displeasing. In age, there was less than a season between us. We came together because we lived together. We sat out upon the same summer fields and watched, lazily, over the same stock. We ran, a-feared, from the same raiders, raised the hue and cry. We ate from the same table, burned our faces at the same fireside. Bloodied our noses against the same hard ground and broke ice from the same stone water trough. And we each caught the other looking, without a blush, when we washed ourselves, naked, in the same stream.

Notyet would often hide herself away in some secret woodland dell, where she would play awkward tunes upon the crude wooden whistles she made. I would listen, and follow after her simple music. I liked to find her there, in hiding. Was she my heart's meat? Was she? Ha! Upon Graynelore! If it were true, I would not have admitted it. She *was* my kissing kin, but . . . (And *but* is enough to condemn me, and us.)

Little more than babbies, we made a babbie together. She did not carry the infant well. It was dropped too early, born a feeble weedling; and un-cherished, it was soon dead. *Birth is such a bloody struggle. Life is such a difficult trail to follow, while death – the sudden stop – so very easy.*

My friend, I have given you these awkward childhood memories; these fleeting glimpses of Graynelore, not because of their individual worth, but because together they might give you a sense of the world into which I was born. For the most part, they might appear to be nothing better than the gathered pieces from a broken clay pot! A handful of shattered fragments, a few, no doubt, so cruelly sharp they can hurt still, but, at best, incomplete.

Indeed, there are pieces missing. There is another memory I must share with you. I must take us to another day, and to a meeting with a Beggar Bard.

Chapter Two

How the World was Made

I can still see him, standing before an open door on a winter's evening. He appeared out of the darkening shadows, just as a cold sun fell out of a weathered sky. Just as the bars were about to be drawn and the wind-eyes battened against the night. The old man's back was stooped, his yellowing skin so dry, so thin, I was certain he was something of a wych's trick; a bag of old bones somehow kept whole. Though he remains forever nameless – he offered us none and history does not recall – I remember him cadging a supper and a fireside in return for his story. All my family, from the eldest crone to the youngest babbie, quickly gathered there, eager to receive him. (For there is no luck in turning a Beggar Bard from your door; ask any who have tried, any still living.)

When he began to tell his story, he began mine. For he told us the tale of how the world was first made.

How easily that frail old man stole a fireside. For as long as he talked he kept his bones warmed, and his audience believing every word. And such a performance! He never stood still. His fragile limbs jerked and twisted in time to his every phrase. His sallow eyes, alert and sharp, even in old age, fell upon each of us in turn and seemed to reach into our very souls. He scared the babbies witless. He had grown men and women cursing and bellowing like cloddish fools. At my side a boyish Notyet was caught sorely stiff afraid. In my excitement I let my fists fly, made her yowl, banged her on the ear to bring her back.

'Hoy!' she cried, returned her closed hand, and cuffed me back.

And I? What did I make of this Beggar Bard? When he spoke, it was as if time itself ran at a listless pace, against its nature. Rogrig was . . . spellbound, beguiled. The Beggar Bard drew us all into his dark tale.

'Look sharp, my friends. Look sharp about us,' he began. He spoke through rotten teeth and with a rasping, ailing breath. 'We are at the beginning of all things. So come and watch with me, as a single scratch of light appears out of an eternal darkness.' The old man's withered hands enticed, beckoned to us, all the while drawing magical, fleeting pictures in the smoke-filled air around us. 'Pass through this stagnant swirl of ageing yellow mist. And come upon a tall grey figure, standing motionless before a great stone tablet.' The Beggar Bard's open fingers and narrowed eyes signalled a caution. 'Make no sound! Keep deathly still. This man before us is a Great Wizard, a Lord of Creation. He must not see us here.'

From somewhere among our gathering there came a gentle roll of knowing laughter. (This childish Rogrig mistook it for simple pleasure.) There were many there who already knew this tale by heart, and the manner of its telling. They were content to play their part and hear it told again, but they took the Beggar Bard's performance for what it was:

common trickery and simple amusement. Sleight of hand to baffle Tom Fool, not a faerie's Glamour, worthy of the gibbet. The Beggar Bard continued his tale, unabashed.

'Now, my friends, watch carefully. Do not blink! Or you will miss the first of it!' He gave a waggle of his bony finger. 'See? The stone tablet, its surface, quite plain and unadorned, in an instant is deeply cut: incised and embellished by its master's hand. The form is a map. The image is a pair of islands – one great, the other small – set upon the broadest sea. Notice how its waters glisten, even upon the stone. And the smaller island: it is such a strange curiosity. What magic is this? See how it moves . . . marking out its course as it cuts a swathe across the surface of the tablet.'

Again and again the Beggar Bard's fingers made magical pictures in the fire smoke. The stone tablet . . . The Great Wizard . . . The map . . . The islands . . . The sea . . . I was so convinced of what I saw there that night I can still see it all, vividly. Every detail, everything conceived.

'And *why* was the stone map made?' asked the Beggar Bard, rhetorically, expecting no answer but his own. 'It was like a great eye that looked out upon the whole world and saw everything. An Eye Stone,' said the Beggar Bard, 'an Eye Stone, created, that all creatures everywhere should know their place in the world and marvel at its splendour. Nothing was missed. For a Great Wizard knows his task and his world quite well enough. And if his concerns were for design and skilful ornament, rather than for accuracy and scale, then he made up for its lack with an indubitable certainty.' Now, the meaning of many of the Beggar Bard's words was often lost to the ears of an ignorant child (aye, and the contradictions too) and yet this only added to their mystique and to my unwavering belief in their authority.

'He made a mark for the Stronghold of The Graynelord; the Headman of all the graynes . . . And a mark too, for the bastle-houses of lesser men,' added the Beggar Bard, shrewdly. At which, there came a great stamping of feet and a roaring of approval. 'There were marks made for the mountains of the gigants, and for the dwarven holes. Marks for the elfin forest dells; for the lakes and for the mires, where the kelpies lie in wait for unsuspecting travellers; and for the broad grasslands of the unifauns. There were simple marks for the hills and the vales; for the roads; and another for the great River Winding that comes out of the mountains and finds its way into every part of this land. All manner of things were cut upon that stone face: the marvellous and the mundane.

'And when, within the making, the Great Wizard found himself at a loss – after all, if he knew his own homelands best, and other, stranger parts at the world's furthest corners hardly at all, can he be blamed for his enthusiasms and omissions? – he simply cut these words and wrote: The Great Unknown, or Here Be Monsters.'

'And what of this curious moving isle, Lord Bard—?' The interruption came from the Headman of our house: Wolfrid, my elder-cousin, eager to have the story told. He spilled wine from the mouth of his stone drinking jar as he spoke, left a spattered trail upon the earth floor at his feet.

'You do well to ask, my friend,' replied the Beggar Bard. His fingers continued to draw fleeting shapes upon the smoke-filled air. 'It is, of course, the Faerie Isle. Never yet seen by any mortal man, I would swear; only ever believed in. For such, you will agree, is true faith?'

Again there came the knowing laughter from among our company, if slightly less certain now. The Beggar Bard continued.

'Just as surely as he knew the Moon moves across our night sky, the Great Wizard knew the Faerie Isle moves across our sea (if, ever and always, just out of sight). He knew it was there, and so he marked it there upon the stone as best he could; adding waves and ripples in want of movement and effect. And he was well satisfied, for he also knew that it was from the Faerie Isle that all the creatures of the world first came.

'Finally, and with flourish, all around the edges of the tablet inscriptions were made, numbering the natural laws of this land, though in a symbol and tongue known only to the Great Wizard himself; that no common creature might challenge their worth or seek to interpret their truth to its own advantage.'

Here the Beggar Bard was forced to pause and take a breath. His sallow eyes briefly passed over us again, as if he was looking for the measure of our understanding. He smiled – at us, not with us – before continuing.

'With that, my friends, the Great Wizard's work was all but finished. The Eye Stone, almost complete. The world unmade, was at once a world made. Cut upon cut, line upon line. Only, in that very last moment of its making, he marked it with a name, and called it – Graynelore.'

There were sudden, fervent cheers. Wolfrid hauled himself upright, applauding loudly (if his wine-sodden face carried something of a befuddled look). At my back, men and women in a jolly drunken fashion, clashed their drinking bowls together, slopped and splashed a rain of warm ale down upon our heads. Notyet yelped and jumped at the excitement of it, which only encouraged the Beggar Bard to more.

'Now then . . . there came a solemn day, when The Eye Stone was at last revealed to the creatures of Graynelore. And, all at once, they believed in its truth and in its accuracy.

They believed without question; because they believed in the Great Wizard without question. And, just as these things occur, just as the Great Wizard had set it in stone, so the world at large became . . . and still is.'

The Beggar Bard fell silent, and for the first time stood suddenly stock-still. Though, his eyes continued to sharpen themselves upon us.

As if it was a given signal, the elder-women of my house quickly stood up. They offered the Beggar Bard a bowl of the best wine and a board of fresh meats, which he quietly accepted and sat down upon the stone hearth by the fire to consume. Out of courtesy, he was also offered a young woman for his own close company, which he politely refused.

Our general gathering sat on, unmoved, waited in eager anticipation of his return. Fortunately, his was a meagre appetite, soon sated. It was not long before he set his bowl and board aside.

In his own time, and beckoning both my own mother and Notyet for their support, he carefully stood up, and prepared himself to continue. It was obvious his great age was getting the better of him. 'That ancient stone tablet, The Eye Stone, stood out upon the exact spot where it had been created and weathered countless centuries. Until, at last, its guardian and creator, the Great Wizard died . . . (Aye, for even the greatest of wizards was not an immortal, whatever other men might tell you).

'Across the ages many Great Wizards have come and gone. There were those who, when they came upon The Eye Stone, believed in its truth. Though there were just as many who came upon it and did not believe. In the fullness of time, The Eye Stone seemed lost to history. Perhaps it toppled, or crumbled to dust, or else was stolen away.

'Copies were made from its memory, sometimes cut upon stone, sometimes scribed upon parchment, or woven into the threads of great tapestries. Though some believe the real Eye Stone was eventually found again . . . Lost, and found.' The Beggar Bard drew out the last of these words, lightly rocked his cradled hands as if he was passing them between one and the other.

Then his tone grew more sombre.

'Upon a day, there came a calamitous moment in our history when, all at once, several Great Wizards claimed to be the only true descendent of the first. And each solemnly declared that the image of The Eye Stone in their possession was the only one made after the true original. Be it marked upon stone, or upon cloth, or upon parchment.

'Their eager debates turned to sour arguments, turned to open conflicts . . . and war! Aye, and with truth and right on all sides and many—!' The Beggar Bard smiled ruefully at this last remark. Around him, the light of the open fire grew suddenly dim. Its smoke belched black and thickened about his crooked form, leaving only the image of a ghastly golem in his place.

Still, grown men laughed, babbies cried, and the eldest crone wailed her distress.

The Beggar Bard's performance was coming to its dramatic height.

'I beseech you all, my friends. Turn away! Look no more upon me! Or else, if look you must, see only darkness here. I did not intend slaughter for an entertainment. We do not need to witness the destruction of war, need only understand its outcome and recognize the utter loss at its last battle's bitter end.'

Even as the Beggar Bard spoke these words, within the fire-smoke filled air a great turmoil erupted. The shadows of men and beasts came together and did gruesome battle. Dark elfin creatures with beating wings, goblins, gigants, and dwarves rose up together in great clashing swathes only to dissolve again into wisps of smoke. Thundering herds of unifauns bolted from the depths of the fire crying their distress. Spitting flames became the fiery breath of angry dragons. The sound of crackling wood became the clash of iron war swords, the death cries of men, the breaking of bones, and the voices of despair. And among it all, in their fury, the feuding wizards cast their bolts of magic and laid the world to waste.

To my childish eyes it was all very real. In all my short life – though I had witnessed much – I had never experienced such pitiful dread. Between us, Notyet and I grasped at each other's stiffened limbs and held on tight. Still the men of my house laughed and stamped their feet, and spat their approval, and demanded more, and more, and worse, and worse. The women wept a dreadful sorrow; and yet were still filled with eager anticipation. The babbies pissed themselves.

The Beggar Bard gave us one final spectacle to behold. At the very last, as I gaped open-mouthed, with the battle of the wizards still at its height, all across the heavens a great shade, a tumult of raging black cloud, descended. A rolling blanket of darkness . . . Then the rain fell, the black rain. It was not water, but dust: Faerie Dust. Each drop as fine as a grain of sand, as sharp as a fragment of broken glass. And as it fell it smothered all before it – even as creatures and men battled on – covering great swathes of the earth, and finding its pinnacle upon the heights of Earthrise, a distant mountain . . . only, now and forever more, to be known as the black-headed mountain.

And then – suddenly, quickly – it was all over and done with.

With a simple shrug of his arm the Beggar Bard dispersed the smoke, as if he was tossing aside his winter cloak. It drifted upwards, a thing in itself, coming to rest against the wooden joists of the ceiling. And there, the skulking loathsome mass, seemed to hesitate, only to seep quietly away between the gaps in the wood and the broken stonework, until it was quite gone up through the house, to the very rafters, and out into the night. And the clash of battle, and the storm of war, and the black Faerie Dust, went with it.

Our gathering hushed then, though whether through dread, or understanding, or anticipation for what was to come next, Rogrig, the child, did not have the wit to tell.

The Beggar Bard waited there a long moment, as if to catch his breath; standing quietly, head solemnly bowed, until the silence was complete. Then, only then, he spoke again in hushed tones.

'All the wizards are long dead now . . . and gone forever. There is little enough left of their true magic here. And if our world . . . if Graynelore survives still, the Faerie Isle, its ethereal partner, was utterly broken by it, grounded, never to move again. A landed wreck, left a mere earthly prominence: you need only look to the furthest point of our own eastern shores – to the forgotten March, the Wycken Mire.' For the first time the Beggar Bard hesitated in his speech, almost at a loss for words.

'Out of the chaos of that war came a chaotic peace . . . a new world order was made, but without magic or rule of law. A world without reason, in which only blood-ties and the strength of a man's arm has any worth. The ways of faerie diminished and quite faded away . . . Much that was good and true, much that was light and fair, faded with them. The warm hearts of men turned to cold, cold stone.'

Was the Beggar Bard looking only at me when he spoke then? I was certain he was and shuddered for it. It was as if he had looked into my own stone heart and laid it bare; a thing to be despised. I tore my hand free of Notyet's grasp, and roughly set myself aside from her. Upon Graynelore, the soft-hearted man is soon dead!

The Beggar Bard's eyes moved on; and his mouth . . .

'What few poor faerie creatures remained soon disappeared from sight. They hid themselves away among the beasts of the fields and the birds of the air; or else among common men. Until, as the ages passed, neither was distinguishable, not one from the other, and little remained of faerie other than their names. Names the great families of this world – the graynes – stole, and took to wearing as their own. Names . . . And the taint of black dust that still lies scattered upon distant fields and covers the head of Earthrise, the black-headed mountain.'

Sullen and forlorn, the Beggar Bard suddenly brightened. He stood up boldly before us, as a final twist to his tale came into his mind.

'And what, you may well ask, became of the tablet that was the true Eye Stone of Graynelore? It has been told that it was destroyed. Already badly weathered through the ages, it was broken up and scattered to the ends of the earth. Symbolic of a broken land no doubt. But, see this—?' The Beggar Bard thrust a withered hand inside his cloth and drew out a blackened shard of stone: a talisman, which was bound to his neck by a leather thong. (All Beggar Bards carried such a relic.) His was too distant, and the shadows too deep to see clearly. 'This old-man's Burden is, alas, only the smallest of broken fragments of the true stone. But do not despair for its safety; I am quite certain of its majority

. . . You see, one day, a man they called Sylvane, who was the first Graynelord of the Wishards, built his Stronghold upon the very spot where it lay, forgotten. His stonemasons, not recognizing The Eye Stone for what it truly was, chose it for a foundation stone, built it into the very fabric of their walls. Which gave the building a great strength: greatest of all the Strongholds throughout Graynelore. An advantage the Wishards still make best use of. Though more lifetimes have passed since then than can be easily measured.'

Unable to control ourselves, and for one last time, his willing audience erupted into a furious display of abandoned approval. How very easily we took the sweetmeat he so generously offered.

Here, finally, the Beggar Bard's tale came to its end. He quickly put away his stone talisman, tucked it out of sight within his cloth. And, suddenly exhausted by the telling of his epic tale, all at once lay down before the fire and slept.

Chapter Three

The Beggar Bard's Burden

If there had been any truth in the Beggar Bard's words (which there was) there had also been nonsense: honesty with lies, fact with theatre and make-believe. Though, which was which mattered less, when none of it could be either reliably proved or disproved.

Long into that night, there was much wild carousing and rough love-making among the men and women of my house. And there was enough warm ale and petty frolics to indulge its youth. Notyet and I took on too much drink between us, and were compelled – with a well-practised relish – to throw it up again, before we each found ourselves a piece of floor and a rag of cloth to call a cot and flounder upon.

We were not a learned people; the Beggar Bard's tale was truth enough for us. It was as good an explanation of our history as any (when we were in want of any other), and worthy of celebration and repeating. The more his story was retold – and it was often retold thereafter – the more it was believed in, until in the retelling it became the certain truth. And if its ending had been a deliberate bribe, a passing gift to satisfy his audience – a gift the Beggar Bard no doubt bestowed upon all his customers of a cold winter's eve – it was a contrived entertainment, gladly accepted and revelled in.

In the early hours, I was woken from my drunkard's sleep by the sound of raised and worried voices. By the dim light of the night-fire I could see the outlines of men standing over the prone body of the Beggar Bard. He was still asleep, I thought. Someone was prodding at him, as if to wake him up. Only, the old man would not stir. There were a few more anxious, telling words; though the truth of the matter was becoming self-evident, even to a bleary-eyed child.

The Beggar Bard was dead.

Clearly, he had not been killed. He had not been murdered: upon Graynelore, a common enough method of dispatch. How fortunate the man . . . He had simply died, quietly, in his sleep.

For the first time, the only time in my memory, the night-fire was quickly dampened, and in the sudden darkness the body of the Beggar Bard was lifted and removed to some other place beyond my knowledge.

I was never to see any sign of him again; though the impression he had made upon me stays to this day. He had stirred something within me. A light was kindled. A curiosity uncovered. He exposed my own stone heart. But more than that; a truth was hinted at, if not fully revealed. I have heard the Beggar Bard's tale retold many a time since, and with many an ending, yet it is with his voice and in his manner that I do best to recall it. I had seen it all so clearly: as real as the day. Or at least that was how I remembered it. And that was the same thing, was it not?

In the morning, with the first light of day creeping under the door and through the battened wind-eye, I searched the spot where the Beggar Bard had stood and performed, and the place next to the fire where he had slept. In my childish way, I was searching for his illusions: his sleight of hand, the source of the tricks he had played upon us. Evidence he had left behind, only for me. I even raked about among the clinker: the snuffed out embers of the night-fire.

What I found lay abandoned upon the ground. In among the rough, straw-strewn earth that made up the floor next to the hearth, something glistened. It was a roughly formed piece of stone, no bigger than the palm of my own hand. Much blackened, its jagged edges had been rubbed almost smooth with countless years of eager handling. It may well have been a broken shard from a much larger piece. The Beggar Bard's Eye Stone? There were the faintest of lines marked upon its surface, and highlighted with real gold as if they were important, but if they had any literal meaning they were meaningless to a child. I could not make them out. Whatever the object was, it was obviously cherished. A sturdy metal clasp had been fashioned at its narrower end so that it could be hung safely from a chain or leather thong about the neck or wrist. I had seen nothing like it. The Wishards – Graynelord and his house apart – wore only base jewellery, cut from animal bone, or else we made do with staining our skin for decoration. Certainly, the object had belonged to the Beggar Bard; it had fallen from his body, been dropped unseen by the men who had roughly carried him away, in their eagerness to remove his remains. And if this treasure was the Beggar Bard's to lose (even in death) then it was mine to find, and to keep to myself. I picked it up and quickly put it away out of sight.

Soon after, I dug a hole and I buried the thing. It was too great a treasure for a common child to hold about his person. A thief and a liar, among a house of thieves and liars is soon found out, cannot keep a secret well. I marked the spot and let it rest there, hidden and untouched.

Enough of this now, my friend! You have indulged Rogrig Wishard quite long enough for a fancy. Here my childhood stories end. After all, this is forever Graynelore. Its children must grow up quickly (if they are to grow up at all). And with this certain knowledge: there is no magic in the world; there is no faerie, real or imaginary, neither lost nor later to be found again.

Remember this: Graynelore was a land continually – habitually – defiled. It was not a good land gone bad it was a poor land made ever poorer (and kept so). Men preyed upon men; family upon family; grayne upon grayne. It was a sore continually picked at; so much so its wounds could never quite heal properly. It was a scarred landscape; a broken scab, ever enflamed and sore.

The fabled beasts of faerie – if ever they had lived – were far beyond the memory of any common men; long since dead and gone. There remained only the bereaved.

Part Two

The Bereaved

Chapter Four

At the Mark of the Wishards

Graynelore has but two true seasons and a year equally divided by twelve months. Yet it has *four* Marches. How so? It is a simple babbie's riddle, my friend. Look to the north of the country and to the south, look to the east and to the west. Mind, the naming of the Marches was not a strict territorial division. Rather, it was more the geographical convenience of a label. Every hill, every valley, every woodland dell had its recognized families: its graynes, both major and minor. And there were numerous surnames, if there were only four principle graynes. The Wishards kept themselves mostly to the South March; the Elfwych mostly to the West March; the Bogarts to the East March; and the Trolls to the foothills below the black-headed mountains in the North March. That said; this was not a settled land with hard and fast rules. There were no permanently fixed boundaries – except perhaps in the minds of a few covetous Headmen. Most men would have been hard-pressed to explain precisely where one March ended and the next began. Nor would they have greatly cared. Reivers did not draw lines upon the ground.

They needed only the memory of what they believed had once been inscribed upon The Eye Stone. And if they were, more or less, always in bloody dispute because of it? So be it. It was a way of life.

In the long dry summers, the Marches of Graynelore were noisy; for it was then men preferred to fight. In the cold wet winters, the Marches were largely silent; for then, most men preferred to stay at home and rest at their firesides.

It was a morning in late summer. Winter was only a short step away. A great crowd of fighting-men had already gathered at the Heel Stone by first light that day. Many more would follow on. There was a handful of blood-tied Wises, Hogspurs, Bogarts, and other lesser kinsmen among the throng, though they were mostly Wishards by name, answering to their grayne. There were Wishards of the Three Dells: Tyne Dell, Fixlie Dell, and Dingly Dell (who were my own closest kin). There were Wishards from as far away as Carr Law. Wishards from Flat Top, and Wishards from Arch. They had come from all parts of the South March, and further. Many had travelled a long way already that morning and yet the real journey – whether it was to be a Long Riding or a Short Riding – had not yet begun.

The Heel Stone, the meeting point, was a giant solitary rock that lay toppled at the corner of Pennen Fields: a sweep of open moorland above Dragoncliffe, almost at the southern edge of the Great Sea. It was the Mark of the Wishards: a historic place of gathering.

Old-man Wishard, Headman of the Wishards of Carraw Peel, and more importantly, Graynelord of all Graynelore, had called his surname to the Mark.

Almost to a man, they sat upon their sturdy hobby-horses: the small, stolid and sure-footed fell-horses, native to the land. Creatures so lacking in height they left their rider's feet and the tips of their rider's iron war swords – that hung from their waists – dangling close to the ground as they rode, in what appeared an almost foolish manner for full grown men. Each man wore a reinforced handmade jack of leather or of rough cloth, as they could afford, inlaid with irregular scraps of metal to serve as make shift armour (more for show than an effective defence). In their saddle-packs they carried griddles with flour enough to make their daily bread. Some, skilled in the art, also carried a hunting wire to snare fresh meat. Only the poorest of men, or the unluckiest, those who had recently lost their mounts upon a frae, stood a-foot; and they gathered together in small packs, ready to fight at each other's back.

Each fighting-man there was virtually the same then. Yet each man was different. These were homemade soldiers. This was a homemade army of reivers . . .

Among them you must look hard and find me out again; Rogrig Wishard, now fully grown to manhood. There was as yet nothing obvious about me to distinguish me from my close companions. I was still quite the ordinary man. Unexceptional, except perhaps for this: I, alone among the gathering, sat *not* upon a simple hobby-horse but upon a unicorn. I fear, I must explain. Do not be impressed. I . . . exaggerate (as is my want). My unicorn was not of flesh and blood. Rather, for a fancy, I had fashioned my mount a stout leather mask – a head-guard – struck through with a single metal spike that stood a full sword's length proud of her nose. My hobb seemed an awesome sight to look upon.

If only she might learn to use her weapon upon the frae. Still, she was a good man's pack animal, and more than capable of carrying a full day's toil.

I named her for another foolish whim and called her Dandelion (Dandy for short) with no better reason in mind than I liked the title.

I was sat upon Dandy then, a little away from a closed huddle of my nearest kin; nearly, though not quite, out on my own; I was keeping the wary eye. There was mostly silence here, expectant if thoughtful silence; only the rough breath of the hobbs, the odd clump of shifting hooves . . . hacking coughs, the breaking of wind. It was too early of a day for beer-fuddled heads (and there were enough). Where a few serious words were passed about, it was done in tight whispers. Otherwise it was an idle banter between scared men trying to talk themselves up to the fight ahead of them.

'Mind, this Riding is to be no deadly feud . . .' said one.

'No . . . How so?' answered another.

'We must not blunt the sword, cousins – it is a simple, common lust!' returned a third.

Now, though all of these men were well known to me, and spoke openly within my earshot, I chose only to listen . . .

'They are saying the Old-man means to find himself a new wife this day.'

'Aye, and it is rumoured he is after taking the daughter of Stain Elfwych.'

'What, are you serious? Norda Elfwych? If it is a fighting wildcat he wants he will need to be at his guard.'

'Aye, well . . . he will be taking her by force if he must.' There was a spurt of careless laughter among the men that did not quite convince. Then a clumsy silence fell again.

In truth, whatever the cause, among the Wishards it was generally considered healthier to turn up when the Old-man commanded. Only a fool ignored the call of The Graynelord, would openly go against his grayne; man or woman. At best it left you for an outcast, a broken man without kith or kin, though more than likely it left you for dead.

That this raid was also the perfect opportunity for many a Wishard to settle old arguments of their own – to steal from their distant neighbours, to plunder, to pillage, to do murder, to set blackmails and kidnaps – is a cold dry meat. Excuse your narrator's common bluntness. I try to speak plainly of these things. A call to the Mark was a familiar event, and this foul business a day-to-day routine. Upon Graynelore, there was nothing unusual in our gathering.

This day it was to be a Wishard riding against an Elfwych. Tomorrow it might be a Bogart riding against a Troll. Each was a grayne ready to take advantage of its lesser guarded neighbour – when the opportunity arose, or when needs must. And the Headman of every house among them would fancy himself The Graynelord; and every Graynelord was *The* Graynelord of all Graynelore (self-professed). Excepting, let any of these conceited men stand before Old-man Wishard and deny him his rank this day. It was a simple calculation; a balance of numbers. Try it. Count the swords at his command.

However great or petty the cause, whatever the nature of the risk, the Old-man, by virtue of holding the balance of power between the graynes (real or imaginary), was ever required to make a show of his strength. If he himself did not carry the sword to his enemies then at least he must deliver the swords of his blood-tied kinsmen to ring out a resolution. For if he did not, among others, there were two younger brothers who would make a dreadful noise over it, who would each look to their own advantage and aim to take The Graynelord's place. They were both stood upon Pennen Fields among our number. Unthank Wishard, who was called Cloggie-Unthank, and Fibra, the younger . . . both faithful to their grayne this day; but what of tomorrow? I fear neither would be beyond planting the assassin's knife, leaving the Old-man the gift of the dagger's arse. It was their blood that tied these men together, not their love. It was likely blood that would separate them, in the end.

Whichever way I looked at it, I could safely say, more than a few men would surely meet their deaths this day, and as many return to their houses with sorely broken bodies, new scars in the making. It was ever so.

We were all of us waiting upon the Old-man's arrival.

I was already growing restless, not eager for the fight; but it is better to be about the business than to be standing in endless contemplation of it. I am not a thinking man. On a whim, I let my eyes carry up towards the heavens. The sky looked burdened and worried this day. A long way above the Heel Stone, a ragged, windswept horde of black birds, winged scavengers – crows most likely – wheeled silently between broken banks of steel grey cloud and patches of glaring sunlight. It seemed the birds were already well aware of our gathering, already expectant of things to come. I saw their presence as a good omen. They were welcome company. Whatever the outcome for men this day, theirs would be a feast and nothing left to waste. It was more than easy pickings; it was a gorging fit for the fortunes. And the fortunes liked a spectacle.

On the ground there was a sudden new commotion, new arrivals, and come at a measured trot.

Here, at last! I thought.

Bright, silvered armour caught in the sunlight. A sword unsheathed, glinted. There were a handful of hobby-horses in this Riding, but there were many more full-sized horses. And not warhorses; but white and grey prancing ponies, stretched out in a formal line. Upon these, men were sat, not dressed for war, but rather like . . . well, like women, in their fancy drapes and embroidered finery. Their multicoloured skirts tailored for the show.

At the head of this procession, with his war sword lifted from its scabbard, rode The Graynelord, Old-man Wishard, upon his immaculately groomed silver-grey hobb. Immediately behind him followed four men-at-arms, with brightly coloured banners waving from their spears, demanding attention. The remainder of the line, the greater number, was his Council. These were the men who sat at his dinner table, who took shelter in his Stronghold, and protection from his arm. These were his advisers, his cunning men. These were his politicians, scholars, and scribes. Not a true bodyguard then.

None of the Council was dressed for a battle. Rather, gentle men, in want of a frivolous day's sport. They were never meant for a fight. This arrival was more of a pageant; a cocksure display. The Graynelord was showing off to us.

Around me, part of the general throng began to fall back, to make way, allowing The Graynelord's entourage to advance and take up a position on the elevated ground just beyond the Heel Stone, where everyone could see them.

Only Cloggie-Unthank and Fibra, the Old-man's younger brothers, stood up on their hobbs and held their ground at his approach. This was not meant as a threat. It was a statement of rank, rather than a signal of defiance. They were not about to confront him. An unspoken gesture of acknowledgement passed briefly between the three. There were no words of welcome.

I sat quietly upon my hobby-horse and waited for the address I knew would soon follow. (There is a strict order to these events.) There was another flash of sunlight against silvered armour as The Graynelord turned his hobb about to face the gathering. And then, in a strong voice, he began to bellow:

'What is the Graynelore?' he asked. 'Let me tell you . . . I am the Graynelore.' The Old-man paused there, looked about purposefully, perhaps to catch the eye of his two brothers, as if he expected an argument. When none came he repeated his statement more loudly: 'I am the Graynelore.' Then, another gap, not for a response this time, but for respectful silence . . . 'This sword I carry is the Graynelore!' He lifted his war sword above his head and held it there, steady, for all to see. 'The Graynelore is not a place, though the land bears its name. It is not a matter of lines drawn upon a map. The Graynelore is not a belief, nor is it an ideal . . . I am the Graynelore.' Again he deliberately paused. '*You* are the Graynelore.'

This formal announcement was the signal for every man there to lift his own arm: his sword or his staff, his axe or his spear, and return The Graynelord's cry.

'I am the Graynelore!' We all bellowed as one.

'Upon Graynelore there is *no* king. You will find *no* queen, here. There is no law, but that which the strength of your own arm can impose upon another. It is the sword you carry. Upon Graynelore you answer only to the grayne . . . your surname, your family, your blood-tie. Make no idle friend here. Make no common ally. Make no enemy, unless he is a dead man. For either is as likely to stab you in the back.'

'I am The Graynelore!' cried our gathering to a man.

Emboldened, the Old-man swung his sword about his head and bellowed ever louder. 'Upon Graynelore we take what we need or else leave well alone. We do not kill the poor wretch for the sake of the killing. Why would we? And if, all things considered, we do not live long, at least we all live well! Eh? At least, we all live well!'

Another silence. Who among us would have dared to argue with him?

Banners began to flap noisily, attacked by a sudden breeze. Above us, far above us, the black birds had turned about and turned again, swooping impatiently across the sky. They were eager for the Riding to begin.

If it was I who spoke then, it was a muttering under my breath meant only for myself. 'We are not so much at constant war with everyone, my Graynelord . . . only there is never a day when we are quite at peace with ourselves. Where does that leave our tomorrow?'

'I suppose things might look differently tomorrow.' The retort came from my elder-cousin, my Headman, Wolfrid, who was sat upon his hobb close by. I might have answered him, only never got the chance. The Old-man's ranting was not quite done with:

'And on this day,' he cried, 'on this day, we are to go a-courting, you and I. There is a wild lady in want of a Graynelord's close company, who must be taken well in hand. And there are Elfwych in need of a reminder of their faithfulness.'

Our jeering laughter in reply; our contempt for our enemy, was real enough. The Wishards hated the Elfwych. I hated the Elfwych. The Elfwych hated us. Why? Perhaps there was no reason good enough. None better than this: it is convenient to hate the men you are about to steal from, the men you are about to kill. Though in truth, it was an endless blood feud, come out of time, and without redemption. This was ever the Graynelore.

The Old-man's address ended there without further explanation or demand. It was obvious he had enjoyed his own speech, its grandeur and its pomp. He also believed in it implicitly. At least, he had to be *seen* to believe in it implicitly. Without that he knew he could not command men. That was the real trick of his leadership.

Others might pretend that The Graynelord ruled by right of birth, or because he was bequeathed the symbol of power that made it so. The Eye Stone . . . the favourite of the Beggar Bard's tales. The stone tablet that so many men here believed rested within the walls of the Old-man's Stronghold at Carraw Peel (though not a single one – outside of his trusted Council – claimed to have seen it with his own eyes). In truth, symbols were just that: symbols. Made of stone, or cloth, or paper: symbols. Solid reality or simple belief: symbols. He was only one man. His rule was a mortal fact, and he knew it.

Old-man Wishard lowered his sword arm, but did not sheath his sword (another symbol). He took the reign of his hobby-horse and, turning the animal about, began to ride out slowly, off Pennen Fields. He made a display of checking the sky for the position of the sun before turning to face the West March: the homeland of the Elfwych.

At my back, to the rear of our gathering many of my kinsmen had not heard a word of the Old-man's speech; only the sound of his voice carrying across the wind. The great bellowing noises he had made. The show he had put on. In truth, it did not matter to them what was said only that he had said it.

He led, they followed.

Chapter Five

The Elfwych Riding

The immediate reaction of our greater gathering to the Old-man's departure was not what you might have expected of a faithful grayne. Certainly, his personal bodyguard spurred their hobby-horses and, banners waving, followed quickly after him. His brothers too, Cloggie-Unthank and Fibra, took their guard and, each very aware of the other, began their Riding. Not so the Old-man's trusted Council. Casually, they turned their prancing ponies aside and, without a look behind them, began their long ride home unattended. Their parading was done with, and their usefulness was at an end here. And if there were a few solitary riders among us common men who started after The Graynelord's party, the majority deliberately stood up their hobbs and stayed their ground.

There was one last ritual to be performed before we were ready to set out.

In almost revered silence, groups of women, youths, and young girls began to appear among us. They walked quietly between the massed ranks of mounted hobby-horses, giving each man there a small present as they went, or so it seemed. Old Emma's Notyet came to me. She held a young babbie in her arms (not mine, I hasten, nor hers) and he offered me up an empty leather pouch. Another man took a single spur from his wife, while yet another was given a sharpened dagger, and so on . . . These things were not given as keepsakes. Rather, they were tokens of encouragement, demand, and expectation. Their meaning was simple and clear:

If we were to return home safely, we must none of us return home empty-handed.

The leather pouch was given to me that I might fill it with coins or seeds or trinkets, or some other treasure procured upon the Riding. I took it without a single word passing between us. Notyet and I had already made our goodbyes. And if, as she turned away, she threw me half a kiss, I did not catch it, or return the other half. Though I did watch her closely as she took her leave; and for far longer than I might. A fully grown woman, there was nothing special about her, no obvious or distinctive mark. She was a weedling still, and did not stand out in a crowd. Less than average of height, weak of pallor, not well bred. There was a trace of silver and blue in the shadows cast across her skin, especially evident in the folds of skin on her hands, between her fingers and her toes, and unevenly around her eyes and mouth, but these were common touches. I am neither describing great beauty nor a freak of nature. I, and all my kin from Beggar Bard to babbie, carry many of the same traits. Upon Graynelore, we are each of us the sum of our collected ancestry. Notyet might have been described as endearing, but never pretty. Her ears were long and slightly high, slightly elevated, but there was no elfin point. She wore her coarse hair plainly. She brushed it back off her face, letting it hang loosely at her shoulder and down her back, as was the custom. Her clothes were simple and functional with no hint of conceit. She wore a long dress, made of several loosely cut pieces of cloth sewn lightly together: it found its own bodyline and allowed for easy movement, let her skin breath.

Do you think me self-indulgent? Or do I betray myself? Have my eyes lingered too long upon her? Would you have had me already in the frae? Have a care, my friend. Faced with death, who among men would not pause for a moment and risk a look back towards life?

When, finally, the greater body of the Riding set out to follow after the Old-man, it was a cold road we travelled. We needed no clues, no scented trail. We knew well enough where we were going: Staward Peel. The Elfwych Stronghold, stood at the centre of the West March, within a great meander of the River Winding, and at the foot of thc hills thcy called The Rise. It was a well-placed tower-house, and easily defended at full strength.

Only, Staward Peel was *not* at full strength.

Its tower was already broken and badly maintained. Its walls, once as thick and strong as any in all Graynelore, had been breached many times in recent conflicts, and more poorly mended upon each event. The Elfwych could not depend upon it for their defence. They were a grayne in trouble; a surname in decline. Whatever gathering forces they could bring to their aid, we knew they would want to make their fight out in the open and on the run. In almost every way their misfortune was our advantage. And where it was not, our sheer weight in numbers would easily make the difference. For every fourth man Stain Elfwych could fetch up The Graynelord could fetch up ten. There would still be a hard fight, and killings, of course – no surname upon Graynelore would have it any other way – but the purpose of the Riding would be served. Old-man Wishard would get exactly what he was after.

I, Rogrig Wishard, had ridden the raider's trail often enough. I knew what was expected of a Riding. Ours was not an army of rank and file. This raid was to be far less a considered attack than it was a free-for-all. We did not advance in the way of a single tutored cavalry. Rather, we straddled the fells and the moorlands: a series of loose rabbles. Close kin preferring to rely on close kin for their aid. The members of each house making their own way and in their own time. (And as often as not . . . with their own intentions and intended victims.) Sometimes long chains of men sprawled thinly across the fells, steadily making their way on their hobby-horses (only a very few a-foot). Sometimes a thick knot of fighting-men moved together as one body: finding their strength and their bravery in their tightly gathered number. This had ever been Cloggie-Unthank's preference. Each house had its own particular fighting tactics and stuck to them rigidly. On the principle that, if something had worked once before, it was certain to work again. (Not always a sensible provision, I fear.)

For certain, there was to be no single great and glorious battle. What was expected here was a scourging. A series of melees and skirmishes taken up wherever they happened, rough-shod Ridings, and individual combats stretched out upon the day.

Without a doubt, there were men among us who liked this fighting business a little too much – aye, and on both sides – fighters who would give no quarter, killing to the last man or woman . . . or child. Then there were those who would openly buy or sell their lives with whatever means they could offer if their sword arm could not do it for them. Sometimes a handful of coin was enough, or the gift of a horse or . . . or else the shaming of a young girl.

It was in this way the Wishards were to answer the call of their Graynelord, and to make their mark upon the grayne of Stain Elfwych.

I rode among members of my own house, with my greater cousins, and the elder-men of Dingly Dell. Together we made our own fighting band. By choice we rode, not in a close formation, but strung out at a distance; each rider keeping a watch for himself, but in sight of his nearest kin. We preferred having open ground between us – enough to swing a sword arm freely. Fight and flee; hit and run; the quick skirmish was ever our ploy.

If I am to be truly honest, this Rogrig remembers very little of this particular Riding; the first of it that is: the setting out. (It was much like any other.) I can put scant detail to it.

I must have ridden many a fell. Crossed and recrossed the many roots and stems of the River Winding. I must have passed settlements; each almost identical, with their heavy-walled farmhouses; their bastles, ugly and squat. (The men of Graynelore are not builders, not creators by nature. They are *all* fighters and thieves. What was made was of necessity – if it could not be stolen.) Their wary, weary occupants shut up inside with their few rescued animals. Stone-cold faces, catching the sun, winking at their shutter-less wind-eyes, ever watchful; wanting, hoping, praying – no doubt – that our Riding would pass them by this day.

I must have trodden streams and skirted about the edges of the west marshlands. Or rather, let my hobby-horse lead me stubbornly across its secret paths. My tough little Dandy, who could carry not only her rider, but the whole world upon her back, it seemed. Pots and pans, wooden implements, swords and weaponry, sticks and stones, blanket rolls and stolen booty. She would carry it all, overloading the tiny workhorse; and yet she always stood her ground, made her way without protest.

I must, on occasion, have stopped to relieve myself, or to take a drink of fresh water from an upland stream. I must have done . . . only afterwards I did not remember it. Not any of it.

Not even the first fierce call of alarm.

Not the first ringing of iron upon iron as swords clattered and clashed. Stones thrown, hitting their target. Riders suddenly taken to the gallop in hot pursuit . . . The smell of fear – as acrid as a slewed piss pot – distinct, yet oddly indescribable.

Not the first brutal killings. Nor the unmistakable crying . . . The frantic calling . . . The pleas, the oaths, the terror . . . The escaping last breath of a man already dead . . . The blood . . . The torn flesh . . . The shattered bones.

I remember none of it.

How so?

I was a seasoned man. All my senses were taken up from the first. Not numbed, heightened by practice. I had allowed a red shroud to descend upon me, suffocating all else . . . Nothing was near at hand. Everything was distant . . . Not indistinct I say, distant. No natural colours. No life. The world was set apart, put aside. No pity. Humanity utterly abandoned. Even fear . . . Even a pounding heart – there could be no heart, except a stone heart.

What was I thinking? I did not think. There was no place for thinking here. Thinking men got themselves killed. There was instinct. There was violence. There was the bloody act of war. There was the doing of it. Only the doing.

Suddenly Dandy was moving at the gallop beneath me. I might have tried to rein her in, only to have her protest and give her back her head. When she slowed again, it was of her own account.

I must have dismounted.

From somewhere the world was trying to get in, to make contact again . . . to find me out. One moment, surely, I had been with my close kin, waiting at the Heel Stone. The very next I was standing here, in this strange place, upon this open scrubland, with nothing in between. My sword was in my hand and already notched and running with blood.

And then I became fully aware.

There was a slight movement close by . . . of all things, a butterfly alighting upon a grass stem.

There was a face in the grass. There was a human face.

And I understood what had passed.

Chapter Six

The Killing Field

Her eyes; they were a blue that startled, invited, demanded. They caught hold of me, drew me to her like a lover. Still wet, they glistened. Not with tears. Nor fear. There was no stain on her cheeks. Her white cheeks . . . White skin . . . She was a beauty yet. The wind was playing lightly across her face, moving a single frond of auburn hair. She had caught it upon her tongue at the edge of her mouth. Open mouth. Red mouth . . . Surely she was teasing me, smiling, whispering. No . . . yes.

I tried to put Notyet's face in the way of hers, only I could not seem to find it. Vague, hidden as if veiled; its image would not come to me.

'Rogrig,' she said.

Again.

'Rogrig . . . '

Did she really speak my name, then? No . . . yes. No. It was only the voice of the wind.

'Rogrig . . . Rogrig . . .?'

But this last was not a woman's voice, nor the wind.

'Watch this, Rogrig!' It was a clumsy youth who had spoken: Edbur, my elder-cousin Wolfrid's whelp; his laughing cry was thin with a disguised fear.

Then there was violence: the sweet scent of fresh blood spilled; the kicking.

I was suddenly released from my stupor, and the woman's spell was broken. Instinctively I gripped the hilt of my sword, but let it rest at my side. There was no threat here. I recognized the boy's smell. Edbur, Edbur-the-Widdle – It was a fitting nickname. He was old enough and big enough to fight, but the whelp soiled himself at every skirmish. Still, there had been killings made here, and if wounded pride was the worst of his injuries he had served his surname, his grayne, better than many. The fortunes would soon forgive him for it. And if they did not, well, then I would forgive him in their stead.

The boy's swinging kick sent the severed head of the dead woman tumbling. Edbur-the-Widdle laughed outrageously as it thumped and thudded between grass and gulley, as it broke heavily upon stone, spilling teeth, spitting blood.

Not a woman now.

Did I wince at the act? . . . Surely, not I.

The youth was only playing at the Old Game. I had made the same sport myself often enough. Why should it bother me now?

Only, upon this day, and without good reason, it did.

I feigned some trivial act of pillage. I wanted a moment to myself. I was still breathing heavily with the effort of the ride, and the early fight. There were several members of my grayne picking over the remnants on that killing field. Both surnames lay dead there: Elfwych and Wishard, though they were mostly Elfwych. This skirmish had been more a one-sided rout than an equal fight, but then, it was a family matter and you take the advantage where you can. After all, there was a Graynelord to serve. That was reason enough, if you were looking for a reason. It had always been enough.

And yet, upon this day Rogrig *was* troubled. I was feeling . . . what was I feeling? I could not place it.

What was this seed of doubt, this nagging intrusion? What had I seen in the face of a dead Elfwych? What had I heard in the calling out of my name? Something here had changed, and upon a moment; something within me, and I suddenly knew it could never be undone. There was no return. I did not like this revelation. Certainly I did not understand it. I felt as if my feet were standing in two different places at once, though neither was planted firmly upon the ground. A field of battle was the wrong place for confusion, and this the wrong time for doubts.

Close to, bodies lay rudely scattered. They had been bludgeoned . . . hacked . . . mistreated beyond mere acts of savage violent death. Some stripped naked, worse, to the raw bone. Torn apart; their meat left for the scavenging birds that wheeled patiently overhead, awaiting our departure.

At a distance, out on the open fells behind me, there was a ragtag; a broken string of figures still running away . . . for certain, more Elfwych. Well, I would let them run, for now. I was never a good man (who upon Graynelore was?) but neither was I so bad, and this was not annihilation. Rather, it was a warning, more a statement of intent. The Wishards are coming for you.

The Wishards are coming!

Some of those poor wretches might well have made good their escape and found their looked-for safety; either going to ground or else hiding within the walls of some near kinsman's secure bastle-house. Others, I knew, we would catch up with later. There would be yet more killing, more death, more hurt before the end. But then, let the thought rest easy, my friend. I did not worry for either outcome. For certain, both life and death were welcome there. Do you not see it? If all our enemies were to die upon a single day, who would we steal from tomorrow? It is a reiver mantra, and a fitting sentiment you will, no doubt, hear again often repeated.

The image of the dead woman's face came back to me then: her untouched beauty. Her dismembered head; how incongruous it had seemed lying among the bloody gore. Yet, why the sudden pity for an Elfwych? Why this nagging doubt, Rogrig Wishard, Rogrig Stone Heart? Perhaps I had been responsible for her death, in the heat of the fracas. But then, what of it? She was my natural, my hated enemy. And yet, still I hesitated, and would not shrug off the thought. I hated her even more for it.

'A stone heart does not melt like a winter's ice. Indeed it cannot be melted. But broken? Aye, maybe that . . . Only, what is this foolishness? How is it done?' I thought my words were spoken only to myself.

'How is more than obvious, cousin . . .' This was Wolfrid, now standing at my side. On his approach he had mistaken the meaning of my question.

'All right. Why, then?' I said, turning the conversation. 'Tell me why?'

'Why?' Wolfrid seemed amused. He pulled distractedly at his thin beard. 'Upon Graynelore, a sword with a conscience will not live for long. Look around you, Rogrig . . . Put a weapon into any man's hand, give them an easy opportunity to use it and an advantage in doing so, and see how few do not.'

'That is not a reason,' I said. 'That is . . . bloody stupidity.'

'Quite,' he said.

We both laughed out loud (and meant it). Then, Wolfrid returned to the matter in hand. He grunted heavily as he turned the body of a man on the end of his sword, making certain he was dead before lifting both his purse and the small crust of bread concealed within his jack.

'We kill or we are killed, it serves us all well enough. See?' Wolfrid broke the bread crust in two and offered the greater half to me. 'And this day is not yet done with, cousin. Nor the fighting.'

Wolfrid was right, on both accounts.

I was quick to remount Dandy, and began to follow the line of my kin across the rising hillside. Within a few moments, there was a thick knot of Elfwych breaking cover, coming down upon us. They were flailing their swords, trying to use the slope of the hill to increase the power of their swing. It was a good notion. Though they were come at us a-foot, if they struck us head on it would make for a bloody show; and us the victims.

I knew the ploy. Fortunately, I also knew the counter. I gave cry. Instinctively, my kin broke up our loose line and we scattered ourselves. We rode across the hillside; each of us deliberately moving in a different direction. And we went slowly – enticingly slowly – we wanted our enemies to follow after us.

That they did was their mistake. It split their number and broke their momentum. Once more on a reasonably even fell we could use our hobbs to drive our victims back, push them into gullies or up against outcrops of rock (as, on another day, we might have driven our shabby herds of fell beasts). First cornering them, then the slaughter: a man who has nowhere to run cannot hide.

Did I kill then, in the thick of it, in the heat? Yes, I killed, if I would bring it to mind . . . twice, at least, and in quick succession. My greater sword arm held the advantage, easily found its mark where panicked men, unwisely, left themselves open to it. Aye, and I quickly rifled the bloodied carcases, took what spoils I could to fill my empty leather purse.

Not yet done, I turned Dandy about. I saw there were three figures ahead of me, backs turned, running down through a deep gulley. They were a youth – a mere boy-at-arms – an ageing man and, judging from the gait not the attire, a young fighting-woman. *Another* girl . . . For pity's sake; was the fighting strength of the Elfwych so very much depleted? I gave a quick look for Wolfrid or his whelp, or any other friend, but found myself riding alone. Confident still, I spurred Dandy on. The Elfwych appeared to deliberately move apart when they realized they were being pursued, and I was gaining on them. The rough grass among broken stones, the deep cut of a stream at the bottom of the fall, was making it difficult for them to keep to their feet. Aided by Dandelion's greater pace and sure-footedness, I would soon overtake them. (There was no need for me to guide her. Dandy would only have protested at the pull on the rein.)

Ahead of me, the fleeing woman turned her ankle, she pitched and fell, though I gave her scant notice until she scrabbled awkwardly to her feet again and turned to face me.

Why did I stop at her? Why dismount then? All three were easy victims. I liked women, of course. But this was another Elfwych and I was a Wishard. I felt the first unwanted physical stirring of my body. But then, violation – was that really my intent? – was such an impotent weapon upon a killing field.

I might have smiled at the paradox. Violate them with your sword. Cut off their heads. Rip out their bellies. Do not try to fuck them. They will only fuck you first.

Yet, there I stood.

And there was something else . . . something far more curious: a connection between us I was at a loss to explain. What was this? A fleeting shadow, like wild bird flight, crossed my mind. For the second time that day I felt as if I was standing in two places at once. I was become an unwilling partner in some waking dream. The real world was less solid than a drift of smoke. And this Elfwych woman was my accomplice. We were conjoined and could not easily step apart. From somewhere there were questions, words were spoken, but so softly, I could not make them out; or their source . . . if they were not hers.

It was enough to hold my sword arm.

'Shit!'

Kill her. Kill her and be done with it, Rogrig Wishard.

She was yelling at me now, but still I could not make out what it was she said . . . only understand the anger, the fervent anger showing on her twisted face, the fierce warning in her voice.

Her kin – the youth and the old man – were already well beyond my reach; above me at the top of the gulley now, only legs moving against a still blue sky, scrambling out of sight. If they were meant for a bodyguard, they did not intend to stay and make a fight of it.

I must use my sword. I must not look her in the eye . . . before or afterwards. One quick, clean stroke would finish it, Rogrig Stone Heart. She had led herself into the frae she must take the consequences of it.

Only, I held off. Only, I did look her in the eye.

And I will swear this to you: it was *her* . . . the dead woman. Yes. Impossibly, it was the same dead girl I had killed already. Living again, breathing again. Her eyes, her hair, her skin . . . they were the very same. Of course, there was a simple answer to this riddle, if only I could truly believe in it. Surely these two were close kin. This was a sister, then, or a cousin at the least? Though, my obvious inaction began to reveal my doubt.

In truth, I did not yet understand or recognize just what it was I had been privy to here. What I had witnessed – no, something more than that – what I had unwittingly become a part of. I might have guessed, and called it wychcraft – wychcraft at the hands of an Elfwych. Or else, it was some other unearthly masquerade . . . a trick; a faerie's Glamour, or the work of a fell-wisp. Though, none of it was likely in a world that believed only in the certainty of a cold sword. I, a grown man, was far beyond faerie tales!

'I saw you dead . . .' I said.

'You mean you wanted me for dead, Wishard!' she returned with a fury.

'I saw you . . . your head was broken, taken from your shoulders, played with for a bloody football!'

We had begun to sidestep each other. I was already holding my sword between us. We were circling warily about it.

'What think you? I was in hiding,' she said. 'What better place to conceal myself upon a killing field, than in among the dead?'

Only, there was an obvious deceit in her voice that betrayed her.

'I think you are an unpractised liar,' I said. 'And this is impossible . . .'

I raised my sword to make my stroke. What did she have to lie about?

'Oh please, not now!' she cried. 'Not him!'

'Eh?'

Her outburst seemed nonsense. It was not a response to anything I had said. Yet she repeated herself, with even greater venom.

'Please! Not now!'

Then I felt the heat of the blow. My hesitation had cost me. She had struck first. She had stuck me with a short knife. My loose leather jack, sewn with its paltry strips of hammered iron, was always a poor man's armour.

'Shit!'

It was experience moved me then. We were at close quarters. I turned the edge of my sword and instead of using the blade, drove the pommel down hard upon her head. The contact drew blood and tore a sliver of hair and skin from her scalp, knocked her sideways. But it was a poor, glancing blow; I had meant to break her head open.

I hit her again and she collapsed already senseless.

'Shit, shit!'

I too was bleeding. And though I should have finished it then, still I held back. I did not kill her. I . . . could not do it?

Stupidly – there was the noise and the threat of fighting all about me on the fells – I lowered my arm, sheathed my sword, and knelt down beside her. How might I explain this? (How might I explain *any* of this?) I wanted to touch her. Not a touch that would hurt her, not like that. Hurting her again would have been easy. I wanted . . . well, if I could make any sense of what I wanted . . . I wanted to prove that she was real, ordinary, human. And not some deluded man's fetch; some foul whimsy brought up out of a night-torment.

She was wearing the common breeches and reinforced jack of a fighting-man, and yet at her throat there was a gold amulet. It was a single piece and simply fashioned, but this was enough of a conceit (or perhaps a mistake) to mark her apart . . . only a damned fool or someone confident, in both her rank and her sword arm, would openly wear such an obvious badge of privilege in the frae. I was a soldier-thief. She was my worst enemy. I should have stolen it from her, taken it as my prize; added it to Notyet's growing purse. I should have loosened her breeches and stolen more . . . gone on my way and thought no more of it.

Her arm had fallen into the stream. The closed hand still held the knife. I took it up, threw the knife aside. I lifted her arm and laid it down, clear of the stream. I cupped my hand and, taking water, gently bathed her brow. That was all. As I did I heard the babble of the stream. I would swear this to you; it was speaking to me. Though it whispered, I could plainly hear its call. And I suddenly knew that if I would only listen to its voice then I would understand its words.

This Elfwych and this Wishard . . . they are the very same . . .

'What?'

When I looked again I saw the stream was turning red.

'Fucking, shit!'

I was still bleeding. I ran my fingers across the cut. The wound was long, but it was not too deep. Yet it had been a deliberate thrust. What was this Elfwych about? Trying only to injure me, to distract me rather than kill? And why would she do that?

Then she was moving again, her hand grasping at a tuft of grass, trying to pull herself upright.

I watched as she slowly dragged herself to her feet.

There was a moment of indecision. She stood almost within reach of me. What was it? Was she going to come at me again? (Even without her knife.) I lifted my sword, only to stay my hand before it ran clear of the scabbard. She turned slowly, almost invitingly, towards me – but invitingly of what?

Afterwards, a long time afterwards, I remembered there was an instant then when our eyes briefly met. What *did* we each see there? What was there between us?

I could so easily have felled her.

I could so easily have let her go.

I did neither.

Upon the moment, the distant, random clatter of swords striking against swords, the cries and counter cries of men in the frae, was usurped, overlaid by the sudden toning of an iron bell. First there was one, and then came a second in reply, off at some great distance. And then there were many. Each of them, languid, almost soporific in tone; it was a deep and sonorous sound. Their beat was deliberately regular and no sooner heard than the gathered crows – our constant aerial spectators – seemed to scatter above our heads, spiralling ever upwards into the very heights of the sky.

All around us, near and far, men stayed their arms; the fighting was instantly done with.

I let go the hilt of my sword, without a care, let it run freely back upon its scabbard.

The toning of the iron bells was an obvious signal. There were to be no more killings made this day. For it bore all the notes of surrender, and a defeat accepted. Perhaps even the death of a Headman.

Chapter Seven

The Unspoken Voice

When the Elfwych woman turned her back on me and walked away, heading towards The Rise, and Staward Peel, I did nothing more than follow after her.

I walked a-foot. Dandelion came trailing behind me, her ears pricked but without complaint. If there was any danger remaining, it was far enough away now and of little enough concern to ignore.

The toning of the iron bells accompanied us.

'You have another name, Elfwych?' I called out to her, raising my voice to be heard.

For the briefest moment she faltered in her step, as if caught, surprised to find me still there. 'Use your eyes and look about you, Wishard,' she said. 'Upon Graynelore people die for their names.' There was a slow drawl to her speech that told me her head was still befuddled by the blows I had struck. Though it had not blunted her tongue; the way she spoke dared me to make an argument. It was a mute point.

'Aye, well, listen to the bells . . . There has been enough

of death,' I said, honestly enough. 'What do you say to an equal trade instead . . . a name for a name?'

'Ha! Does that not depend upon the goods offered being of an equal value, and the trader not simply a common thief?'

'Are you a thief then, Elfwych?' I was goading her.

'And is my name safe with you, Wishard?'

'Rogrig . . .' I corrected her. If I did not answer her question (I did not wish to lie). It seemed she did not want one.

'I am called Norda,' she said, without inference.

It was my turn to falter in my step. I turned my head aside, certain I could not easily conceal my reaction to her revelation. I knew the name, of course. Who upon the West or South March of Graynelore did not? This woman was Norda Elfwych, the elder daughter of Stain Elfwych, Headman of his grayne. It was she that Old-man Wishard had set his eye upon (aye, and his lust). She was the prize we were fighting for this day.

Suddenly the iron bells stopped their toning. One by one, they were quickly stilled. Their message was delivered.

The silence they left behind them lay thick and heavy upon the air. No natural sound was willing to intrude upon it. It seemed the world had taken a deep breath, and now held it, waiting upon an outcome.

We continued to walk on together, if always at a safe distance from each other; still wary enemies and adversaries, and neither of us quite willing to take our hands away from our concealed weapons. (No fighting man – or woman – wears but one.) Though I carried my sword sheathed.

'I did not ask you for an escort home, Rogrig Wishard,' she said, at last, determined to break the uneasy silence between us.

'I did not offer you one, Norda Elfwych,' I returned.

'Am I to be your prisoner then . . . is that it? Or perhaps you are to be mine?' She tried to laugh, only to falter as she stumbled again.

This time I did not move to help her – though she was not expecting me to – I was being deliberately cautious of her now. She shook her head as if to clear her befuddlement, put a finger to her ear as if to stop the ringing. There was blood. Her pain was more than obvious. Certainly, she must have endured more serious injury – she was a fighter, and by reputation more than equal to many a man – only the last strike of my sword had knocked her cold. That had, obviously, annoyed her. I could read it in her face each time she glanced my way. She was, after all, the daughter of a Headman, and a privileged member of her grayne. (A grayne that, no doubt, felt it had a rightful claim to the title of Graynelord.) In her eyes, she had been brought to ground by a clumsy, common fell-man, a poor soldier-thief without distinction. She had managed to stick me with her knife and could well have finished it. Only, I sensed there was still something more to this than her common annoyance alone.

You are not even aware of your own true nature.

Did I say it, did I even think it? Or did she? She was looking my way, but her mouth was not moving. There were no words spoken. I will swear to it. I am a plain man, but I am not an idiot.

It might have been the voice of the babbling stream (all this time we had continued to follow its course), or else it was the movement of the leaves on a tree, or the scuffling of a breeze as it ran off through the long grass.

For certain I had felt a connection between us, but I had not understood it for anything more than, what? At best a weak man's physical desire for a woman. She had roared at me. Why? Was it for my ignorance? (I did not know.) I had mistaken that too. So she had wounded me and I, in my turn, had struck her down. We both might thank the fortunes I had not the wit to take my advantage of her while I might.

Again I heard the whispers of an unspoken voice:

How long have I waited upon another . . .

'What?' I said.

Look to Wycken . . . You must look there . . .

'Wycken? What did you say, there? What is this trickery?'

But that was the last of it.

Before me, Norda Elfwych looked suddenly ashen. Her face had drained white. She fell to her knees and let go the contents of her stomach.

I chose then to stay silent. I chose to remain Rogrig Stone Heart yet awhile. I waited with her until she was done and had cleaned herself up, then we walked on. We remained always just out of arm's reach of each other. I deliberately followed a few steps behind her and let Dandy make her own way, free of her reigns.

We were not travelling alone, nor had we been for some time now. There were many others coming off the killing fields, instinctively covering the same ground. Some were riding, but as many men went a-foot now, driving their overladen hobby-horses before them: the hobbs made to carry more than their full weight of dead men slung across their backs. Elfwych and Wishard moving in the same direction . . .

The fighting was done with. The day was won and it was lost. We were nearing The Rise, and close to the tower of Staward Peel, where we would wait upon the pronouncement of the manner of our truce, that we might all take ourselves safely to our homes again.

Chapter Eight

The Broken Tower

All settlements throughout Graynelore, though loosely planned, were broadly similar, often built upon lonely and inhospitable ground. They grew up higgledy-piggledy, sometimes upon exposed hilltops, sometimes hidden away within closed valleys, or kept a secret within dense woodland, as the country allowed. The best houses, though small and squat, were always made of stone, with walls so thick that, from within, you could not hold an ear to the world outside. Lesser dwellings were huddled together, with perhaps a patch of land for pasture, or for grain fields, or for root fields; the staples of our diet. All the graynes – great or small – set their houses as close to the Stronghold of their Headman as familiarity would allow. They maintained them in this manner, not out of any real desire for close community, but rather for mutual safety: common defence against the raider. In a moment of crisis, close kin were in eye sight and earshot of close kin, and might more easily raise the alarm, go to their neighbour's aid, or make good their escape.

The Elfwych bastle-houses of The Rise were great in number. Only, as we began to pass them by, it became obvious that many of them were already long abandoned, and others, if still inhabited, were sorely ill-repaired. Strings of fell beasts were being led off nearby pasture, and Norda's own close kin stood by and watched as Wishards brazenly took them. These were the first spoils of the Elfwych Riding then.

The weight of men about us steadily grew in number. There might have been as many as two hundred men waiting upon the breach in Stain Elfwych's broken peel tower. Both sides still held their arms, as was the way of things, but it was more than obvious where the surrender lay.

At least no man there tried to hinder Norda's progress. Perhaps aware of her rank, riders shied their hobby-horses aside and gave her way as she approached the door of the broken tower.

She looked back towards me only once more. I will admit it; I had already deserted her. I had deliberately slipped away into the growing crowds, was already lost to her eyes among the throng; Dandy too. I caught a glimpse of the question on her face. Had I been making certain she was safe . . . or safely delivered? I dared not disclose myself and attempt an answer. The job was done, either way. Beyond the Riding I, a common fell-man, had no further part to play here. Neither Graynelord nor Headmen sought my opinion of the terms of any truce. Certainly, it was not my place to interfere with the Old-man's . . . conquests. Save for this: I was more than curious of that strange connection between us two; that ethereal bond that even now left an Elfwych and a Wishard somehow hopelessly conjoined. I made a vow then. I would play the spy and keep an eye out for

Norda Elfwych. Within that broken ruin of a tower there were many vantage points a nimble man could choose to make his perch.

I used Dandy's back for my first platform, climbed the broken stonework with ease from then on, and soon found myself sitting pretty within a, largely collapsed, arched wind-eye. The perfect spy hole! The spot gave me the advantage of overlooking both the inner Great Hall and the outer courtyard. The truth of the Elfwych decline had not been overstated. Staward Peel was in a ruinous decay. Its weakened face lay open to the sky in several places it should not have been.

I carefully watched Norda's progress through the crowded courtyard. Among the throng I recognized my own close kin, my elder-cousin Wolfrid, and caught sight of Edbur-the-Widdle some way behind the Old-man himself.

The Graynelord was still mounted upon his beautiful silver-grey hobb, still dressed for show in his best finery and polished body armour. I had last seen him at the head of his grayne leading us into the frae, though I could see no mark of battle upon him. He was looking Norda's way, staring avidly after her as she approached the breached doorway. His face and balding head stood out bright red with an unhealthy excitement. Suddenly, he stood up in his saddle: another deliberate show of his manhood. There was no disguise here. And if he made no movement to bar her way, content yet, it seemed, to stay his hand and wait upon the moment: he was making his intentions more than obvious.

When Norda walked across the threshold of the tower she was immediately faced by the remains of her own family . . . both the standing and the fallen. From the vantage of my perch, I could see by the way she pinched her nose and gagged at the throat – which she tried to disguise with her hand – it was the stench that first caught her attention. Though, I am certain, she was well used to the smell of the bloodied dead, forgive her reaction. After all, the sack of butchered meat presented to her was all that was left of her own father. I do not make the description frivolously. The tolling iron bells had not lied. If they had called for a truce, they had also warned of a Headman's death. Stain Elfwych had been killed in battle. For the sport of it – and some small souvenirs – his enemies, *my family*, had crudely hacked his body into little pieces.

'Ah, my dearest sister, thank the fortunes, she has returned safely to us.' It was Iccara, Norda's younger brother, who made the greeting. His face was tight with worry and thick with sweat, though there was no sign of a blood wound upon him. He had been in a heavy fight or else he had been running. With the killing of his father it seemed he was now the Headman of the Elfwych. A feeble weedling man, it was a title he did not want and was not best suited to. Let other men lead; let him alone. Of course, he had no choice in the matter. He may have been Norda's younger sibling, his beard still a shadow of soft hair, but no woman was ever a Graynelord.

He pushed his lank hair away from his face and gave her a weak smile.

Norda appeared to sway, as if her legs were about to give way beneath her, and she might well have let them and swooned, but this was not the time to show a woman's weakness. She feigned strength, and stood firm.

'This day is lost, then?' she said, desperately trying to keep emotion out of her voice.

'Aye . . . lost my hen.' There was a twitch about Iccara's left eye. 'Though not perhaps without a little hope; and even some advantage to it . . .'

'Advantage, how so?' she asked, confused. 'And speak plainly brother, if you can, this day is already sorely long and ill-used. What are you saying?'

'Old-man Wishard, The Graynelord himself, is . . . waiting outside for you. We have already spoken and come to terms. He has made us a proposition.' Iccara broadened his weak smile, revealed his crooked teeth. It did not improve his look of obvious insincerity. 'After the . . . unfortunate killing of our father, he wishes only for peace between our kin. He seeks but a simple Pledge from us this day.'

'A Pledge?' she returned.

'Aye, well . . . All right . . . a Pledge *and* a union, then. He wants a union of our surnames: Wishard and Elfwych. A marriage would suit us both at this time, dear sister. Eh? What better symbol of our good faith.'

'A marriage . . . between an Elfwych and a Wishard? Do you really think the man wants a marriage? Have you seen him out there? Have you? A strutting cock-bird! All *he* wants to do is fuck! And have a care my brother, his blood is up! I do not think he has a mind to where he buries his manhood!'

Iccara held his tongue still between his grinning teeth, as if in careful consideration of his answer. Across the years there had been so many Pledges, so many unions between the graynes. There was hardly a pair of fighting Headmen in all Graynelore who were not already cousins, of sorts. So much so, that that particular leash had become too long a measure to make effective political unions. And marriages, the strongest knots, close to incestuous. If a man took his enemy for his wife (though more likely for his whore) it was little more than expediency; a winner taking his spoils; a way for defeated foe to make up the balance of their loser's reparation when other resources were scarce. What would a Headman prefer to forego: the little gold he possessed; the few stock animals that remained to see him through a winter, or would he rather give up a sister to a letch, a full grown mouth to feed?

'Our own brother's trampled body was brought home sorely broken apart. We needed four strong men and a blanket to carry the . . . the remains left of our father. There are at least two hundred men-at-arms waiting on an answer at our shattered door. You have seen all this for yourself, sister. Need I go on?' Iccara was spitting as he spoke. There was neither sentiment nor any sense of personal loss. He took hold of Norda's hair, pulled her head up, bringing their eyes level. (A better man than I might have drawn his sword and intervened. I only held on tighter to my perch and let the scene play out). 'Believe me, sister, if all it was going to take to resolve this matter was a quick jack-up, I would hold you down myself and help him to it . . . Be assured. This is not a private affair. There is the well-being of our entire grayne to consider. Now, find me an alternative – preferably one that does not involve us *all* being butchered – or else make your Pledge and let us have done with this.'

'Iccara, my beloved brother: ever the diplomat and defender of the grayne.' Still held fast, Norda stiffened resolutely. 'How he always looks out for the best interests of his family.'

'Enough! There is no room for negotiation here.' Iccara raised his arm. His sister's sarcasm had not gone unnoticed. He lifted her off her feet by her hair. 'I will not ask you again. Nor, I fear, will they . . .'

Norda fought back. She tore herself free of her brother's grip, leaving a clump of red hair in his clenched fist. The pain drew tears. She blinked, pushed them away with the back of her hand. Her eyes were searching elsewhere.

For the first time I became aware – Iccara was not the only member of her close family waiting upon an answer. There were three younger siblings – all sisters – hardly visible; a miserable shrunken huddle, backed against a far wall. One, I guessed, was little more than a babbie still, grasped tightly in the arms of her elders. There was no sign of a nurse . . . or of a mother.

'Very well, then,' said Norda, still looking toward her sisters. 'You may tell Old-man Wishard, Headman of the Wishards, you may tell The Graynelord of all Graynelore, we will meet his terms. For the sake of my kin, I will Pledge to him . . .' She turned to face Iccara. 'And the fortunes damn you for it, brother.'

I stayed within my wind-eye perch and studied Iccara as, without ceremony, he watched his sister borne away among a horde of my kinsmen. Aye, and roughly managed. Was there no sign of regret there? I fear little, if any. He well knew his house could not afford to lose more fighting-men. And though Norda was as good as many a man, prejudice was alive and well upon Graynelore; it was ever wise to keep watchful of wagging ears that might prick at such a thought. His sister was an easy sacrifice for him to make.

After this day Old-man Wishard, my Graynelord, would be content to leave the Elfwych untroubled; for a while at least. He would give them the time to bury their dead, to lick their bloody wounds and repair their shoddy walls. Though for certain there were others upon Graynelore who would not. A badly wounded animal becomes a prey to its lesser foes. It was to his own close neighbours Iccara must look now and worry over. Less powerful graynes they may well be, but ever watchful of finding an advantage. As word of the Elfwych defeat spread they would surely come to Staward Peel in search of easy pickings. How were the mighty fallen. The Elfwych reduced to little more than a scavenger's carrion.

Was my own stone heart suddenly gone soft for an Elfwych? Does the conflicted man reveal himself? My friend, I am merely reporting the facts of the matter. I felt no sympathy for the Elfwych, or their losses, however severe. They were, forever, my sworn enemy.

There were few options open to Iccara. It is a cliché, but attack is always the best defence. If the man had any sense, he would quickly plan his own raids. Choose easy targets. Show, by example, there was strength yet in the arm of the Elfwych. There were isolated settlements out of favour with The Graynelord and without protection. There were unwary travellers. There were the poor houses: the makeshift shielings of defenceless or broken men. The Elfwych would become the sneak thieves and the night-murderers. And if there were few goods or chattels to be had, if there was little blackmail to be raised, Iccara would take his victim's children alive; the extra pairs of hands (and small stomachs) to make amends for his own losses.

Norda was carelessly stripped of both her clothes and her arms, though her gold amulet remained about her neck. She was dressed again in a plain white shift. A crown of weedling flowers was placed upon her head. Her feet were left bare, as a sign of her subjugation. Cloggie-Unthank and his younger brother, Fibra, were leaders among the group of men who clumsily took her up, wantonly pawing at her, before sitting her down again upon a great white pony. Young girls and youths were set in a line behind her, and made to follow after her a-foot. Deliberately staged, it was a poor mockery of a stately procession. Her meagre baggage was draped across the back of a single rider-less hobby-horse.

This day, Norda Elfwych, daughter of Stain Elfwych, was to be the Old-man's prize; his first lady, and his night's entertainment . . . With an obvious, wanton swagger he spurred his hobb and rode to the front of the line, took up his rightful position there. The Graynelord was showing off to us again.

Before Norda's parade was even out of sight of Carraw Peel, I watched Iccara beckon to a serving girl over some trivial domestic matter. How quickly he turned his back upon his sister, and shut her out. How soon she was forgotten. If not by me . . .

Nor did I ever see the man give any comfort or succour to his remaining siblings.

Chapter Nine

Aftermath

With the fighting done, and The Graynelord appeased, the remaining Wishards quickly drifted away from The Rise. Reivers do not care to tarry at the end of a Riding. They have no wish to occupy the lands of their enemies (it cannot be carried away). Rather, they go home again, laden with their gathered spoils! And if some travel by the shortest route, most go by way of settling their private feuds with their defeated foe.

There is muck to rake.

Killing Fields leave men enraged . . . knotted to the core, and not easily undone. The aftermath of a Riding is not a worthy spectacle. And the Elfwych were sure to bear the brunt. (Aye, and any other poor troublesome sod who happened to get themselves caught up in it along the trail.) There is no chivalry. There is no civility either. Only the cloistered fool would argue otherwise. Or else the politician: who thinks there is some advantage to be gained by it.

Did cowards force themselves upon unwilling company to soften up their manhood? Were the lives of already beaten men and women taken for coinage and idly played with for a sport? I will not condone our despicable actions with an attempt at reasoned explanation. Indeed, I would not wither my clumsy pen to report it further. Unless it was to admit my active part – freely remind you of my poor breeding, my own worst character – and leave it there.

If that was strictly true. It seemed the blood-soaked reiver who had made the outward journey to Staward Peel was not quite the same man who now made his return home.

In truth, if I feigned interest in the crude blood sports of my companions, and even lent a half-hearted sword to their bloody assaults upon the event, I did so only to disguise my troubled brow against inquisitive eyes.

Nor would my body care to entertain the distressed young women who held their skirts stiffly about themselves and in full cry ran wildly away at our approach, inviting the chase.

Even the hoard of small silver coin Wolfrid and I lifted, unexpected, from the jack of a beaten corpse upon the trail was not enough to excite my interest.

That strange meeting with Norda Elfwych upon a killing field had seen to that. Aye . . . and the distant calling of a shadow-tongue that even now reminded me:

You are not even aware of your own true nature.

And again:

Look to Wycken . . . You must look there . . .

We made our way slowly home, then; our return journey far longer than our outward trail. By the time we came again to Pennen Fields and passed by the Heel Stone, I felt we had all but regained our full measure. That is, for the most part, we had become ourselves again; only common men in need of the comfort of a fireside. If we had, each of us, lost just a little more of our souls, perhaps?

Be cheered, my friend.

We were all well met upon our return. The houses were decked out with fine sprigs of holly and blossoming winter roses . . . There was good food and wine; fresh vitals served upon a homely table! And Dingly Dell echoed to the sounds of sweet laments and merry laughter.

Bleeding men were, at last, fully repaired. Dying men, alas, there were a few, brought kindly to their end. While the fallen-dead were recounted, their loss fiercely celebrated and briefly mourned (whether Wishard or Elfwych it has to be said).

Wolfrid eagerly boasted of our exploits to all who would listen, spilled his gathered spoils upon our table, and drank himself into oblivion.

For a short while, Edbur-the-Widdle became a simple boy again. He took his warm ale thankfully, aye, and the edge of his mother's tongue for being a lazy son, for returning, out of the frae, with little of value.

. . . And, I, what of Rogrig on his homecoming?

Without a word – a game she was most fond of – Notyet came to me. She shamelessly searched my person – my boots, my cloth, and my intimates – and took back her leather purse, now fully laden. When I flinched at her touch she pulled open my bloodied jack to reveal the single knife wound in my side. She clicked her tongue, playfully . . . 'Be still, Rogrig!' she said. 'That is nothing but a babbie's scratch!' (In truth, it would soon heal and without a scar.) Content with her finds, and my safe, full-bodied return, Notyet took several full swigs from a great stone wine jar. In jest, she offered it up to Dandy before me. She roughed the hobb's ears, as the beast drank it greedily down . . . And began to tweak a simple tune from an old wooden whistle, to catch my ear (and my eye, no doubt). Then she took herself on a lover's walk, a deliberate enticement, bid me to follow after her.

Did I?

And did Rogrig Wishard at last stay gladly at home with his Notyet?

Sadly, the sweet distractions of that merry day were not enough to hold me there for long.

Above my head, the weathered sky was streaked blood-red: and there was a constant flutter of birds in flight. It seemed the crows would not let me alone, or cease their frantic calling, one to another. They cast a fleeting shade upon the ground as they passed me by, reminding me of another day and another man who had found he could not set his own two feet squarely upon the ground.

I had been touched. I was a marked man. I had listened to the whispered voices of shadows. If yet unwittingly: I carried the full weight of a faerie's Glamour . . .

Aye, and the man was utterly confused by it. Only I had no doubt, whatever my part in this mischief, whatever my true connection to Norda Elfwych, I knew I was bound to it. There could be no turning away.

I had set my mind upon a task.

I could not easily settle.

Soon fled . . .

Though not before I visited a lonely piece of ground I had all but forgotten; a secret knoll that marked the spot where, as a simple child, I had buried a stolen treasure:

The dead Beggar Bard's relic, his talisman, his so-called Eye Stone . . .

It had lain undisturbed these many years, seemed now like something out of a half-remembered dream. I fully expected to find no sign of it there.

The place was largely unchanged, its trees a little older; a little broader. The object was not so well hidden after all, and easily found again by the grown man. I had wrapped it up in a piece of cloth to protect it from the dirt. Still attached to its leather thong, it gleamed. Only something stopped me from openly examining it. Was it guilt at the theft? Surely not! More like an uneasiness, lest I should be spied upon; a fervent desire to keep it secret still, and solely to myself. I quickly hung the stone about my neck; put it well out of sight beneath my jack.

Chapter Ten

Against the Grayne

I was going against my close kin, going against my grayne. There is no greater sin. I was about to ride out on them. Had I gone quite mad? Had I lost my head, or had I lost my heart, perhaps? For certain, this was *not* love. Something far worse . . . Was I enamoured? A man does not take a fatal poison of his own free will.

I was for turning my hobby-horse away from my home, and away from Dingly Dell. Poor Dandy, she was already trail-weary and wanting only her due respite. Yet she did not protest, beyond a tempered snort, when I led her off her pasture. I could try to tell you I was distracted by a mob of crying black birds that appeared, and flew continually across my line of vision and would not cease their infernal bickering until I took heed of them. I could tell you this for a fancy; one of them as good as spoke to me – if in its own peculiar bird-like fashion. (I know, my friend . . . there is little sense to be had here.) It would be better to tell you that Wolfrid, my Headman and elder-cousin, seeing something of my intention, came after me and tried to dissuade me.

'Is this a jest, Rogrig?' he asked. 'Where are you at?' Wolfrid was uncertain as yet. His fingers toyed with his beard. Maybe he thought I was after some local sport of my own; with a tryst to keep, or a blackmail to deliver perhaps: coins to levee from a neighbour and him not included in the purse. He took his best guess. 'What are you making of this Norda Elfwych? I recognized your – what was it? – your *interest* in her, upon the Riding . . .' He was a shrewd man and a quick wit, when sober. Yet not even he could fetch up the truth from such a meagre portion. 'She is a Graynelord's concubine. A Pledge made and delivered. She will be whoring for her surname this very night.'

I wanted to protest in anger, to defend her honour, only I knew Wolfrid was only speaking as he found. I could only stumble foolishly for an answer.

'I . . . I . . .' I put empty hot air in the way of words.

'What is this, cousin? I see nothing to your advantage here. Does she have you beguiled? Is that it, are you in love?'

'Perhaps,' I said, merely to deflect the conversation. 'Perhaps I am.'

'Perhaps? For the fortunes! The man says perhaps! You are taking to the road alone for a . . . for a perhaps?'

'She is . . . I am . . . there is something between us. Something has happened,' I said, clumsily.

'Explain yourself, Rogrig. Make some sense, if you would! You will remember I am the Headman of your house . . .' I hoped this last remark was not so much a threat, as a gentle reminder. In all my life, from the very day of my father's bloody slaughter, when Wolfrid had become Headman, he had not once used his household rank as leverage. Did my current actions disturb him so?

'I fear I am at a loss. I cannot explain it,' I said, plainly enough. 'Nor can I stay here and do nothing.'

'Then, what . . .? What are you telling me?' said Wolfrid. 'I am trying to listen . . .'

'In all honesty I do not know. There is something to be done . . . I must try to find the others. I must do it.'

'For fuck's sake, what *others* . . .? What is to be done?' He asked, his anger slowly rising now, clearly frustrated by my vague retort.

'For fuck's sake indeed . . .' I said. 'Oh, I wish it was that simple. I really do. And I wish I knew. Norda is . . .' My hesitation was prolonged.

'She is what?' Wolfrid demanded.

'She is . . . touched. She is . . . *fey* . . .'

'What?' Incredulous now, Wolfrid began to laugh. 'You are saying what? This woman is a . . . is a bloody faerie! She is a throwback . . . Is that it? You'll have her strung from a gibbet next! Listen to me; she is an Elfwych. It is in her name. Nothing more! You have been listening to too many fireside Beggar Bards. Old wives tittle-tattle. And be aware Rogrig, you have been spouting madness ever since you lopped off that young girl's head upon the killing fields. Take heed, and let it go. She got in the way of your sword. Make that an end to it. I will grant you she was something of a beauty. Just do not lose your way now because you missed out on a piece of cat's tail . . . however precious.'

I was already shaking my head.

'No, that is not it, cousin,' I said. 'I must go. I must find them . . .' If I could not explain my actions to myself, how could I possibly explain them to my kin?

'But where will you go?' he asked.

I could not bring myself to say I was going to follow blindly after a murder of common crows. There was a more obvious answer. The shadow-tongues, the unspoken voices, had left me with a name . . .

'I am leaving the South March. I am travelling to Wycken,' I said. 'I am going to Wycken-in-the-Mire, for the Winter Festival . . . for the Faerie Riding.'

'And this is it, then – the Wycken Mire! This is your answer?' Wolfrid looked at me coldly, still wanting a better truth, something he could believe in.

I nodded, brusquely. 'I will travel the trade roads . . . to the town.'

'Towns . . .! What does any Wishard of the South March know of such places? Rogrig, you know as well as I, Wycken is a tinker's town built of wooden sticks upon a shift of mud.' He spoke as if I was already lost and he could see only the broken man. 'And there is not a certain path across the mire that surrounds it, except for those born to it; those petty traders with stinking bog-moss in their blood. The town could not be better protected nor defended if it had its own standing army.'

I turned my back on him. I made to mount Dandelion, took up the reigns. Wolfrid put his hand gently upon my shoulder as if to stop me. I did not recoil, though perhaps I had expected a blade.

'You will not be turned from this foolishness, cousin?' He asked. 'Not for your kin, your blood? Not even for your true heart's meat . . .?'

I knew well enough what he was saying. I shrugged his hand away, before he could say any more. I took to my hobby-horse. Used the spur to move her on.

'I fear I will not,' I called back to him. 'Forgive me for it.

Tell Notyet . . . Tell her . . .' Only my mouth stood empty. There were no words left to say.

'Forgiveness will not save you, Rogrig,' said Wolfrid, 'if you ride out alone this day . . .'

I gave him no answer.

Part Three

The Wycken Mire

Chapter Eleven

Into the Mire

I heard again the voices of the old-wives calling to me out of my own past. 'Mind how you go there, child! Keep off the bloody bog-moss. It swallows grown men whole! It sucks down full-laden fell-horses, carts and all! It will leave us no sign to remember you by . . .'

Would I have listened? Would I indeed!

How do you find the mire? Let me tell you, my friend. In truth, you do not. The mire finds you. My travels took me north and east. But the mire has no constant geography. No certain edge about it. Rather, it comes, and it goes. It insinuates itself upon the land. It creeps upon you, lurks patiently in wait. It conceals itself behind an ever-changing mask; of pelting rain; of meadow mist; of winter fog or blinding snow. It eats up the very path upon which you tread. It steals upon you and hides the weathered trail. In the darkest night it beckons you in, lures, with the light of the jack-o'-lantern.

Indeed, this was already a fool's journey, and I, Rogrig, the greater fool, no doubt, for seeking it out.

As the fortunes would have it, I did not travel quite alone, though I had to look again to the sky for the first of my companions. Aye, to the birds, to that same crowd of black birds – the crows – who, it seems, had taken it upon themselves to be my shadow on this foolhardy adventure. They flew so high they appeared to wheel among the clouds. Pointing the way with the direction of their flight, their vigil keeping my path constant; though it was Dandy's sure footing that held me to the trail.

Fair praise where it is due; without both of my guides I would have quickly been lost. I could neither lead the way through the mire, nor follow the shifting signs.

My third companion was less expected. It appeared I was being deliberately followed. There was a lone rider at my back, clumsily copying my steps, keeping his distance, yet making no secret of his intentions. When the wind brought his scent to me I recognized it at once as belonging to Edbur-the-Widdle, Wolfrid's son. (I told you Wolfrid was a shrewd man.) Was the youth sent to keep an eye out for me? Was he to be a second right arm, or perhaps his father's spy? Time would tell.

I might have called out to the gangly youth, bid him join my party openly. I liked the lad well enough. Only, upon Graynelore, it is best to leave well alone, to keep to your own business once it is settled upon: he to his and I to mine. There is ever a cunning knife eager to make its mark, an owner looking to his own advantage. And there are just as many mistakes made; intentions misconstrued, not worth dying for.

Oh, for the freedom of the open fells of the South March! For clear skies and green pastures! How I hated to be closed about with sopping mists and murk. The bog-moss trails (if they were trails at all) were but a trick to the eye. They led nowhere. Each tempting curve of the path, each broken sod, was nothing but a lure and a dead end. Or else a dizzying circle; a devil of a dance that left this traveller disorientated, with no sense of here or there. And the trodden path was hardly as broad as a single hoof; each sure-footed step poor Dandy took was hard found before it was placed. It was a slow and wearisome trial.

I should have stayed constantly alert, not given up my guard to a flight of birds. I should have held off my breathy cusses, fought the drowsy man.

I should have turned an ear and listened out for the real threat of approaching strangers.

That they came upon me at all was a lucky meet. Then again, upon Graynelore, a man rides his luck when it presents itself. They: a gang of scavenging horse-thieves, or the like, and come hot-blooded. I: a seasoned fighting-man but caught unwary and alone. (Edbur, by chance or design, was too far distant or unawares to be taken into account.) Poor Dandelion broke their path, and to their surprise took the full weight of the leading horse almost head on. The iron spike upon her headdress – meant for a unicorn's horn – was driven hard through the animal's neck. It seems it pierced both the horse and the rider equally. Flesh was split apart. Bones broke. Hot blood spurted. As the horse fell – still skewered – we were brought down with it, rolled under its thrashing hooves. Instinct alone held me to the saddle. It took Dandy's quick wit and stolid presence to save us, as the second and third horses ploughed into the melee. Men cursed, lifted their swords and swung in search of a target. But they were swinging blindly and at an adversary they were not yet certain of.

'Is this bastard truly a man upon a horse . . .?'

'Aye, aye . . . or some foul beast . . . some crude monster?'

Their reticence, their wary attack, was my good fortune; for it was not the time to stand and make a fight. Dandelion tore herself free of the dying animal. She shied, turned herself about, found her footing and, with my eager encouragement, bolted, took off at the gallop. Edbur was his own man; the circumstance dictates the action; I left him behind to make his own fate, as he left me to make mine. (And if I am – among all else – a coward when there is no need of a hero. Truly, who is not?)

If it had been an easier trail and firmer ground my escape would have been certain. But flight is not a game to play upon the bog-moss, nor is pursuit for that matter. The remaining riders – perhaps as many as three or four together – judged they had found themselves an easy prey after all, and came after me. More fool them; their larger, heavier horses, were less suited to the uncertain ground even than poor Dandy. The chase was soon done with.

I did not have to make a fight of it. The bog-moss caught us all out. It found my pursuers first; and I, soon after. It held us apart. I heard the anguished cries of both the men and – more cruelly – their horses, as it took hold of them. They thrashed their limbs about, beating at the sodden earth in a vain hope of gaining a firm purchase and winning their freedom; only hastening their imprisonment. The men's pitiful wails, their horses' desperate whinnies, broke the silence of that failing day, and afterwards, long into the night, coming weaker with every report until, almost at the break of dawn, they were finally extinguished.

In truth, I fared no better than my enemy, and was as quickly stuck fast. Only I stayed quite still, and calmed poor

Dandy's fright with gentle words, when instinctively she would have struck out in want of her freedom. My subtle actions greatly slowed our descent into the mire; though I feared there was nothing else to be done.

Once the bog-moss has you it will not easily let you go again. It grasps at your feet. It claws at the legs of your fell-horse until it finds its hold, and then it binds itself there, in a grip that is unrelenting. It envelops, devours, ingests; it holds your still living body in a tomb of stinking mud until the last breath is drawn out. Then, forever more, it sucks at your slowly decaying corpse until nothing remains . . . and the captive and the mire are one and the same.

So it was, and I would surely have met my own death there, without a rescue.

I might have expected Edbur to come to me, only it was not him who found me out. In fact, I was so close to an endless sleep, I did not see the arms that lifted me from the mire. I only knew their immense strength as they bore my weight and pulled me free, as they led poor Dandy by the reign and guided her to the safety of a sure path. I might have wondered how my rescuer kept their footing. Why they did not succumb to the deadly grip of the bog-moss. Inside my head I heard their soothing whispers, in a shadow-tongue, anxious to calm my fears, if outwardly my ears caught no natural sounds. What I saw, fleetingly, was this: a tall figure, draped in meadow mist . . . she was dark skinned . . . she was lithe . . . for a moment silhouetted against the coming dawn sky. Then, suddenly broken apart, a dozen fragments or more, like birds in flight . . .

No. Not *like* . . . but certainly, birds in flight.

Chapter Twelve

Wycken-on-the-Mire

I had not found my own way onto the mire. I did not find my own way off it. Rather, I would say, the bog-moss released me. It allowed me free passage, kept Dandelion steady upon the certain path without her protest or my direction. When we needed respite – to regain our strength after our night's ordeal – the mire gave way to a sweet, grassy knoll, where there was some firmness to the ground; and we could both stretch out our lengths and rest a while. And later, where the way forward forced us through a meandering thread of the River Winding, well, the mire let me get my feet wet. How might I explain it? I cannot. Perhaps the mire was well satisfied with the victims it had already claimed? (Poor souls . . .) Or perhaps it was something else, something more, like a (dare I say it?) like a faerie pact. Ha! I might still laugh at the thought! Only, for certain, that dark figure among the meadow mist, that shadow-tongue whispering inside my head, that scattering of black birds had been no common thing.

Notwithstanding, the remainder of the trail I followed was long, and it was tedious, and it was grim, the going always difficult. When at last the mire relented, and I saw beyond a rising mist the town of Wycken before me, and felt good, solid earth resisting the movement of my feet, in all the world there could have been no more joyous a man than I. If, in truth, I had never before seen the town, nor did I have any real understanding of why I had come upon it now.

Norda Elfwych had beseeched me to find the place out, was that not it? (I was still having difficulty believing that the unspoken voices I had heard upon the killing fields belonged to any other than to her.) The murder of crows – circling in flight, high above me, even now – had helped signpost the way. More intriguingly, I had felt myself, inexplicably, drawn there. I had become a seeker, and here in Wycken I might find answers . . . if only I knew the questions to ask, and of whom. Or else I was a simple lost fool, who long before now should have been at his home, sitting at his own table, resting by his own fireside.

I will tell you this: I was not a man made for towns (nor was poor Dandy). Give us open fells and the bliss of solitude. I let her run loose beyond the first houses. She would come to no harm and find her own grazing. She had earned it. When I needed her she would surely find me out again. There was a good head and sharp eyes upon those old shoulders. And I had no fear of horse thieves. A Wishard has a private trick that keeps only his own arse upon his hobb's saddle. If any man was tempted by the mount he would soon know himself delivered of a forceful rebuke.

I walked into the town alone.

In Wycken I was a stranger, an outlander, and aware of it. And any outlander who lingered in the town – with or without intent – would be revealed soon enough. I would be looked upon with suspicion. No man could expect to travel completely unchallenged. With that in mind I kept my hands openly filled. Not with the hilt of a blade, but with a bulging leather bag, a poke, lifted from Dandy's back. Before setting out I had filled it with trinkets, and rag-cloth, and who knows what else (mostly, the latter), topped it off with a few loose coins, for this very purpose. I understood Wycken for a place where men traded. Everyone there was sure to be a merchant of a kind, and it might easily be assumed I was out to do some honest trading of my own. And if there was any argument I could claim to be there to see the spectacle of the Winter Festival; reveal my loaded purse. Money to spend was enough of a reason to let a man be. Mind, it would not do to remain too long. This was ever Graynelore! There were sure to be tempted men, who might happily dispatch an outlander for little more than the price of the clothes upon his back and his copper coin . . .

In Wycken there were more buildings standing together in one confined space than I could possibly count – certainly, I had never seen its like – and not a single one was built of good stone or visibly defended. Rather, they were all loosely made wooden shacks, each one leaning heavily upon its neighbour for support; the wood blackened with an oil or a tar, it seems, against the creeping bog-moss, and always lifted up on short stilts to keep them clear of the ground. From every rooftop, fire-smoke drifted. At every wind-eye, light blazed. The taverns were full. There was the sound of raucous laughter and excited banter. And there were people out in the streets . . . there were crowds of people everywhere.

By simple fortune (good or bad) my arrival had coincided with the first day of winter. In Wycken-on-the-Mire this day was traditionally marked by the festival they called the Faerie Riding. All across the town, though it was morning still, people were on the move. Their celebrations had already begun. Every door stood open in welcome. Trailing processions, of men and women, of youths, old crones and babbies, were snaking their way steadily through the streets. This was a day of joy then, a time to frolic and make merry. There would be no serious work done: fields would go untended; animals would go unwatched. For some it was a holyday, for all it was a day of truce. It was a moment, an opportunity for the local graynes to play the fool together; bad blood and deadly feud temporarily forgotten.

Though, a caution, my friend . . . Remember it. This was not a *real* Faerie Riding. This was only the people of Wycken *pretending* . . .

I stood by and watched it all.

And if for the first time in a day my belly protested for the lack of vitals, I took a small coin from my poke and offered it to a street vender in return for his warm bread and hot meats. Aye, and was forced to share it too; with the greedy mouth of some prancing urchin who cheekily tore off a piece, openly laughed at the affront and, with a full mouth, skipped merrily on his way. I, a man who had used his sword for less, only laughed in my turn at the thief in the making. This was a strange day indeed.

Small bands of young boys chased after young girls who were dressed in faerie frocks. There were tall-ish men pretending to be gigants. There were short-ish men, carrying decorated wooden axes, pretending to be dwarves. Handsome women, dressed in flowing white garments, their hair braided with fake gold and silver thread, rode upon fell-horses dusted with white chalk – that they might appear like graceful white ponies – and they threw small coins to the frolicking crowds who followed at their horses' tails.

Already jovial drunkards lay by the wayside, lost in a stupor.

It was a day for false ears, fake wings, and faces stained bright blue or green or red.

Young women stood purposefully at street corners, singing sweet melancholic ballads that told of old histories. Ancient battles lost and won. Love and hate. And there were sad, tearful laments for wasted youth.

Young men drank beer, swaggered, and bragged to each other of their conquests; real or make-believe.

Here and there, in the light of open doorways, Beggar Bards held eager crowds in raptures of delight as they told their mythical tales: of the making of the world, of the death of wizards, and the grounding of the Faerie Isle.

The babbies laughed and skipped, and scattered handfuls of black soot – scraped from the insides of chimneys – upon the unwary throng, in the pretence that it was Faerie Dust.

Handmade rag flags, dyed bright blue and red with the juice of berries, hung from roof tops and from the branches of trees along the way. While long rag ribbons decorated the hair of both young men and women alike. Often trailing the ground in the way of a tail, or a lure, encouraging the boldest among them (depending on who it was they were trying to attract) to make a chase of it.

Every now and then, small bands of revellers would break away from the main processions and, dancing hand in hand, form a human chain: winding in and out among the trees and the bushes, the standing boulders and the tethered animals, the horses and carts; cheekily coaxing friends and foes alike to join in with them as they went.

'Oh, won't you come, dance? Oh, won't you come, dance and sing?'

'Oh, won't you lift your feet in time and join our Faerie Ring?' sang the prancing fools to the pretty young girls.

I stood and watched it all . . . and did not believe a moment of it.

'What is all this, eh? What is it?' I called out, trying to take a hold of a dancing pair as they passed me by. 'And where are you all going?'

What did these revellers reply?

'We are on a Faerie Riding! And we are making Faerie Rings, of course. Then we're off to raise the Faerie Isle!'

'Oh, of course!' I returned, with a shake of my head.

For a fancy, the young man I had hooked released himself and gave me an extravagant bow. The young girl with him took his lead and curtsied, lifting her skirts . . . too high. They laughed together, without shame, danced their ring around me and fled on.

I let them go, and looked again towards the seething crowds.

It seemed an open competition, for no two bands of revellers were moving in quite the same direction. Back and forth they danced and back again. This way and that way – at cross purposes. Some threaded their way towards the banks of the River Winding. (There is nowhere upon Graynelore where some part of its watery fingers have not stretched; great or small.) Others were seeking out the market square, or a particular outcrop of rock, or else a particular area of open green. Each human string, each family grayne was making its own way, regardless of the direction of the greater crowd, heading for its own favourite place of gathering where they could finish their dance, and complete their Faerie Rings.

Would I have joined the throng? Perhaps, upon another day, only I was more curious than I was enthralled by the unfolding events.

Wycken-on-the-Mire; here was the very place where the Faerie Isle was supposed to have floundered. Ha!

Well, there was not *one* Faerie isle here. No. I could see dozens of them, at least! No two quite alike and all of them make-believe. How so? The townspeople had built them for the purpose out of gathered windfall, dry grasses, broken wooden furniture and household rubbish. And they had set many of them upon make shift carts that they wheeled before them. I knew the children's tales; the Beggar Bards held that eight true faeries were needed to complete a Faerie Ring . . . a Ring of Eight. But not here! Not in Wycken-on-the-Mire, on the first day of winter. For certain, *every* faerie dancer among them held hands and joined in. Even as I watched, people began to set their wooden Isles alight, one after the other, raising huge bonfires. Roaring flames quickly reached up into the sky (scaring off the gathered crows). And the brave, or the foolhardy, or the drunks among them tried to keep the carts moving as they burned. The heat scorched their hair, the flames licked at their hands and faces, caught hold of their ribbons, set fire to their clothes. Until they were forced to let go and roll upon the ground to put the flames out before they were badly hurt. Abandoned, the burning carts ran to a standstill. Though more than one toppled over, spilling burning embers into the throng of people that surrounded it: and far too close to the wooden houses for safety.

The fires were symbolic of what the Beggar Bards called The Raising of the Faerie Isle. A time when the Faerie Isle would be restored to its rightful place upon the Great Sea, when all things faerie would return again into the world, to make it complete: as it had been on the very first day of its creation. Of course, that was just another foolish children's tale. It was a story to delight the babbies. More to the point, I think, the great bonfires kept the Wycken revellers warm on a cold winter's day.

All the while the fires burned the people danced and played. The market traders came and set out their stalls and bartered their wares. In a drunken haze, the local Headmen – who, no doubt, fashioned themselves Graynelords – held their private courts, renewed old alliances and resolved old differences. In hidden corners, beyond the firelight, star-crossed lovers kept their secret trysts.

As for Rogrig Wishard, I confess I was now at something of a loss. Standing among this sham, I felt like a ruddy fool at a fool's parade. Had I really made poor Dandy suffer so, for this? Had I gone against my grayne?

It was only then, through the fake trappings of the make-believe faeries, through the crowds of bawdy players, the dancers and the singers, against the light of the burning bonfires, I began to see them for real. Faeries that is:

Aye, Faerics . . .

Chapter Thirteen

Faeries

Faeries . . . My madness was complete. I felt myself lost within a living dream and I could not wake up from it. In that moment they appeared quite vivid and clear, while the people around them became the shadows and grew dim and grew vague. Intriguingly, none of them looked remotely like the dressed-up versions with their fake wings, their painted faces, and gaudy ribbons. What can I say? Faeries –The real thing looked a lot less spectacular (even to the eyes of an enamoured madman). And yet, somehow they were more real than reality, more normal, more ordinary even than the ordinary.

In truth, there were not that many of them. I could count them upon my fingers. I tried for six, gave up at five (it seems they would not stand still long enough to be counted). They were transient creatures. But believe me; they were there, all the same.

What was my proof of their pedigree? I did not have any – none that you would recognize, my friend. Nor did I need any. Let Beggar Bards do tricks, let wizards cast spells. Fey creatures are what they are. Does a wolf need to tear out the throat of a fell beast before you recognize a dangerous wild animal? Does a dog need to hear another dog bark before it recognizes its fellow?

What truly was become of Rogrig Wishard? It seems I had travelled so much further than the physical miles that separated Dingly Dell from Wycken-on-the-Mire. So much was gone behind. Fleetingly, I recalled the face of the dead girl upon the Elfwych killing fields; the look in Norda's eye when we were first met; the exchange that had left me a man no longer balanced. I saw again the silhouetted figure of a woman become a flight of birds. I heard the whispers of the unspoken voices, the shadow-tongues beseeching . . . that were certain to be calling to me still if only I would listen out for them.

Those faerie creatures, now before me, were no less flesh and blood than you or I, my friend.

Among them, there was an ancient grotesque . . . a crone. She held a long wooden pipe to her mouth that burned badly. Its intermittent flame singed her wiry grey hair. She blew draughts of smoke out through her nose. There was a young boy, or rather, a fat youth. There was a pair of young women, strikingly elegant, beautiful, who held each other's hands coquettishly, tossed their hair in the way of manes. And there was a black bird (of course there was) . . . a single black crow.

No matter where I looked within the crowds they seemed to be always there. Though, I swear to you, I never saw them move from one place to the next. There was an odd, worried-yet-startled look upon each of their faces.

The crone was suddenly in front of me, at nose length (and still blowing smoke). It was I who turned away, looked deeper into the throng; only to find her there again.

I first saw the fat youth sitting upon a fence, and then again, in between two frolicking babbies. He seemed far too heavily dressed. He was draped in reams of raw linen. He had a face like a half-cooked pudding and skin as soft as river clarts. While the crow kept flitting between the branches of trees and the gables of houses and gate posts. Oddly, I felt I knew it best of all.

And if I had suddenly noticed them, I was just as certain they were all aware of me. They were watching me, in an obvious rather clumsy way, I thought. There was no secret, no threat either. Rather, they looked at me longingly, as if they were expecting something from me, a response or an answer to an unasked question. Or was it simple recognition? Eh?

Now that I knew them to be there, there was no mistaking them. They were the image of each other. By that, I do not mean they looked alike. No. Indeed, they could not have looked less alike! Nor, if I am to be truthful, less like I ever imagined true faeries! Forgive the paradox. I fear there never were two quite physically the same. Rather, it was something else they shared between them. They all possessed it. There was an aura about them. There was an intense, a profound sense of self: a deep shared knowledge; an understanding that was greater than simple truth. It gave them stature, a distinct presence, whatever their physical size or form; whatever they looked like.

In essence then, plain and ordinary was their make-up, their disguise. It was part of their faerie Glamour; a mask to shield them from common men, no doubt. They were all of them in hiding, hiding in full view of the world. And yet I had found them out there. And they knew it. And they in their turn had found me out, it seems. Perhaps that had always been their intention . . . or mine?

They continued to move self-consciously among the crowds; never together, not as one, but always aware. It occurred to me, they were behaving shyly, almost as if they were as much strangers to each other as I was to them. I had been lured to Wycken-on-the-Mire, drawn there by an overwhelming desire I was still at a loss to explain. Was it the same for them? Was it? That same desire drew me towards them now, and so fervently, with such emotional force that the attraction – it was an attraction – physically hurt. It took my breath away. Even if I still refused to understand what it meant. Again, forgive your narrator's infuriating reticence.

I began to feel a desperate urge: I wanted to go to them, to be among them. Only I hesitated. I was still just this ordinary man; this Rogrig Wishard. And they were . . . they were real.

Left to me, the reluctant stand-off between us might have gone on forever unresolved.

Someone was suddenly at my side, asking questions of me.

'Sir, we are strangers, I think? And yet, do I not know you, my Lord?' The introduction, the flattery, was clumsy at best. My lowly rank was obvious enough. I was, after all, dressed in a crudely armoured peasant's jack, and no doubt smelled of mire and fields, fighting irons and . . . the stale blood of dead horses, and men.

'Er . . . no,' I answered lamely. Only then did I look towards my inquisitor.

I thought I had found my sixth faerie.

It was a young woman who stood there. She was looking at me in earnest, as if to put more weight into the meaning of her first words, and yet her face was flushed. She was obviously embarrassed by the pretence in her approach. That: or else she was simply unpractised at the common tongue.

'Yes, I do think I know you . . .' she said. Even as she spoke she took a deliberate step backwards, which left her standing in the shadows of a tree; as if, even now she was not quite ready to reveal herself fully to me. Around us, fires burned and the bright, childish processions of make-believe faeries continued to flow past.

I could see her clearly enough. She was tall and lithe, handsome rather than beautiful, and stood rather in the way of a man; without swagger but assured and capable. She was dressed completely in black – Everything about her was black. From her black pointed shoes, made of soft black leather, to her black skin-tight breeches that accentuated her bony hips and slightly bowed legs. Her woollen jerkin was black, with its sleeves pulled down over her hands and loose threads hanging wistfully from the ends (as if her fingers had deliberately unpicked them). Her face was flawed ebony. She had thin, slightly vague, black lips that were always wet. Long dark eyelashes, that hid her never more than half open black eyes. She left me with the same impression the other faeries had given me: she was trying to hide herself in full view of everyone. Everything was about hiding.

'Who . . . who are you?' I asked. I was being deliberately slow-witted. For I had no doubt now; it was she I had first encountered upon the mire. However improbable, this strange woman, this fey creature, had saved my life. I had seen no transformation, yet I knew if I was to look about me now to search out the crow I would not find it there.

'You do not recognize me yet?' she said. She spoke thoughtfully, with no hint of impatience. 'If you are in want of a name, I have two. Which one would you prefer? Indeed, which one would you believe? I am both Lucia

Hogspur and I am Lowly Crows . . . And you . . .?' She began a clumsy unpractised bow, when she found herself rudely interrupted.

'And you will be Rogrig Wishard, if I am not mistaken. And I never am.' This was a statement not a question. The stubborn old crone had reappeared and stepped between us.

'And how is it that *you* know my name?' I asked rudely, in my turn.

'Well, you look like Rogrig Wishard,' said the crone, dismissively. She took a deep suck on her pipe and blew out an extravagant plume of blue-grey smoke.

'Our Wily Cockatrice can, *see* . . . She *sees* . . .' said Lowly Crows, drawing out the repeated word, wincing slightly at the awkwardness of her explanation (and finishing her bow). 'She knows something of us all . . . Sometimes better than I would like, if I am truly honest.'

I saw the faint beginnings of a smile forming at the corner of her mouth, only for it to disappear.

'Now please. We must speak together,' she said, again in earnest. 'We are in need of your close confidence. It is important . . . but cannot be done here. I think you understand?'

There were still crowds of dancers in the street. There were drummers. There were pipers. People were singing nonsense songs. There was a juggler, drunken men reeling, and a throng of babbies dressed as impish faeries. There was nothing to stop me from simply moving in among them and walking away.

Only I was not certain I wanted to walk away. (I was not certain of anything.)

'So, what is it to be, are you coming with us or not?' The old crone, who Lowly Crows had called Wily Cockatrice, spoke abruptly, yet softly now. 'You must make up your own mind . . . One way or the other. Yes or no?' Her words were an inquiry not a threat, but the implication in her tone was clear enough. She was the ancient grotesque and I the battle-worn reiver. Yet it was I who had reason to be wary of her; not the other way around. A thin wisp of white smoke escaped her nose.

'Yes,' I said. 'Yes, I will come with you.'

Chapter Fourteen

Joining the Dance

Wily Cockatrice made us take a hold of each other's hands, as if we were to play some frivolous game, deliberately leading us into the throng of Wycken revellers. She snatched at a tail of fluttering ribbons hanging from the backside of a passing drunk, and began to dance a kind of reckless jig behind him. We could only follow after her and joined his reeling procession. It struck me, these were *real* faeries: among a masquerade. Real faeries: pretending to be pretend faeries. (Though, I did not regard myself among their number.) In fact it was all quite ridiculous. I tried to feign enthusiasm for the dance, but each foolish, prancing step we took was badly placed and ever mistimed. The crowds were actually laughing at our lame attempts. Among it all, my leather poke, complete with its oddly assorted contents, disappeared. It was swiftly lifted from my person by some clever unseen hand. And there were random insults, if spoken in jest and not badly meant.

'You'll need steadier legs old mother, and better masks, if you mean to fool the babbies with that display!' Someone called out to the ancient crone.

'Aye, right enough . . .!' added another. 'Or else you'll all be slapping your arses against the ground!'

Lowly Crows and Wily Cockatrice stoutly ignored the rebukes and put on brave faces – which meant them fixing rigid smiles, holding them stiffly in place. Mind, they kept up their unruly stride, unabashed. The fat youth, whose true name was Dogsbeard, only coughed and spluttered as if with some childish complaint. While the pair of coquettes took no mind of the insults at all. The reverse of it! They curtsied regally before our protagonists, and played up to the greater crowd.

'Should we dance for them my, Fortuna?' asked one of the other.

'Indubitably . . .! We should dance for them my Sunfast.' Together, they hitched up their skirts and, encouraged by a sudden spontaneous applause, flung their hair about in a furious abandon.

For perhaps another hundred clumsy steps the drunkard's cavorting procession snaked forwards, to the wild beating of drums. Then, on reaching a division in the street, the teetering line gave an awkward lurch and swung abruptly in that new direction, spilling several of its members, losing them to an oncoming crowd as they fell over, tumbling together. Wily Cockatrice saw her chance and, at the same moment, let go the drunken man ahead of her. She turned sharply aside, taking us off that street altogether, and down some crooked covered back lane (only there because the wooden hovels rested shoulder to shoulder at that point, leaving an irregular gap between them on the ground).

The procession had let us go without a fuss and once out of its sight our company quickly stopped their foolish dancing and fell into a, more or less, steady walk. The drop in pace allowed us all to catch our breath a little – and straighten our faces.

I remember coming out of the crooked back lane onto a narrow, but widening, cobbled courtyard – its stones broken and loose – badly kept and overgrown with weeds and mosses. A few thin, ailing willow trees grew up among them. There was a shallow pool of stagnant water. Further in there were greater ruins. Tumbled stone slabs, and the remains of stone arches; all neglected, long abandoned in earlier times, and strangled with creepers. There were no crowds here. No lighted fires. No cheer.

'Where are we going, Lowly Crows?' I asked, not impatiently. 'I mean . . . where does this all lead us?' I was feeling for the right question.

'You will know soon enough,' she said.

'I would know *now* . . .' I said, and stopped walking. It brought our company up short. Fortuna and Sunfast drew quickly aside from me, as if startled by my outburst. I had not meant to speak so sharply.

'What? Is this a tender trap then? Is that what you are thinking?' Wily Cockatrice, quite recovered from the dance it seemed, had turned upon me in an instant and was hissing. The ancient crone was not to be trifled with. 'Is our Lowly Crows the sweetmeats; a temptress to ensnare you?'

Beside her, Dogsbeard, the fat youth, sniggered into his hand. 'Is she luring you away from welcoming company, leading you into the unknown darkness?'

'No, I . . . I did not mean to . . .' I stumbled over my words.

'Understand this, Rogrig Wishard. What we are about is no trivial undertaking. Go back to the prancing parades if you would. Go and warm yourself by its fires. Get drunk; find yourself a whoring woman; plant your worried manhood where you think it safe, and forget us . . . It is all the same to me.'

'There is not far to go.'

Lowly Crows had stepped between us. Her black eyes shone coldly, unblinking. Her finger ends picked at the loose threads on the arm of her jerkin in the way of a bird preening. She might have been angry with me. She was certainly ruffled and looked anxiously towards the crone.

'Pah! Speak again with this cautious man, if you would,' said Wily Cockatrice. 'Tell him a little of what you can. He tries my patience too far.' She passed a meaningful look between us and withdrew to find herself a temporary seat among the fallen stones. 'Just be quick about it. We will wait here but a short while.' Her pipe was instantly between her lips. A great plume of black smoke rose up to engulf her.

Only a tempered sigh from Lowly Crows broke a prolonged silence.

It was I who spoke first, if in thin whispers. 'Give me a sword. I can tell you what to do with that. But this, this vagary – where are the answers here?'

'We all desire answers, Rogrig,' said Lowly Crows, her black eyes still shining. 'Only we pussyfoot . . . and dare not put a name to our dilemma, though we all understand it well enough, I fear.'

'Not I!' I said; again I spoke more sharply than I had intended.

'No?' She looked at me balefully. Then, considered a moment. 'And there are others.'

'Others?'

'Others, who are the same as us . . . *Like* us. Just like us,' she said. 'They are close by.'

'How so?' I said.

'You are a stubborn man, Rogrig Wishard. You will not easily let yourself see what your own eyes are showing you.

You will not allow yourself to believe what you know in your heart is true.'

If she wanted a stubborn man, I would show her one. 'And do you pretend to know me so very well, then: though we are hardly met at all?'

'Who is pretending now? I know myself and I know my own kindred,' she said. 'I have followed after you for long enough. Be honest with yourself. We are not so very different.'

'No?'

'No . . .' she hesitated. Her look was become close to anger. Though she was inwardly annoyed; as if she was uncomfortable with what she was about to say, and I was solely to blame for it; had given her no choice but to reveal herself and offer up her private testimony.

'As a young child, when Lowly Crows was Lucia Hogspur, I always loved to dress up as a faerie. What little girl does not?' She let her voice drift lightly with her words, although there was something in her tone that hinted at disguise . . . or perhaps, regret. 'On the first day of winter I always wore my faerie gown – homemade from rags and tatters – just like my mother before me. I braided my hair with bright ribbons and dressed it with wild flowers. I loved the processions and the storytelling, the singing and the dancing, making Faerie Rings; burning the great bonfires in the pretence of raising the Faerie Isle . . .' She paused, with a sigh. Then she took a short breath as if to steel herself, before continuing.

'But a childhood soon ends. We must all stop believing in faerie tales and grow up. Or at least, that is the way it is supposed to be. Only, not for me; for Lucia Hogspur it was very different. I stopped believing in childish things when I discovered, to my horror . . . they are real. I saw them – faeries – if only glimpses at first. Tantalising glimpses . . . Fleeting moments when I recognized them for what they were. I saw through the Glamour that hid their true selves. It was like seeing a mask slip out of place, watching it hurriedly readjusted.

'Worse, I came to realize . . . this gifted sight was mine alone. Among my whole family it was only I who possessed it. In all honesty, what innocent child can carry such a weight? And why me—? Why did I see them when no one else did? Not even Martha, my dearest cousin. No one! That would have made what I knew to be true, bearable . . . acceptable even. But no . . . what I had seen had only been revealed to me.

'In the end, it was the wind brought about the revelation . . .' Lowly Crows paused again, looked at me to gain my reaction to this seemingly odd statement. When I gave none, she continued. 'When I was still quite small, the wind began to carry voices to me – the voices of the birds, that is. It carried their whispered secrets all the way to my ear. And I, without reason, fully understood their meaning.

'Upon a day, I was out walking with my mother and my cousin. The voices of the birds came to me upon the wind and quietly warned me of a change in the weather: rain was coming (though there was not yet a cloud in the sky). It was such a simple thing, especially to a child. I thought nothing of it and so I told my mother what I had heard. Surely everyone could hear the voices of the birds in the wind? It did not make a changeling of me, did it? My mother and my cousin did not want to get caught out in a rainstorm, did they? Moments later the rain began to fall in earnest . . .'

There was another marked silence before she would continue.

'I was beaten with a stick for it. I was beaten until my bones were bruised, and the welts upon my skin bled freely. But worse, much worse than this; I was cursed by my own father for the shame of it. Sworn to keep it a secret, threatened with a cut tongue.' Her face became suddenly tight, as if with pain. 'In my dreadful loneliness, in my despair, it was not long before I looked again towards the kindly birds. And, as is the way of faerie, thought I saw my own true nature, my own true kindred there . . .'

Her eyes stared through me to some far distant place only she could see.

'Is not this Winter Festival a perfect irony, Rogrig? And how it hurts—' Her voice began to lift with anger. 'Once a year it is quite the thing for everyone to dress up in their ridiculous outfits and play at make-believe. They can pretend and paint their faces and put on their paper wings and fly. It is considered . . . *normal*. Just do not dare say any of it is true. Do not ever say that, whatever your belief. If you do they will only come for you; take you away in the dead of the night. They will hang you for a changeling, a throwback. They will burn you for a wych! They will burn your family too if they have a mind!' She was glaring at me now, eye to eye.

I was at a loss. I wanted to say something that might help her, only I could not find the words for it. I held her gaze. It was the best I could do.

'It is better to stay silent,' she said. 'What the world at large does not know does not exist. Was it not ever so? Like the true faerie, it is best to hide your reality behind a shaded mask.'

At this, she ended, turning her eyes away. I was still at something of a loss. Uncertain of what I believed? Or uncertain of what I *wanted* to believe?

'And this is your tale?' I tried to speak kindly.

'Enough of it for now . . . At least, to see me hung upon a gibbet if it reaches the wrong ears . . .'

'Ah, yes,' I nodded my understanding. 'And enough to calm the suspicions of a foolish man?'

'Aye, that too, perhaps . . .' she said.

Almost unnoticed between us, we had begun to walk again. We had caught up with Dogsbeard, and with Wily Cockatrice, who was already on her feet, and with the pair of coquettes who kept a-pace, if still cautiously shy of me. And then, for the very first time, we were all of us talking quite freely, and without embarrassment.

'You know, I thought they were all just stories,' I said. 'Make-believe. Faerie tales! I did not think any of it was real. Well, why would I?'

'Indeed, why would you, Rogrig?' said Wily Cockatrice, without humour.

'We can spend our whole lives alone – so very many of us have – without knowing the truth,' said Lowly Crows. 'I worked it out . . . though it took me long enough. The fey . . . they can feel each other's presence. How else might I describe it? On our own we are incomplete, are nothing, in fact; less than nothing, perhaps, when we cannot know our true selves. But once together . . . when like-minds meet, that is something else. Faerie-kind need their kin. It stirs something within them, rekindles a dormant state. It makes them stronger. More, it breathes new life into a hollow shell. Of course, you know of this already . . .'

'Eh?' I turned my head away, found myself unnecessarily distracted by some flying insect that was suddenly a bother to me.

'I hear their inner voices . . .' she continued. 'It is like a distant echo, like a song being sung; only the words are faint and the language is indistinct. Anyway, the point of it is this: there is more than one voice calling, more than one song. And I know you can hear it too. Surely you must? It gets stronger even now . . .'

'What are you suggesting, then?' I said. 'Are we all to go and live in Faerie-land? Are we to speak to the wild animals and eat flowers for our breakfast?' I was being deliberately flippant now, trying in desperation to remain the ignorant, common man. 'We are not going to pretend to be trees, are we? I positively refuse to go and live in a lake . . .'

I stopped there. It was only now, distracted by the ludicrous tone I had allowed into our conversation, that I realized where Lowly Crows was leading us.

We had reached another area of broken stonework. It was as much overgrown and loosely scattered by time as the first, but here and there were the partial remains of walls still standing at the full height of a stout man, and perhaps four or five full paces in length. In almost a thousand years, no builder upon Wycken had used stone to make his dwelling houses. These were far more ancient ruins, then. At their centre was a group of even larger stones – some hand-cut, some natural boulders – leaning heavily against each other, as if they had been set there on purpose to mark an event. Either that, or to disguise a secret opening in the ground . . .? Certainly, there was something of that kind there.

I had a sudden fancy; the opening I could see was obviously the entrance to an underworld, perhaps a circuit of tunnels that would lead us on to the Faerie Isle, or to a dwarven hole, at the least.

(It was neither.)

Without hesitation or debate, one after the other, my entire company stepped through the opening. How could I, the only grown man among them, not follow their lead?

Chapter Fifteen

The Secret Meet

We stepped into what I sensed was a cavernous chamber, though one completely taken up with the dark (and unnaturally so). Outside, a veil of heavy cloud had begun to creep upon the town. At best it would make for a poor grey evening. Nevertheless the remnants of the daylight should have seeped into that greater space. It did not. It stopped at its entrance, as if deliberately shut out. The darkness was a solid curtain, or else the mark of a closed door. This was a private place; an otherworld where even the fading light of day had no business without a firm invitation.

The cavern remained always just a cavern, only I had no sooner stepped across its threshold and into that utter darkness than it began to change – not avert, but transform; the stuff of faerie. What happened was this: all at once I could see a way through the darkness. Not in the way of my eyes becoming used to it. This was altogether different, if immediate. Without the use of my eyes, I was *allowed* knowledge of that dark space. An enchantment was lifted or the gift of blind-sight was bestowed upon me. Either way, I was made aware not only of its extent but also of the nature of the welcome that awaited me there.

This enlightenment did not make me any the braver, nor did I feel better for it. Rather, it reminded me of how little control I had over this foolish adventure. Since the very outset I was never the guide, but always the guided; a beguiled man, blinded by my own ignorance and left groping in the dark – like a weedling babbie – until I was shown the way. I did not like it. Nor did I yet truly believe in it.

Does your narrator's continued nagging doubt exasperate you, my friend? Would you have me eagerly embrace this shadow-land? Is the knowledge of a lifetime so easily dispelled by the passing of a few hours among a company of strangers? I say not! I had heard Lowly Crow's impassioned testimonies. I was *trying* to come to terms with these bloody fey creatures! Only theirs was the miraculous transformation, not mine. Do not expect it so easily of me! Rogrig Wishard was always the man first, and ever so!

I was become wary. My inbred instincts were beginning to reclaim me. Should I have followed Lowly Crows? I had the sense of there being numerous figures in that cavern – certainly more than I knew – standing or sitting about in the darkness. I was aware of their presence. And if I could not see them naturally, I could hear them. Their breathing . . . A fidget was scratching. There was the sound of movement, as someone shifted their body weight from one foot to the other. And there was a bird – no, more than one – birds now! I could hear the slight raking of their claws, as they moved about upon some rocky perch; hear the gentle pecking of a grooming beak.

And the air was filled with a mixture of common smells . . . the sweet odour of a woman's sweat . . . old clothes, too long unwashed . . . rusted iron (was someone holding a sword?) Cold stone . . . cold, cold stone . . . anxiety . . . even fear? There was the leather of worn boots . . . rotting wood and damp . . . It was a dank cave, its floors, no doubt, constantly awash . . .

It was not a sweet hole, then.

We had all been drawn to this place separately and yet together. (And now inseparable, it would seem.) For me, it had begun with the Elfwych, with a severed head, and Norda . . . that was the first connection . . . I had felt it again when I met with Lowly Crows upon the mire. Even now, as I stood there in the dark, that mystic bond between our gathered company was growing ever stronger. If I was still fighting hard to deny it! After all, this was just the sort of careless mess my whole life's training had taught me to avoid. Had I really allowed myself to be lured here? Was this not simply a robber's ambush after all? It bore all the marks.

'Did your father never warn you? You must not follow strange young women into dark enclosed spaces.' This first voice was mocking – a faerie slight? It was as if its owner had plucked my thoughts out of my head and thrown them carelessly back at me. But there was a caution there too. And with the voice there was suddenly extra light in the cavern: again, no common thing, not light to be seen with the eye; but ethereal light without a natural source. Almost as if it had been spoken into being; was a part of the words. Though, not yet enough light to reveal the protagonist, only enough to ease the darkness a little.

Other voices began to join in.

'Maybe this man is an idiot?'

'Maybe he is a great warrior, come to show off his sword!'

'Well, you know what they say about Wycken girls, especially upon the Winter Festival. Maybe he thinks our Lowly

Crows is up for it? And him only a poor innocent lecher led astray?'

'Maybe you have got the guts to show your faces?' I said. Though I knew myself bated, I could feel my anger rising above my trepidation. 'So I can knock your teeth down your throat—! Lowly Crows, where are you?'

I heard the flapping of a bird's wings.

'Patience, Rogrig, and rest easy, I am here. My companions only jest. They are making fun of you.' With the sound of her voice, yet more of that ethereal light filled the cavern, enough now to expose something of the figures standing there. Wily Cockatrice and the youth, Dogsbeard, were clear to see. Though there were others still only a vague mass, perhaps keeping deliberately to the shade? I supposed that was where I might find the pair of coquettes . . .

There was a short ripple of not so innocent laughter. Could they *all* read my mind? Or maybe, if they were among the shadow-tongues inside my head, was my voice but a shadow-tongue inside theirs?

'Enough of this foolishness! We are each of us come to this place in good faith. Let us get down to our business here,' demanded Wily Cockatrice.

As she spoke, I felt the mood of the whole company change. The laughter, the mocking jollity, was suddenly gone. The very air was thick with concern. 'Is this gathering complete? Are we enough for our common purpose, at last? We have waited long enough for it. Can it be done?'

'Business? What common purpose?' I asked.

'Oh my . . . Tell me he knew. Lowly Crows, tell me he knows why he is here?' Wily Cockatrice rolled her tongue, gave a deliberate rattling hiss. If her pipe had been in her mouth there would have been smoke billowing.

'Aye, and be mindful, crow – There are many among us now, whose prowess is so diminished, so diluted by the passage of time, they can do no more than bear this company witness.' An elder-man had stepped out of the shade to speak. He was stooped with age, but was also crooked and wiry, in the way of a tree as it naturally grows. 'Yet they came to us all the same. All the same!'

'There was little enough time . . . I—' the crow began to explain, only to be crossed by the elder-man.

'It was dangerous enough for each of us on our own,' he said, his annoyance rising. 'Aye and ever so! Meeting together . . . in a company of strangers . . . was a greater folly.'

'What sense, Wood-shanks? How else were we to do this? None of us are powerful enough on our own,' said Lowly Crows, matter-of-factly. 'We must complete our Ring. Only then—'

'*Our* Ring?' I interrupted their growing argument. 'What? . . . Are you trying to say this is a Faerie Ring? This is another bloody meeting of a Faerie Ring upon the Winter Festival?' I let my hand rest heavily upon the hilt of my sword (if only for its comfort).

'This is not a game we are playing, Rogrig,' said Wily Cockatrice. 'We are not here to dance around a bonfire! Unless, of course, you know better; then you can tell me—'

'You still jest, I think . . .' I said. 'You are after the makings of a Ring of Eight? Is that it? You are putting on a show! . . . And then what? Do not tell me! Let me guess the end of your riddle. You are going to raise the Faerie Isle and restore the world to its former glory . . .' I could not disguise my contempt, nor stop the deep sigh rising in my throat. 'I know this story well enough. Upon Graynelore, what three year old babbie does not? For fuck's sake! It is a Beggar Bard's tale. It is a ridiculous fiction.'

The strength of a growing anger – not all of it mine – seemed to resonate physically in that dark hole. Inside my head the shadow-tongues were groaning with despair.

Several *real* voices began to speak together. 'How long have we waited, how many lives . . . eh? Wasted . . . unknown . . . forgotten . . . unlived . . . How many fruitless generations has it taken us to find each other out? Just to hear this fool of a man insult us?' There was a sense of frustrated, agitated movement among the shade, if I could not place its whereabouts.

'Too many and too long, no doubt . . .' replied Wily Cockatrice. 'Only, be at peace with this, Wishard . . . This place is protected yet, I think. For certain, no *ordinary* man can pass within its boundaries. The darkness will not open to them. They do not see us hidden here . . . soon lose themselves within the cavern's deepest chambers.'

Though the ancient crone was speaking in my defence the implication of her words only fed my growing anger. 'Pah! You mean you leave good men and true to wander in the dark here. Until in utter despair and certain madness, they expire! Is that it—? And why? To keep, yourselves *secret* . . .?'

'In truth? This was not of our doing, Rogrig,' said Wily Cockatrice, momentarily contrite. 'It is a safe haven stumbled across, not made. There is an ancient spell at work here. Not so subtly crafted, perhaps, but far beyond any of our skills. And it works. It has served its purpose, these many years.'

'Though I fear not for much longer, if this common man has found his way among us,' said Wood-shanks. The elderman drew back into the shade as he spoke.

'Oh, I am certain this is no common man,' replied the ancient crone. 'Rogrig Wishard belongs here with us. He just does not want to admit it.'

'I am not so sure. Perhaps he is only a lost fool after all, or a broken man? Worse . . . is a bloody spy, for some arrogant, petty Headman.'

'I am no spy!' I said, turning myself about, trying to find my accuser in the shade.

'There is a way to prove it . . .' said Wily Cockatrice, quietly. The weight of her comment was a far heavier burden than it might have appeared; for there was a long moment of uneasy, thoughtful silence.

'What . . . you mean, you show me yours and I will show you mine?' For the first time the fat youth had openly spoken. His voice was thin and bright and unbroken. His words sounded in jest.

'How childish of you . . . Oh, but forgive me, I forget, Dogsbeard, you are a child still, are you not?'

'Aye . . . I am a child still and childish with it, no doubt, but I am also right, I think!'

'And still conceited with it too, I see. However, I agree with you,' said Wily Cockatrice. 'If a greater proof of our worth is required, it is time for our gathered company to fully reveal itself; each to the other. We are, all of us, well aware of our Lowly Crows, who long since threw off her mantle . . .' At the mention of her name the crow, shifted upon her perch. There was just light enough around her form to reveal the movement. She turned her head aside and pecked self-consciously at her ruffled feathers. 'Now is the moment for us to match her candour.'

'But my, Wily Cockatrice . . . Such a revelation is a dangerous thing!' There was more than one voice of dissent come out of the shade. 'Aye, if knowledge of our true worth were ever to be openly revealed to a greater world we would, all, be risking our lives upon it.'

'Do not worry yourselves so,' said Lowly Crows. 'If this Rogrig Wishard proves himself, false, after all . . . we can always kill him.' There was no hint of humour, no faerie slight.

If my hand stiffened about the hilt of my sword, I chose to remain silent.

'Then let us not waste any more breath upon words,' said Wily Cockatrice. 'If we cannot put our faith in ourselves, who are we to trust?'

It seemed the decision was made.

There was an immediate change to the darkness. There was neither more nor less ethereal light, only a difference within it. At several points the darkness resolved itself into another nature. Put more simply, I might have said that together the figures in the shade let go their faerie Glamour and revealed themselves (which is the truth). Only – sometimes neither words, nor even the truth are quite enough.

Lowly Crows aside, where before I presumed the darkness was hiding only an oddly assortment of grown men and women, a grotesque crone and a conceited youth, the vision before me had inextricably altered.

(Forgive me my friend, I will hesitate here, for fear of you not believing this revelation so simply put.)

There was now . . . a pair of unifauns . . . an elf . . . a dryad . . . and, most spectacular of all, a dragon. Aye and other fey creatures too, besides, if less well defined . . .

To speak their names is to see them all.

Surely, if ever you had an imagination, my friend, you know them well enough – if only from some childish dream. Yet, to stand before them in reality is not to be compared. What I saw of them was perhaps only a glimpse against the changing feral light of that cavern, but what I did see, and remember still, is most vivid. The flesh and the bone of them; the fur and the cloven hooves; the pointed drawn teeth and the scales: with all the weight and stature of true wild beasts (and yet not wild beasts at all, but each of them a greater breed apart).

The single-horned unifauns, Sunfast and Fortuna, stood together, instinctively a pair; their every slight movement made in perfect unison. Fine boned and elegant, a mirror of their human selves, they stood fully naked but for their braided goat's hair.

In the fey light of the cavern the green skin of the elf appeared grossly rough and gnarled, yet his eyes remained childishly young. While the dryad was less manly wood-nymph than a stout living tree. And Wily Cockatrice was the image of her namesake; standing four-square upon the ground, an ever coiling tail endlessly wrapping itself around and about her.

'You . . . are truly . . . a . . . a, dragon, then?' I said, clutching for the words.

'Oh, do not look so innocently shocked!' A slight trail of smoke drifted from her elongated snout as she spoke. 'We are all of us the same here. Whoever we are, whatever we are. The very same! We all seek the same answers . . . And technically, I am a wyrm, Rogrig, not a dragon. I do not fly.' She slowly turned the great mass of her body, exposed the scales upon her wingless back.

'More to the point, we now see you, as you were intended, Rogrig Wishard,' said Lowly Crows. 'Now that you have removed your veil and taken off your disguise . . .'

'But . . . but I was not wearing a disguise,' I said, truthfully enough. 'I cannot . . . I am not . . . I have never—'

There was renewed laughter.

'Rogrig, we were all of us wearing a disguise . . . some of us more than one, I think,' said Lowly Crows.

'She means your Glamour,' added Wily Cockatrice. 'See, you have let it fall.'

I was confused. I was not mindful of having done anything at all. In front of me were these astounding, most wondrous of creatures, and yet it was they who were staring at me! I tried to take a look at myself, though there was no mirrored pool to reveal a change. There was nothing unusual about me that I could see.

'But I am what I am . . . It is just . . . just, I, Rogrig . . . Nothing more, nothing else . . .'

'Of course it is just you. It always was *just* you.'

Did I feel any different? No. Was I more powerful or stronger for this supposed feral transformation? No. I can tell you only this – and for want of a much better explanation – in that moment, whatever I had become, I knew myself a man complete; no longer a blundering lost fool standing with his feet in two places. (Take it or leave it, my friend.)

When the very last disguising veil of Glamour fell away, I swear, I heard a sharp intake of breath, a mark of awe perhaps, come out of the shade.

It did not last.

There was to be a most dreadful end to this uncommon event.

For then, I felt the pain of it. Come suddenly and unrelenting. All consuming and absolute . . . Alike a crushing death blow, yet nothing so mundane. It took away all hope from the world. It left only despair.

I fell into an utter darkness.

Life stopped. The very earth collapsed upon itself. And there was nothing more to it.

Nothing at all . . .

Part Four

The Faerie Riding

Chapter Sixteen

The Changelings

I woke with a start, out of the depths of a night-torment, only to find myself caught within another; and the worst of foul dreams.

Windblown grass was tickling my face. I could smell the cold earth. I could hear the movement of trees, the creaking of their branches, and the discordant chatter of distant birdsong. There was no daylight as yet, nothing to see . . . an uncertain pattern of shapeless shadows. I think someone was talking, if indistinctly.

I tried to sit up, only my arms – suddenly too feeble – would not support me; and my body was too heavy, and too numb, to move of its own accord. I remembered my infancy, and a broken iron war sword I had not the body strength to more than drag across a cold stone floor.

A sudden stab of uncommon pain racked my head. I fell once more into utter darkness where, in my torment, a cruelly smiling sun rose quickly across a pitch-black sky only to set again. Still smiling . . .

When next my eyes opened it was into a kind of sullen, grey daylight.

A huddle of people sat over me. I was certain I had known them once. Among them there was a fat youth, and an ancient grotesque. Only what they had been before – something magnificent – was no more than a vague allusion, much less a memory. I have seen death on the faces of men. I have never seen living faces so drained of life and yet still living. If these were not ghosts, mere apparitions, then they should have been. They were a pitiful remnant, and failing still, I feared, by the moment.

There came again the lull of discordant birdsong.

I spoke a name I seemed to have upon my tongue. 'Lowly Crows, is it you? Tell me, what has become of us?'

The crow was sitting in a tree close by, I think among a number of her kin. As I spoke, the birds stopped their chatter and fell silent.

Then Lowly Crows answered me. She spoke for what seemed a long time, and without interruption, trying to explain, never quite explaining. Her speech was soothing and yet without real worth. Only words washing over me, over us. The best of it was this:

' . . . The enchantment has broken . . . Our ancient refuge has fallen . . . is done with. We thought together we might be strong enough . . . Only, it was all too much . . . too much and the magic too old and feeble . . .'

In all my life I have never felt so weary. I thought perhaps it was the time for all of us to die. Can you die inside a dream?

Only we did not die, not then; at least, not those of us who had managed to come this far . . . who were a party to this torment.

I had thought I was the ignorant one, the foolish infant among the ever knowing adults. The lone simpleton who, stumbled about trying to make patterns in the dark, could make no sense out of a disturbing world.

Not so, it seems. I was not alone. Whatever the so-called fey talent of my present company, it had been come upon by accident: trial and error. It was not certain knowledge but simple good fortune. We were *all* of us the same here. All fools. And my waking dream was not a dream at all.

What a sorry looking company we were. I let my eyes pass discretely across each of them in turn. The ancient crone, who was nothing more than that . . . she had taken to pacing in small circles, in an agitated, distracted fashion; her dry pipe, passed endlessly between her hand and her mouth. The fat, irritating youth, his skin so pale it was stark white, and his eyes distant, withdrawn into himself. The pair of coquettes . . . mock now . . . their beauty sorely withered. There too, a failing elder-man (I hardly recognized). He was tousle-haired, tall but bent in the extreme; stiff of limb. And the flock of birds . . . rather, a bloody murder of crows! Just birds then, among a handful of ailing and decrepit men – neither gods nor graces, nor fabulous beasts! Though it was not their general form, it was not their physical age, or even their weariness that most concerned me. Rather, they all looked diminished, and fragile, as if much of what they had been had fallen away and was lost.

Was I the same? Was I . . .?

And what had become of *all* the others? The lesser creatures, who had meant only to witness the making of the Ring of Eight, not become its victims . . .? And the owners of the shadow-voices I had argued with . . .? Certainly, there had been more full-bodied fey within that fated cavern than stood among our company now.

Their absence told its own tragic tale.

Not for the last time I wondered what I, Rogrig Stone Heart, was doing among this strangest of companies. Was I truly for turning home then, towards Dingly Dell? Eh? After all that had been revealed? My friend, if I had so lately found myself a man complete, I was, yet again, a man sorely divided! Neither one thing nor the other! I see it now. It was that very division that kept me there.

We had begun to take a walk. Wily Cockatrice had started it, giving herself a reason for her agitated pacing. She did not lead us. We were wandering, an aimless huddle, simply moving together. Why? I could see little reason in this . . . this Faerie Road? I only supposed it kept us together; temporarily gave us a common purpose, without further invention. It was only much later I came to understand that such a thing is quite second nature to fey creatures; they prefer the ordeal of an endless road when there is no safe haven to be found.

We were already a mile or so outside of Wycken. We had found our way to the banks of the River Winding – if it was little more than the width of a broad stream at that point – and were following its course south and east, towards the Great Sea. In this way we stayed safely off the mire and walked away from the town. We had had our fill of winter festivals and false mockeries.

What we had hardly begun in that cavern – what we had attempted – should have been our deliverance. Instead it had almost proved to be our end.

Who were we really, if not merely ourselves? A man might know his own story. But no man can know everything. Do not expect anything different of me. I thought I had seen dragons, and wild unifauns, dryads, and elves . . . *I thought.*

There was nothing majestic about any of us now.

The ground beneath our feet was loose and dry, even close to the water's edge; as we walked our steps were lifting dust that marked our passage, revealing our position to any curious eye that cared to take a look. It was then I noticed an extra trail of dust rising not far behind our own trail. It might have disturbed me, if I had not soon recognized Edbur-the-Widdle. The sight of his familiar figure even raised a smile. The whelp had not been lost upon the mire after all. He had come after me, found me out again; become my shadow. Only now there were two hobbs in his party. He was riding one, and leading the other. The audacity of the youth! There was *my* Dandy, and the beast was not best pleased with the constant restraint or the careless handling.

I wondered then . . . was Edbur holding her *for* me, or *from* me. What better lure to keep me constantly constrained? He knew that, given the opportunity, I would endeavour to take her back. I would not be long parted from my hobb.

I wondered again . . . was it perhaps the time to slit a young man's throat? (Old instincts die hard, my friend.) Remember, a dead enemy is as good as any friend. I decided to trust in what I could see. The youth was riding in full view, making no attempt to hide himself from our company. I would rather think him an extra pair of eyes for Wolfrid, his father, than an assassin; better a constant sentinel and a reminder of my fealty than a threat. How much he understood, how much he gathered from what he could see of us, was unclear. Though I suspected – and hoped – it was little enough.

When we reached the edge of the Great Sea there was no further to go. Reason enough to stop walking.

I took myself aside to empty my bladder; and to watch a distant Edbur upon a lowly cliff top, leading the hobbs to pasture, until he passed from my view. When I returned to my company they were, all of them, sitting upon the sand, among the washed-up driftwood near the tide line; each one gazing out upon the endless waters of the Great Sea. If they were looking for answers there, evidence of a Faerie Isle, I could see none.

Did they really suppose it had ever been there? Had been . . . would be . . . could be . . . was . . .? The Faerie Realm, fixed for all time upon one single piece of earth. An island that, to escape the eyes of men, kept always on the move and ever out of sight. What can never be seen is so very easily invented.

And yet, perhaps our aimless walk had had more purpose to it after all.

'What happened?' I am not certain who asked the question, it had surely been on all of our lips, and for a long while. It was Wily Cockatrice who made an answer.

'Do you think any of us truly know any more than any other?' she asked. She was still looking out upon the Great Sea. The sunlight glistered upon the moving waters. There was no sign of a ship, no Isle, no timeless otherworld.

'I hope so . . .' I said.

The crone laughed dryly, shook her head. She spat upon the sand to clear her throat. Fetched out her wooden pipe and relit it, was soon puffing smoke contentedly. Aye and she looked the better for it.

'Do not let my stubborn manner or my great age deceive you, Rogrig Wishard. I may have lived far longer than you . . . and you might think I fit the part, only . . . I fear I have merely played at the role.' She pointedly tapped the end of her pipe against her own head. 'There is nothing more in here. I am, sadly, none the wiser for it.'

It was my turn to laugh. 'But I thought . . .'

'I see the things I see!' she said. 'Sometimes uncannily perhaps, but that is all of it; and little enough. There is nothing more substantial to me.'

'Excepting, a wyrm, perhaps?' I offered.

Wily Cockatrice gave no indication that she had even heard the remark. She merely continued to puff upon her pipe.

I tried a different question. 'And what of the cavern?'

'Sithien . . .' said Lowly Crows, suddenly become the dark woman before me, and not the crow. She at least, among us, retained some of her former prowess.

'Eh?'

'It is Sithien . . .' she repeated, 'or rather, it was. A place of faerie . . . The remains of something from another age . . . And truly rare beyond easy measure . . .'

'Magic, then . . .?' I shrugged.

'The last worn threads of an ancient spell . . .' Wily Cockatrice interrupted, rubbing her thumbs against her fingers, as if she had somehow taken it up between them. 'It was enough for us to find it out. Indeed, to hide behind, to shield us from prying eyes while we gathered together and prepared ourselves . . .'

'Though not enough to protect us from ourselves it would seem,' I said.

'I am so sorry, Rogrig Wishard,' she said. 'I . . . apologize. We were conceited, and arrogant. We thought we understood the task. We thought we had the measure of its making.'

'And foolish . . .' I said.

'Aye and that . . . We possess only our Glamour (which we must not underestimate). It is a strong enchantment. We have been using it to disguise our true selves all our lives. We are good at disguise. Hiding is what we do best. Some of us did not even know we were doing it, eh, Rogrig? But to finally let it fall, and to attempt to release our *other* selves was . . . too much, too difficult to command. The threads of the old spell might have born its weight in our stead. Only, it too was no longer strong enough – nor was it meant for it – came undone. It is simple good fortune so many of us survive yet.'

She drew slowly on her pipe. Let the trails of smoke find their own way out again, through her nose and part open mouth. It lingered in her wiry hair.

'We are all of us like children; innocent babbies! But it is ignorance, not stupidity. We have listened to the old stories of the Beggar Bards for too long, and been taken in by them . . .'

I nodded my tacit agreement.

I thought I was beginning to understand what all of this meant. Whatever our . . . talents, we could not simply use them just because we believed we possessed them. There had been no true fey creatures upon Graynelore for a thousand years. None that, upon discovery, had not quickly found itself stretched upon the gibbet, or drowned within a murder hole, or burned. Truly, we did not know what we were about. What knowledge we had was self-possessed; and of our own invention. There was no wise old wych among us, nor any wizard to teach us. There was no book of practical magic, no rules to read, no instant knowledge or instruction. Only faerie tales, meant for the babbies.

'Aye . . . We might all carry the blood of our ancestors within us; some of us might even wear their names,' I said. 'But tell me this, upon Graynelore: of all the men named Smith, how few could we trust to hammer us out a good iron war sword, eh?' I did not expect an answer – talked on. 'Only, there is more to this. *Something* has brought us together. A handful of days ago I was a common fighting man and nothing more. I was a reiver. I do not flatter myself. I always knew exactly who I was, and what I was. And I was certain of it. But now, now I do not seem to know anything at all, excepting . . . I did not choose to do this! (Nor, truly, do I want it yet!)'

'Did any of us choose?' said Wily Cockatrice brashly. 'Indeed, was there really a choice?'

'Can you choose to be your true self?' added Lowly Crows. 'Can we avoid it when it is revealed to us?'

'We could have ignored it, and lived out our lives,' I said, stubbornly.

'Oh yes, we could have done that. We could have kept our little secrets to ourselves. Stayed hidden; dutiful and loyal subjects to our beloved Headmen . . . Lived a lie, and the world none the wiser for it,' said Wily Cockatrice. 'Damn it, Rogrig. Ignoring the truth does not make it any less real. We have to believe; and act upon our belief.'

'Do you then?' I asked, pointedly. 'Do you still believe?'

At this, all eyes there, even among the silent onlookers, turned, if not accusingly, then certainly, inquisitively, upon the ancient crone.

'If we cannot be true to ourselves, what is the point of life?' Her eyes were fixed upon mine. 'Only . . . Do you know something? I am not quite so certain that I do believe any more. But I still *want* to believe . . . Is that enough for you?'

'If it is all that can be offered . . . It will have to do,' said Lowly Crows.

'So, what now?' I asked.

'Now . . .? We must finish the task we have so badly begun. First, there is a Ring of Eight to complete. Only, look about, the strength of our number remains one short—'

'What do you, *see* . . .?' asked Lowly Crows of the ancient crone. 'Is there another?'

'I *see*, what Rogrig, here, has already seen.' said Wily Cockatrice.

'Me? How so—?'

'There *is* another at hand. If only she could find her way to us.'

'She . . .?'

'Her name is Norda Elfwych, is it not?'

I started at the name.

'And she is aware?' asked Lowly Crows. 'She *knows* herself?'

'As well as I know you, my sweet bird . . .' Wily Cockatrice was blowing smoke again.

'And Rogrig, you know of her whereabouts, you can find her for us? More importantly, she will come when you bid her to?'

Inside my head the unspoken voices, quiet for so long, began to call out again.

Norda Elfwych . . . Norda Elfwych . . .

How long has she waited for another . . .

How could I tell them what, I knew, had become of her? 'The Elfwych is at the house of Old-man Wishard. She is kept fast within Carraw Peel.'

'She is blood-tied, then . . .?' asked Lowly Crows, 'to The Graynelord?'

'No. Rather, she is the Old-man's Pledge.'

'Pledge?' Wily Cockatrice lifted an eyebrow, took the word for its worst meaning.

'She is bonded to him, is all!' I could not help my rash defence of her. 'A bond of peace and good faith; between Elfwych and Wishard . . . Upon Graynelore, it is a common enough practice betwixt sworn enemies—'

'If you say so, Rogrig,' said the crone.

'And she will break this sworn Pledge so very easily?' said Lowly Crows. 'She will forsake her own blood-kin and join us now, *because . . .?*' It was a leading question, left deliberately hanging in the air between us.

I took a moment's pause. 'Because we are going to make her,' I said. (It was a clutched for suggestion, my friend, not a considered plan.)

'What? Are we to kidnap her then, are we going to steal her away from The Graynelord's own Stronghold?' asked the ancient crone. There was another long and knowing silence (without so much as a whiff of pipe smoke).

'I, for one, do not believe any of this!' said Wood-shanks, the elder-man, suddenly breaking his silence. 'Suppose this were even possible. What then? When every man at arms upon Graynelore is out for us, as surely as they must be . . .?'

He turned towards the pair of coquettes, as if in want of their support. Momentarily, Fortuna and Sunfast returned his look, only to pass a second look of mild astonishment between themselves, before settling their eyes upon me for an answer.

'Perhaps, the graynes will be too busy with their own private arguments to bother themselves with us,' I said, more hopefully than with any real conviction.

'Ha! And you a Wishard, too!' cried the elder-man. 'Are the best of your kin so easily put aside? I would think not!'

I could only sigh. (Better that, than a blatant lie.)

'How many more fruitless battles must men fight?' asked Lowly Crows, lowering her head.

'At least one more it would seem,' I said.

'And do we not wish to see the Faerie Isle, then; would it not be a true spectacle? And to find our rightful home at last—?'

'I used to think this land here was my home,' I said.

'And now?'

'That is the question . . .'

There was not one of us could find an honest answer. Wily Cockatrice took the renewed silence as her opportunity.

'There would be no sense in us all making this journey.' The crone spoke as if the decision was already made. 'What good reason could a Wishard have for bringing the likes of our mixed company to the Stronghold of his Graynelord?'

This was the truth. Yet I did not think I could possibly do this thing alone (if I could do it at all).

'I would take only Lowly Crows with me,' I said at last. 'We have already travelled a long road together, all be it, much of it unwittingly . . . If she will travel with me again—?'

'*She* will come with you, Rogrig.' The crow needed no persuasion.

'And as for the rest of us – What is to be our part in this unlikely plan?' asked the elder-man.

'We will hide ourselves away, of course, as only we can,' said Wily Cockatrice. 'And wait patiently upon Rogrig's safe return.'

'And how will we find you out again, in hiding?' I asked.

'Rogrig, you are ever a stubborn man. Do you, even yet, pretend to know so very little of yourself . . . and us?' said Wily Cockatrice, without further explanation. Inside my head I was certain I heard distant shadow-tongues laughing, and I was mocked. It was a faerie slight.

I shrugged.

'I will not lie to you,' I said. 'I do not know how this will turn out.' The implication was obvious enough.

'Nor do any of us, Rogrig.' At this, I will swear, Wily Cockatrice winked at me, before turning her back to look again upon the Great Sea, returning to her pipe with a renewed enthusiasm.

Chapter Seventeen

A Brief and Intimate Respite

What were we become – if not lonely travellers, homeless nomads, to be set upon a trail? Wanting only to find an escape . . . My tale was gathering a momentum, not to be stopped without a final resolution. Yet we were not come prepared for a long journey. We had carried so very little between us – it was a meagre vitals we took together that last evening, before we parted and went our separate ways. A few tugs on a loaf of bread passed between us. A swig of warm, sour wine – no fresh meat – We each made the best of our repast, and our brief respite. We all slept a little. A few sat together and talked on a while into the night. Wily Cockatrice sat purposefully alone, to recount her personal thoughts; still nursing her pipe.

I had half a mind to go and seek out Edbur-the-Widdle, to discover what he was really about, only my mood had lifted, I was almost sanguine, now that we were fixed upon a course of action (however unlikely its success). I had no real desire to share further confidences that night, or to become embroiled upon a confrontation that might turn bitter, or bloody. I decided to let that particular sleeping dog lie, for now.

Instead, I took a walk alone, in want of solitude, my own company. A handful of bright, snapping stars studded the black sky. A slice of a winter moon stood out coldly between the feathered edges of the few broken clouds; it scattered a shower of silver light upon the Great Sea, a myriad broken fragments. How calm, how beautiful, how peaceful it was. How lonely, too. I tried to picture the Faerie Isle . . .

In front of me, across the bay, there were short stretches of scrub-like sand-grass, catching the moonlight, dressing the edges of a line of shallow sand dunes. There a man might have made a temporary refuge. I decided to make them my business. However, I had not walked far between them when I found myself come upon two of my own company. The young women, Sunfast and Fortuna; the coquettish pair I thought I had seen, briefly transformed, as magnificent unifauns (if I believed that to be a true memory).

I meant to stand off, to let them alone, undisturbed. In their fragile state, perhaps, like me, they were in want of their own company? Only, I saw they were lying together, secreted in the lea between two grassy knolls, and fully naked now. Their raiment unashamedly cast aside. At once, I understood the meaning. (As I am sure, do you, my friend.) These two were lovers, and a pretty pair even in their frailty – their diminished state. That I lingered there, unseen, is of course without excuse, beyond my own bad character. Still, I *will* briefly report this private scene for the greater pity of subsequent events. (Though, I might add, I see nothing unseemly in the mating of a loving couple.)

They were kissing each other tenderly, and in a close and intimate embrace. Unhurried, in the way of faerie, they let the timeless night rest easily between them, felt no cold it seemed. They gently hushed their rising passions, quietly shared their bodies without shame. When, at last, they broke together they stiffened only slightly. Briefly opened their eyes, and sighed their release.

I fear they saw me there, watching over them.

I would have started away, only they appeared to smile, as if pleased with their find. They reached up, took my hand in theirs and pulled me down toward them. I did not recoil. I was always a man first. And they were women still, if their skin under my common touch was more akin to the soft fine brush of a doe's hair. We exchanged no spoken words. Together they drew me out, and between the pair, gently cradled my first arousal. It was a shared moment tenderly exchanged . . . and purely for my pleasure. Then, after a short while, they drew me out again, only selfishly this second time.

We three freely played together a goodly while.

Amid it all, and in that sorely wanton mood of wild abandonment, Sunfast and Fortuna became again graceful unifauns. I am certain of it. How they galloped in perfect unison! How they pranced and frolicked among the gentle moon-touched waves that tumbled at the edge of the Great Sea. A sight to see! And I, in my selfish lover's stupor, forgot myself. I turned my back against the darkly shrouded cliffs where Edbur surely made his camp, and I frolicked with them.

At the end, when we were all done, Sunfast and Fortuna lay down again. Still closely locked together, the pair closed their eyes, content to fall asleep in each other's arms. I, who had briefly become their lover, was again the outsider, only a companion (though abandoned without malice). It was a sweet goodnight.

I left them quietly, undisturbed.

Though, I was thoughtful still. In my passion I had found Notyet's name upon my lips. Yet I had hushed it. I hushed it again now. I kissed it gently away against the palm of my hand, set it aside. How often men are cruel to their heart.

In the morning, Wily Cockatrice was the first to take her leave of us. She departed without a speech of farewell, quietly slipped away, while others still drowsed.

One by one, if somewhat reluctantly, the remainder of our company began to follow her example. First the youth, Dogsbeard; then together, Sunfast and Fortuna, my ardent lovers (who made not the slightest reference to the incident), and then, Wood-shanks, the elder-man. As they left, each one upon their own road, I suddenly felt the inner pull of their presence begin to weaken. Had we few become so utterly entwined? My gut wrenched. At close quarters, the mental grip we each held upon the others had grown strong – if unwittingly so – and was become as much a part of us as our own thoughts. Its lessening was a physical hurt. Though it did not quite fail completely: even when they were all gone from my sight there still remained a faint, if fragile, link between us; a bonding that did not break. It was enough that I might find them all again – even in hiding – upon my safe return. And with that simple revelation I smiled as I recalled the conversation of another day when the crone had sorely rebuked me for my ignorance of such things.

At the last, I was left alone with Lowly Crows. Beside me, she – now become the bird again – preened her feathers as if to soothe away a discomfort.

I wondered if we would ever see our greater company again.

Chapter Eighteen

Upon the Threshold and a Dream

To look at, Graynelore was always something of a paradox. It was a beautiful land and yet ugly. It was often glorious and yet as often vague and unimpressive. The Great Unknown in the far north was a world set apart. While the black-headed mountains, at Graynelore's heart, stood up like the spokes of a great fallen wheel, with the hard-fought summit of Earthrise – the hub – at their centre. The burden of time may well have blunted their edges and reduced their heights but they were no less a formidable adversary. It took a brave man, or perhaps a fool, to attempt to scale their heights. Looking to the south, where the mountains fell away, and the wheel was broken, there was a great vista, a broad open plateau, only hindered by stretches of feeble, withered woodland – The Withering – that chequered and fringed the otherwise seemingly endless landscape. Beyond this, came the more gentle rolling hills and shallow vales of the Southern Marches. And if the lowly hills could not hinder you, if the trees did not stand in your way, there was always the mud – the clarts – of the stinking bog-moss to stop a man's progress; the mire to swallow up the unwary horse and rider. Or else the never ending waters, the countless threads of the River Winding that cut the great open lowland fells and moors into uneven pieces across the majority of its face. To my mind, it was always a lonely, endlessly wind-scarred earth. A difficult land to love; it left no easy place for men or beasts to hide or find welcoming shelter. Yet it was mine by my birth. And if I were to admit that my heart's meat has always been divided, then surely that land must take its due share.

The Southern Marches were a landscape of attrition rather than extremes. Though there were extremes, even here; and most dramatically where the Headmen had built their Strongholds. It was as if, on the day of its making, the Great Wizard had deliberately drawn the world that way. Perhaps he had, after all?

Making passage was never easy, always a hard and physical struggle, even when the path was clear and the way ahead known by heart. I was ever in need of Dandy, both for her hardiness and sure-foot; aye, and her sense of direction, or else I was in for an arduous journey.

It was time, at last, for me to confront Edbur, my trailing shadow. I set Lowly Crows upon the sky, to find the whelp out. Her flight was brief and fleet. Hardly away, she was at once surrounded by a host of her close kin: birds who appeared out of discreet hiding (if not out of thin air) to deliver her their intelligence. She quickly returned to my side.

'He is no longer there,' she said, without explanation, only giving me an inquisitive rook's eye. (It was an odd mannerism that meant her turning her head upon one side to regard me. A look I was to see many times thereafter.)

'No longer there?' I pressed.

'His camp is broken up; his fire is quite cold. There is only carrion to be seen – a bloody carcass.'

Edbur had encamped upon the scarp of a slowly rising cliff at the mouth of the river. It was not a great height. Though obviously enough of a hide for him to watch over us, within the bay, without being revealed in his turn.

Had I underestimated the talents of the gawky youth?

As I approached his abandoned camp I saw at once the broken carcass of a horse; all signs of leather and iron, saddle and baggage, removed. The animal's throat had been cleanly cut, and it was freshly killed; its meat still bright red, its exposed bone still pink. Some eager scavenger had already been gnawing upon it.

'Dandy? Shit! Shit!' I began to run, lifting my sword from its scabbard though it was a futile gesture. 'Dandy!'

The dead hobb was obviously not Dandelion. Its colouring was similar, but it was much older in the tooth, and its stature too slight. There was a grey mask around its sightless eyes. This hobb was surely Edbur's own. I saw the ploy in it.

Edbur had taken the best animal for himself, and deliberately slaughtered the other. He was a Wishard, after all – he knew the trick to sitting his arse upon Dandy's back without the rebuke. Given the choice, any fighting-man would do the same if his mount was become aged, or suddenly wearying beyond help. There is no pride in riding a dying nag, neither for the man or the beast. Or were there other reasons, other games in play here? Was it done simply to hinder my progress; take my hobby-horse, leave me without? If Edbur was a more seasoned snoop than I had suspected, if he had seen more and understood better what we were about, and was set upon returning to Wolfrid – who was always The Graynelord's man . . .

'Fuck!' (I fear, Rogrig Wishard was become a bloody fool!)

It was only now I recalled the reckless follies of my previous evening's intimate entertainment. How blind the enamoured man!

'Fuck!'

Of course, Edbur-the-Widdle, the scrawny whelp, had witnessed it all. And what – was gone scampering home to Dingly Dell with sordid tales of the faerie-touched man seen cavorting with the unifauns? And what might my elder-cousin, Wolfrid, make of such tittle-tattle? Enough, I fear, at least to wonder at the truth of it. Enough, perhaps, to leave me dangling in the shadows of the gibbet tree? For certain, I would not be easily welcomed at that man's door.

And worse! Nor would I want the waggling ears of the South March to catch rumours of such a fanciful tale before Lowly Crows and I were well set upon our path. The Graynelord was not a forgiving man. We must be quickly away.

And close kin or no, Edbur-the-snoop, Edbur-the-horse-thief, would be made to pay for this! Fortunately, the whelp had made one mistake, which was to my advantage: in abandoning his hobb, he had left behind its meat. I quickly set to work, stripped its bones, taking as much as I could sensibly carry. I wrapped it in a pouch cut from the animal's own hide. While I busied my knife, Lowly Crows watched over me. She shyly took her own share, made a brief repast of the hobb's sweetest entrails; entreated her fellows to come down out of the sky to do likewise.

The road is a difficult companion. It is endless, silent, and a heavy toil. I was a-foot and a man alone when I set out upon the trail to Carraw Peel. And if I exaggerate my burden just a little for the sake of my tale, if the crow took pity upon me and, sometime, gave me better company as the woman – and herself a rougher journey for that – forgive the liar. Shanks's pony was never my preferred transport and I do reserve the right to complain about it as often as I like.

We travelled hard and fast, and upon the less worn path; paused only for the necessity of rest and repast; saw little on our way worthy of account (which was our intent). Though once, when we were sitting comfortably together beneath the shade of a tree – the man and the woman – we found ourselves in a conversation I would relate to you.

'Upon a day, when we were hardly met, you gave me half a tale, I think,' I ventured.

'Mine own, you mean? And the greater half I think it was,' she returned, almost shyly. As she spoke she closed her eyes and held them so. While her fingers pulled at the loose threads of her woollen jerkin. 'You would have me give up its simple remainder?'

I left the answer unspoken. 'I am curious, is all.' I said. 'I have no doubt you saved my life upon the mire, and I would know how it truly came about. Only, I did not wish to offend you.'

'Wishes, Rogrig. Wishes?' Lowly Crows opened her eyes. She shook her head at me, gently smiling now, but gave no explanation of her teasing, her faerie slight. Then she took a breath as if to steel herself, as if what I had asked of her was not such a simple thing after all.

'What have you seen of me?" she asked.

'Seen of you? Well, I have seen the bird alone,' I said. 'And I have seen the Shift. That is the bird become the young woman; and again, the woman become a flock of birds—'

'Ha!' Lowly Crows laughed openly, as if I had made a joke.

'Is it not so, then?' I asked.

'And which of these do you suppose came first?' she returned.

'First?' I shrugged, uncertain if this was only a game we were at; or something rather more. 'You were, Lucia Hogspur . . .'

She shook her head slowly. Then, she drew a circle in the air between her outstretched fingers, as if to stand my answer upon its head.

'Eh?'

'We are fey, you and I. We have long known our own true selves,' she said. 'But it is the shaded face we have shared with the world. Only the painted mask we have openly offered to other men.'

I brought to mind the Beggar Bard's tales. How had they always described the demise of faerie? At the very end the few survivors had disguised themselves, hidden themselves away (wasn't that it?). They had hidden among men, and among the animals of the earth, and among the birds of the air. Only I had always thought of it as, well, simple flavouring, added to the pot: part of the telling of a good story. In my simple ignorance, even now, I had assumed we were all of us men first.

Lowly Crows ran her fingers through her hair, at the nape of her neck, in the same way I had seen the bird use her beak to preen her feathers.

'My true beginning is as a dream to me now,' she said, smiling slightly. 'Though, it is a most wondrous dream.' Again, she picked thoughtfully at the woollen sleeve of her jerkin. 'I was good at what I did, of that there was no doubt. And I was so beautiful, of my kind, and so strong. My flight was perfection. My cry was awesome; enough to ward off all but the most foolhardy of predators. And those I could not scare with threat alone, the rake of my claws or the cut of my beak soon settled.'

I suddenly realized, within those few words, Lowly Crows had transformed herself before me. The retiring woman was gone. It was the crow who stood upon the ground before me now. She gave me her rook's eye, as if slightly embarrassed.

'I was, if not a queen, then a princess among my kin,' she said, without conceit. 'And Windcatcher, a most handsome male, was my prince . . . or he surely would have been if only he had known the strength of my ardour. I was young still, and the instinct to mate – if not the desire – was not yet overwhelming. There was time enough, and I felt safe in the knowledge that it would come about.

'And if he was Windcatcher by name, we were all of us wind-catchers in our hearts. Whenever we heard the cry of the wind we would spread our wings and fly. We were not birds meant to settle, always moving on, ever keen to catch the next wind . . .' She paused, reflectively. 'I knew the sky, then, Rogrig! Oh, how glorious is the sky!' Her voice suddenly faltered. 'Only . . . Alas! I did not understand the tricks of devious men.'

'How so, my friend?' I asked.

'Upon a day, I was caught within a cruel trap,' she said bluntly, with scant detail. There were other dark shadows there she preferred to leave undisturbed. 'I was lured to the ground, and as I took the bait I was caged! I might well have died; it was as much a sudden end. And for what good reason was I imprisoned? To become a pet! A curious plaything, for a babbie's amusement! Surely, not I! Not I, who would have, only, the sky! Who would ever take wing and fly!' She fluttered her wings in an agitated fashion as if she could shake off the unwelcome memories. Then she fell still, took a breath, steeling herself for the last of it. 'Though, in the end, of course, the bird *did* die. You see, I let her die, Rogrig. I let the bird die. It was the only way to escape the cage.'

'You . . . you *became* the girl, then,' I said softly, 'to regain your freedom?'

Lowly Crows gave me the rook's eye. 'In that darkest hour, when all that I had been was finally stripped away, what was left to me? Only at the last, I remembered my true self, my original nature . . . that small part of me which is fey . . . or rather it was laid bare before me . . . So, I let go of my other self . . . And the bird died, and was *utterly* forgotten. While the infant girl who took her place survived . . .' There was a tear in the crow's eye. 'How easily that human child – not recognized a changeling – was taken to the hearts of men and became Lucia Hogspur.'

The crow took off then, lifted herself high into the sky. As I watched she flew in among the clouds where she was joined by a great body of black birds; companions that had shadowed our adventure all the while. Lowly Crows stayed away a long time.

I took the two halves of her story and made it a whole, as certainly as you can, my friend. Lowly Crows never spoke of it again.

Chapter Nineteen

The Gateway

Carraw Peel, the Stronghold of Old-man Wishard, Headman of the Wishards, Graynelord of all Graynelore, lay in a valley surrounded on three sides by hills; the summits of which could be safely climbed from the Stronghold side, but were all steep and broken scree slopes, from the far side. The scree slopes, great and terrible expanses of loose stone and fractured rocks, were unstable and treacherous, impossible to scale. They protected the Stronghold's rear. At its front there was rough moorland and open fell, here and there broken up by dangerous patches of bog-moss – nearly, but not quite as deadly as the Wycken Mire. A single track divided the valley in two across its length, and steered the unwary traveller to the gateway of the peel. Carraw Peel was easily guarded, very easily defended. Our slow approach was carefully watched from the moment we stepped into the valley.

Towards the end of our journey, Lowly Crows kept herself constantly in the form of the bird, and took to perching upon my shoulder (her idea). It was not done for companionship, but was a simple trick, a ruse; that she might be taken, by men, for my pet or constant familiar and given free passage without note or significance. Her kin continued to follow after us, but flew a devious route, at some great height and distance. Lost among the clouds they came on unheeded.

At intervals along the valley I could see a scattering of stone houses – these were bastle-houses, of course. Each one set clearly in view of the next; always a simple but effective defence. If there was ever an alarm to be raised it was easily and quickly done.

I made my approach openly, and noisily. If I cautioned myself; lest there were strange tales upon the air – of a Wishard man seen cavorting with the faeries. There were men and women about: stockmen, mostly youths, in their fields; mothers with their babbies, standing at their doors. They held my eye, cautiously kept their weaponry close by, though, for that, seemed little worried at a stranger's approach. I felt I might yet turn myself about, make a quick escape, if it was needed.

'I am Rogrig Wishard, of the Three Dells,' I called out boldly, as I reached the first settlement. (I would know what I was up against.)

Faces stayed rudely blank at my disclosure. The name meant nothing to them. I remained safely hidden as yet. If, in truth, I had also been hoping to see a friendly face; one I might at least vaguely recognize from a Riding, or a holyday, or a call to the Mark. These were Wishards, and my distant kin after all. Only there was no one familiar to me there.

Most men gave a tacit acknowledgement of my passage. A few spoke in open greeting. One man offered me a clean drink and a piece of bread to see the back of me. Lowly Crows even raised a few smiles: playing tricks; stealing red berries from out of wicker baskets; picking loose hoods off the heads of startled babbies and carrying them away. Though, no one invited me to stay awhile.

I had to walk another good mile along the valley floor, repeat my bold greeting a dozen times, before I came, at last, close to the front gates of the Old-man's Stronghold.

Carraw Peel was indeed a magnificent sight. Its heavy, solidly built outer wall stood at the height of a small hill and surrounded a truly massive inner tower. Its stonework was shear and unassailable and unmarked by hand or battle. As much a statement of The Graynelord's power as it was his defence. (He was showing off again.)

'I am Rogrig Wishard, of the Three Dells,' I shouted without falter. I was calling to a barred wooden door, its face ornamented with black iron nails. 'I seek only a night's refuge in my Graynelord's house.'

The retort came blindly and only after several moments of silence.

'Refuge? I see no raiders in hot pursuit. Or is it that the Marches are bereaved? Are there, so soon, renewed troubles in the south or in the west?'

'No. None, that I am aware of, Keeper,' I said, politely.

Again, there was a short silence.

'You are not a messenger then? For we do not recognize you – or your pretty pet.' It was obvious I was being regarded through some simple concealed spyhole in the doorway. Lowly Crows shook herself, displayed her wings, settled again on my shoulder, with a rook's eye. 'Or are you a Beggar Bard – or a merchant with wares to . . . sell?'

I was certain the Keeper was fishing, with a mind for a bargain, or a bribe perhaps. I had little or nothing to offer him. I carried about me only the remains of a parcel of dried horsemeat. Crushed and tenderized, smoked upon the campfire, but hardly the sum of a trade.

Already this exchange was going badly.

From the moment I embarked upon this trial, I had been vexed – left to ponder this exact stand-off. What good reason could a Wishard of my lowly rank and distant kinship have for gaining access to the house of his Graynelord, let alone secure a personal audience? I was not after a meeting of equals here, far from it. I had only one constant thought, only one possible answer.

'I am no merchant, Keeper,' I said. 'But I do bring my Lord a gift.' At this, I felt Lowly Crows shuffle uneasily upon my shoulder. There was nothing I could do to soothe her.

'And I am not a common fool,' answered the Keeper. 'My name is Wint-the-Snoop, and if you have something to reveal, something *worth* revealing, you will let me see it first.'

I had little choice. I opened up my jack, uncovered the stone talisman that hung about my neck. This was my one true treasure, and kept a secret, always concealed, these many years. I had revealed it to no one. Not even to my own heart's meat.

The stone's gold decoration caught brightly in the morning sun.

'What is *that*?' asked Wint-the-Snoop, impressed but always shrewd, playing up his ignorance. He was well named.

'I fear, you cannot tell? It is a true and honest fragment of The Eye Stone! My Graynelord would surely want to see this.'

'Would he, now? And you say you are *not* a Beggar Bard . . . what you hold there is their usual device . . . and this door-keep has not long since seen the back of one of that particular breed of men.'

'I am not a Beggar Bard, Keeper,' I said, firmly.

'No? Then I would add; you are not the first common man to offer up such a trinket! I could build a road that would lead you all the way home again with the stones this house has been offered . . . *said* to belong to The Eye Stone.'

'Neither am I a fraud! Though would *you* be my judge?' I asked. 'Is his door-keep making decisions for The Graynelord now?'

'Aye well . . .' This last question seemed to stump the man, or worry him. 'Like I said, I do not know you. I keep this door safe, is all. But then tell me, Rogrig Wishard, so-called, why be so generous with such a precious thing? I can see you are not a wealthy man.'

'I am a Wishard, if distant kin,' I said. 'I want only to return to my Graynelord that which is rightfully his—'

'Surely though, not without some kind of just reward?' he asked. There was a knowing edge to his question.

I was certain I had gained the measure of the man. Wint-the-Snoop thought we had a meeting of minds. I had only to play my role straight.

'Ah . . . Now, if my humble gesture was to put me in my Lord's good favour and he wished to express his thanks in some manner; by way of gold coins, or barrels of wine, or salted meats perhaps. Upon Graynelore! Who am I to refuse it?'

'Hah! Now there is a man who speaks the truth . . . Wait upon me.' There was movement behind the barred door, though I was left standing there: and long enough for the sun to be briefly shaded by cloud, for the cloud to briefly spit rain. This was not a threshold lightly crossed. Behind the walls of Carraw Peel my unlikely entourage was obviously the subject of a very long and serious discussion. Until:

'Help me to unbar this door!' called out Wint-the-Snoop, 'And bid the man to enter here.'

Chapter Twenty

The Faerie in the Tower

As the door to Carraw Peel swung open I saw, at once, that the Keeper was afflicted by a natural deformity, a kind of stoop, which left his head forever bowed, and particularly, his large hooked nose travelled always before him. It gave the impression that he was forever pushing his nose squarely into the next man's business. Without further conversation, he briefly looked me over. He used his hands freely. And then, finally satisfied with my worth (or, rather, its lack), he openly stole the last of my dried horsemeat and bid me to follow after him.

Wint-the-Snoop led me first through the outer courtyard: a bright, open space, surprisingly noisy with people and the bustle of the day. Bored men at arms stood lazily about the outer walls. Youths fed and groomed their hobbs. A carpenter worked wood. And while servants busied themselves at their chores, a stonemason, with his apprentice, loaded a cart in preparation for his departure. This last man was overly tall; a Troll for certain, never a Wishard, only give him no offence, my friend. A mason is always a man to be fed and watered; if you can afford his services. More precious even than a Beggar Bard, for his magic is real. He rebuilds walls that will not shift again. He makes good what the hand of a reiver, and his sword, cannot. So, I will let him pass. And follow Wint-the-Snoop through a heavy wooden door and into the first great chamber of the tower-house.

Once inside, and with the door closed behind us, we appeared to be alone. The room was ornately vaulted, its ceiling made of stone that it should not burn in a siege. There was a thick mass of clean, dry straw upon the floor, and a full store of grain, and water pales, and upon the walls horse leathers and irons, all apparently for the use of sheltered beasts in a storm. Only there was no sign of a storm and there had been none here for many an age. This house was best prepared, but quite obviously, expected no threat.

There were wooden steps (permanently fixed) that took us up through the stone ceiling and into the Great Hall. Here, at last, Wint-the-Snoop stopped. He left me standing at the foot of The Graynelord's long table; and without another word he withdrew, returning to his own business. Oddly enough, with his departure, I had the feeling I was being abandoned by a friend. Though, I was not left on my own, after all. Far from it; there were a dozen or more people in the Great Hall, only I was being ignored for the moment. On my shoulder, Lowly Crows ruffled her feathers. It was obvious she did not like the enclosed space, or the strangers. She turned her eye about, made a brief study of the Great Hall's narrow wind-eyes, its chimney and fireplace, its balustrades and high ceilings. Seeking any route that might make an escape, or a safe perch, out of harm's way – as needs must.

I allowed my eyes the same extravagance. I saw no hint of threat, exactly. Only, there *was* a strange smell at the table;

and strong with it. Something . . . stank. It was not a gentle aroma, not simply the forgotten remains of old food discarded to the floor. Not bodily function even, but a body, maybe? Yes: this was more like rancid, unhealthy, rotting flesh – It was not unfamiliar to me. I might have expected it if I had come upon remnants on an old killing field, or the corpse of the murdered man at the side of a road. But not here, not in this place. In truth, I had noticed the stench the moment I entered the tower. It seemed to linger about the walls and the doorways. It insinuated itself from nooks and crannies, seeped from the very stonework. It had obviously been disguised – expensively disguised – judging by the ever-present bowls of rosewater, the hanging sprigs of herbs, and the open boxes of fresh spices. It had been disguised, but still not hidden.

I did not dare meet the gaze of The Graynelord who was seated at the top of his table. He appeared to be in a deep conversation with a pair of his advisers. I looked instead toward the other men and women who stood about the Hall. This was not a house under siege or threat. This was a home. The Graynelord did not need armed men at his own dining table. There were servants, young girls, old men. There was a single guard. And if any other man there carried a sword it was only out of custom; he was not expecting to use it. Servants apart then, this gathering was, mostly, members of The Graynelord's Council. They were huddled together, somewhat awkwardly, in tight groups, their backs turned firmly against the walls – unnecessarily careful? They were, to a man, still dressed in their ridiculous fop and finery, their embroidered cloth and brightly coloured skirts, just as I had last seen them upon Pennen Fields, on the morning of the Elfwych Riding. I do not recall any of these gentle men having a name of their own. Excepting the common title they were forced to share between them. The Council always appeared to be a full set, rather than individuals. Only one stood apart. An aged man, who held himself so rigidly, and moved about as if he were sure to break apart at every step; I could not help but call him Stiff Brittle. Anyway, they gave me no clue to the source of the foul air. They were politically polite to the very last.

I caught only a brief mumbled apology from a servant as he passed me by – about problems in the kitchens – but if that was so, why was the smell stronger in The Graynelord's Hall, and at its very worst at his table? And why did no one else remark upon it?

Mind, the foul stench was not the only curiosity here. This was obviously a soldiers' Stronghold – the bare stone walls were decorated with arms and armour still notched and carrying the marks of combat – it was a fighting-man's abode, and yet, somehow it had the feeling of being carefully dressed by a female hand (and an unusual one at that).

I tried to look about for Norda Elfwych, the purpose of our endeavour – I could not see her. There was no obvious visible sign. And yet, among all this, I seemed to sense her presence . . . in that *other* way. Inside my head, distant shadow-tongues were again whispering to me, if incomprehensibly.

I felt the sudden stab of the bird's claws digging into my shoulder, breaking my train of thought. It was as if she too sensed something of what was about here.

'I think the man is a drunk!' whispered Lowly Crows.

'Eh?'

'I think he is a drunk. The Graynelord, drunk. Can you not see it, Rogrig? He keeps slipping out of his seat and he cannot keep his eyes open. And look – his words are not even timed to the movement of his mouth.'

Perhaps I should have recognized the truth; only, if the crow could but make guesses and be well off the mark, it was no surprise that I did not yet have the understanding or the guile to comprehend what was before me. There was a kind of Glamour at work here, and it was a clever deception. Someone, somewhere, was cheating. Though I was blind to the detail of it and saw there only what I expected to see.

'Never mind that he is a drunkard,' I said, under my breath. 'I think I would be the same, if I had to put up with this constant stench!'

'What have they been doing, leaving their dead unburied?' suggested Lowly Crows.

Behind us, on some unseen signal, the only visible guard suddenly rapped his wooden staff against the stone floor. Its resounding echo instantly silenced the Hall, and brought it to a semblance of order. The Council, with their backs already set firmly against the wall, stiffened further. Then, slowly, and in his own time, Old-man Wishard looked up from his table, and at last appeared to see me standing there.

This man was my Graynelord and my kin. The Old-man . . . nicknamed not, as you might expect, for his great age, but simply because he was largely bald. In fact he was almost a young man still. There were, perhaps, only a dozen seasons between us. I knew him then, though I was never a member of his household. I had seen him often enough – if at a distance – on many a Riding. And yet, as I looked at him now, close at hand, I hardly recognized him. Certainly, he did not know me. But then, why should he? I was part of a greater crowd and his kin in name and duty only, as were so many others. If it were not for our similar looks and common family traits we were virtual strangers.

'Rogrig Wishard?' he said, using my full name as if it was a question.

'Yes, my Lord,' I said.

'And this other – this bird, you bring into my Hall, and with it play upon my generous hospitality. Not our kin, I would fear?' There was a faint shadow of a real smile.

'She is only my common pet, and well trained for an amusement.' I said, lying without hesitation. Bird or not, upon Graynelore, to give any less of an answer would likely have been the cause of her instant removal, and probable death. There was, indeed, little trust among men.

'Then, if the bird amuses you, she amuses me also,' he said.

'Er . . . Thank you, my Lord—'

'I am told you have something of mine, Rogrig Wishard. Something, about your person, that rightly belongs to me. What is it that you want here?' The statement and the question were both suddenly blunt; the pleasantries were obviously done with – and there was no hint of shade.

'Want? I have brought you—'

There was a further interruption, only this time it came from one of the members of the Old-man's Council, standing at his side. 'Yes, yes, you have brought . . . Quickly now, quickly; what is it that you have brought? Show us and be done with it!' This man was elderly, his face wiry, and his eyes narrow and cold. He appeared anxious, though not, I think, because he had spoken across his Graynelord. Oddly, the Old-man seemed not to have noticed the slight.

I quickly opened my jack, and displayed the talisman that hung from its leather thong about my neck. The light from the fireplace in the Great Hall touched the slivers of gold within its face.

'Ah!' The reaction, an awkward mix of surprise and thinly disguised delight, came from more than one member of the Council. Yet still the Old-man appeared unmoved.

'What is it, cousin?' he asked, squinting as he spoke. He appeared to be having trouble seeing it clearly. His head bobbed involuntarily. He slipped slightly in his chair and was forced to correct himself.

'I told you the man was a drunkard,' Lowly Crows whispered under her breath.

'It is a present for you,' I said. 'It is a gift – a true and honest piece of The Eye Stone, my Lord.' A truth is often the best part of a lie.

'A true and honest piece, you say?' Again it was a member of the Council who spoke for The Graynelord. 'Be very aware of your answer!'

'As I speak . . .' I said, inclining my head toward the Old-man in a gesture I hoped was something close to subjugation. It was so rarely practised.

'And where in all the world did a . . .' the Old-man seemed to falter briefly, only to regain himself, 'where did a man – such as yourself – come into possession of such a rare device? I do not see them growing on the apple trees!'

Suddenly everyone in the hall was laughing; if too loudly for the jest.

'I took it from a Beggar Bard!' I said, honestly enough.

'Ha!' There was more laughter. 'You stole it, then? The man is nothing but a common thief! Is he to be trusted then?'

I shrugged off the retort with a smile of my own. 'Upon Graynelore, we are all of us more likely thieves than not. And the man *was* already dead.'

'Ah.'

'The Beggar Bards believe the true Eye Stone knows itself and cannot be fooled. I would put my trust and my faith in it, and its true guardian, my Lord. Even if my very life were to depend upon it—'

'Indeed, and well it might yet,' he said, 'if this tale of yours is discovered to be twisted.'

I was beginning to wonder if I was not getting a little too carried away with my own performance.

'What say you, my Council? Do we put him and his pretty treasure to the test?'

'Yes, my Lord. We would put him to the test.' Yet again, though it was The Graynelord who had spoken and a member of his Council who had replied, it was not altogether clear to me who it was had given the command.

'First though, a little . . . repast, I think. The man would share in our board?' asked Stiff Brittle, and though he spoke with the beginnings of a thin smile he was eyeing me coldly. He signalled to a servant to bring forward a tray of vitals already prepared. 'Take a drink with us, at least. You must be long travelled and thirsty for it.' This was not the man being a polite host, nor was it an offer to be refused. Rather, my test was already begun. For a friend who will not drink freely from your cup is not your friend.

The Old-man looked on dispassionately, I thought. Though if I were to recall that face now, I fear, I would see not only vacancy, but also regret.

In truth, I had no choice – and though Lowly Crows cried out in warning – I took the drink I was offered and, with a smile, quickly swallowed it.

Suddenly the armed guard was at my side. The members of the Council were waving politely at me, wanting me to follow after them; Stiff Brittle at their head as they walked towards the back of the Great Hall. I understood their duplicitous gesture was not a request. I felt myself nudged forwards. Instinctively my hand moved towards the hilt of my sword. Only, I let it be, and allowed the indignity. This was not yet the moment for a hero. I was more than the guard's match, but I was uncertain of the full strength of the house; and there were games here not fully played out.

It was Lowly Crows who stirred from my shoulder. She took to flight. She lifted herself toward the high ceiling and found a makeshift perch there; well out of the reach of men, and safe for now. Still . . . This was not the welcome I had expected from the house of my own kin.

I was led back down the wooden steps and came again into the lower chamber. On the floor, the straw had been brushed aside revealing a wooden trapdoor. I *had* seen its like before. It would lead, at best, to a cellar or an underground store; at worst, to a dungeon or a murder hole. The trapdoor was open, a wooden ladder already set in place. Though, I was not to be thrown into the hole nor, it seemed, abandoned there. It was Stiff Brittle who led the way. He took a hold of the first wrung of the ladder and climbed down. I was expected to follow his lead.

Chapter Twenty-One

An Unexpected Murder

The underground space was a small vaulted chamber with a solid, uneven floor of natural rock. I could barely stand my full height within it. Its walls were cut stone but, for the most, if they were well laid they were poorly dressed and blackened with the neglect of an age. This was the very bottom of the tower of Carraw Peel. These were its foundations. A broken man, or a forgotten Pledge, might be left in the darkness to die here (there was old evidence shifting under my feet). Oddly enough, for the first time since entering the house, I could not smell the lingering stench. Instead there was the natural foul dankness that comes with stale air, long absence, and abandonment. This space was never meant for the eyes of visiting dignitaries or house guests. There was no need for the Old-man to show off his wealth here.

Yet I had been brought here for a purpose . . .

I remembered again the Beggar Bard of my distant childhood, explaining how the first Headman of the Wishards had, unwittingly, built his tower-house upon The Eye Stone. Was it only a babbie's story, a whimsy meant for gullible ears, or a real part of the truth? We had heard the tale retold often enough. It had become so. I had offered the Old-man my talisman because of it. How strange it was that only now I should consider my own belief; to chance all upon a fancy. And if this Eye Stone was such a powerful device, why was it so neglected, kept a secret, hidden away in the darkness? This place was more an abandoned tomb than an honoured shrine. I could see no sense in it, nor any advantage to the grayne.

The only light in the chamber came through the open trapdoor. There were three figures vaguely outlined against its weak display. The light ringed their heads, caught in their hair. They were all Councillors; the Old-man was not among them, nor was the guard.

'You will give it up now, your . . . gift.' Stiff Brittle, seemed to have to search for his last word. It was not a question.

'For the test?' I tried to sound as if I believed I was still there to make an offering to my Graynelord. Not walking into a trap I did not understand.

'Ah yes, the test,' said Stiff Brittle. Then he repeated his statement. 'You will give it up.' He held out his hand in the gloom.

I took the talisman from around my neck and gave it to him. (As yet, I had no good reason not to.) How easily something so very important was given away then. There was a sharp intake of breath.

'Is it real?' asked one of the Council.

'We shall see,' answered Stiff Brittle.

He grasped the fragment of The Eye Stone, his hands shaking violently, though whether through excitement or simple old age I could not tell. He appeared to dither, in a way that suggested he might not know exactly what it was he was supposed to do with it. Was this a ceremony so little performed? He turned to face the grimy wall, towards the spot where, I assumed, he would find the keystone of the house – The Eye Stone.

It was then murder was committed.

Mine.

I was poisoned after all. My vitals the culprit, I had no doubt. If I am uncertain, even yet, who it was delivered the fatal dose to my cup. I felt its lethal strength begin to course through my blood. My head screamed with the pain of it and I fell down, at once, dead (the intention, if not – thankfully – the final outcome). It might have been a physical blow. It was certainly enough to kill any ordinary man. That it did not kill me, I cannot fully explain, give only my belief. Do you remember my words at our first meeting, my friend?

I am *not* an ordinary man.

Though I must add, at once, I am not an immortal. All creatures die eventually, each to their own circumstance. Only now it seemed some men were less easily dispatched than others.

When Rogrig, the man, was killed, did that small part of him which is fey survive? Was a faerie trait enough to make a difference? For upon Graynelore, surely every man was a mixed breed. An empty lamp, though its wick is still damp with oil, will not hold a light. Still, I could not guess any better, nor did I need to – only thank the fortunes for it and accept the gift of life gladly.

Chapter Twenty-Two

The Eye Stone

I was dead, then – dead to the world, at any rate – and lying in that dark hole. The three members of the Council were standing over me. They were speaking privately among themselves. If I could not easily see them or set them apart, I could hear them. I guessed the first voice belonged to Stiff Brittle. It was a heated debate.

'Why do you think it is that we dwelt so long and hard upon ancient maps, and the words of long dead men?' he asked.

'You do not believe it, then?' returned a second voice, harshly.

'Belief? Is that it? Ha! You are asking the wrong question of the wrong man.' Stiff Brittle was suddenly scornful. 'The Eye Stone – so-called – is the very foundation stone of this tower. I know that perfectly well. It is solid enough. I neither need to believe in a relic or disbelieve. Possession is everything. And the wall is a wall just the same.'

'Then, The Eye Stone is not real?'

'Real? What, exactly, is real?' asked Stiff Brittle. 'Take away The Eye Stone from where it now resides and tell me, what would happen?'

'The walls would break,' answered the third member of the Council, his voice both languid and supplicatory in its tone. 'Carraw Peel would fall into a ruin, of course.'

'Of course. And is that magic then; is that belief? No, it is a fact. It is simply the truth. And that is your reality.' Stiff Brittle sighed. 'Tell me, my Lords, who is it that most benefits from the wealth of this grayne?' His words were pointed.

'Truly? In the continued absence of a Graynelord, then . . . this Council . . .'

'Indeed.'

'But . . . The Graynelord *is* dead.'

'I know he is dead. At this very moment his rancid rotting corpse sits in the Great Hall above us. If it were not for the intervention of the Elfwych, the Old-man's brother might already be sitting in his place. Our influence usurped. Is that not so?'

As Stiff Brittle spoke these words I felt myself give an involuntary start. If I had not been lying dead at the Council's feet and in the dark I would have given myself away. What did they mean by it? The debate continued:

'Norda Elfwych is a bloody throwback! She is a true fey wych. Magic . . . sorcery is an evil, not tolerated here. It is the common man's law. We have more than encouraged it ourselves.'

'Can you really be this stupid, my Lord?' Stiff Brittle's retort was as dry as ice.

'Throwbacks are slaughtered – put into the fire. Aye and their close kin are slaughtered with them – their companions too, if the angry mob has a mind.'

'Only if they are caught,' said, Stiff Brittle.

'This is a very dangerous game we are playing. That is all I am saying. A very dangerous game, indeed—'

'Ah, yes, well. We are all throwbacks to one degree or another, are we not? It is only a matter of perception, point of view. If a Headman is looking at you and he sees you as a threat . . . well then, he kills you. If, on the other hand, you are useful to him, or you are a member of his own close kin . . .' Stiff Brittle left the implication hanging. 'Ha! What does a man care for pedigree when it is his power at stake? The law, right or wrong, guilt or innocence, politics and politicians – it is all of it, matter-less.'

'But there is no denying the facts.'

'Facts! Ha! There are so few facts. One man's fact is only another man's bare-faced lie. Like I said, it is not fact we are dealing with here, it is simply a point of view.'

'And points of view get people killed.'

The Council's heated discussion had descended into political debate and rhetoric. It seemed, even now, in this moment of extreme danger, they could not resist the temptation to embroil. Were these old men only fools after all? If they had simply abandoned my body to the hole and shut me in, there would have been a sudden end to my tale. Their continued distraction was to my advantage. It allowed me the time to recover sufficiently to act for my life.

'But by rights, the Old-man's brother is his natural successor; as it is written upon the Stone.'

'Listen, my friends. This Council is weak. We are only advisers, simple merchants, and scholars. We count coins and we wring meanings out of feeble words cut upon ancient stone. We play out ancient ceremonies for the eyes of gullible men. We dress up and we act the part. We are politicians, not fighting-men. We are powerless to keep control of the Graynelore without the strength of The Graynelord. We cannot go to war.'

'Oh please! Save the pitiful grovelling for someone who cares!' Stiff Brittle's voice began to rise above those of his fellows. 'However, I do have to agree with you – there is many a grayne that would take advantage of this death. Indeed there are many Headmen whose legal claim to Lordship of the Graynelore comes before our own.'

'Ah! But we have The Eye Stone. Is that not the true Mark of The Graynelord? Is not possession the rule?'

'Oh indeed it is a magnificent symbol, but on its own it can never be enough. Not without the man. So, enough of this futile discussion! We are all of us a party to this act. What is done is done. Has anyone actually been listening?'

The Council seemed to falter there, as if perplexed by Stiff Brittle's words. He continued:

'All right, let us say I agree with you both, in principle. And, what is written upon The Eye Stone is so.'

'Yes.'

'Then obviously, all we have to do to remain on the right side of the debate is to . . . *update* the stone, a little.'

'But that is impossible.'

'Is it, my Lords? Forgive me if I were to disagree with you. Other than us; who else has actually seen it?'

'But every house upon Graynelore knows the story of The Eye Stone . . . and what is written here upon it.'

'Do they? Listen, I am not talking about old men's stories. I mean the original. Have any of them actually *seen* the original Eye Stone, have they read it for themselves?'

'No. Of course not! It is more a question of faith, than of . . . well, of fact.'

'Exactly! We get there in the end. So, let us take a leap of faith of our own, and let me suggest to you that what we have here has, over time, required a certain judicial . . . embellishment.'

'You mean The Eye Stone has been faked?'

'I would prefer to call it . . . clarified.'

'But why? Where is the sense in it?'

'Let us consider a moment . . . Your family, your grayne, are the rulers of the known world. Why? Because The Eye Stone says they are. Your close kin sit at the very top of the apple tree, among its fruits, while everyone else sits at the very bottom and goes hungry. Why? Because The Eye Stone says they do. You have everything your own way, because The Eye Stone lets you. And nobody, but nobody questions The Eye Stone. What is more, nobody asks for the proof of it, which is very convenient. Who could blame a grayne for wanting to further their advantage?

'Looking like a Graynelord, acting like a Graynelord, giving orders like a Graynelord . . . makes you a Graynelord. And who needs paltry trinkets!'

There was the sound of a quick movement. Suddenly, I felt exactly as if I had been stung upon the head by a thrown stone. I might have cried out for it, given myself away to that company, if my voice had been mine. As it was, I was yet mute. My body was still quite inert. There was no life in it to react to the pain. I realized Stiff Brittle had thrown my talisman back at me, as if it was without value. How curious this all was.

It seemed he had more to say. 'And the more ancient your rules, the more they are steeped in tradition, passed down through faceless generations; the more deeply rooted and twisted you can make them, then the more difficult it is for common men to unravel.

'Think of it like this: the more often the people are told, *this* is the way things are, the easier it is for them to believe it: especially when they are not being offered any alternative.'

'Is the world this sad? Is this our best?'

'Ah, now there is a thing. I fear it was ever so,' said Stiff Brittle. 'Indeed, the manner of the rule does not matter, not really. The world works the way it works just the same. A man must be a leader. Others must follow.'

I heard the distinct sound of a hammer blow. Iron upon breaking stone. The rattle of stone fragments hitting the floor. The shocked squeal of men convinced that the earth was about to fall in upon them. Again the hammer fell. Then silence.

'There, you see?' said Stiff Brittle. 'How very easily history is rewritten.'

It suddenly occurred to me; I had been killed not because I had been lying to them, but because they had been lying to me. Why had The Eye Stone not revealed my talisman to be a pitiful Beggar Bard's fake? Because . . . because *their* Eye Stone was the imposter?

I began to feel life returning to my stricken corpse. It was fortunate for me that they had killed me less than dead. I speak of it now as if my recovery was a common thing, and so easily achieved. It was neither. I came to myself slowly, and very painfully; it was an unusual agony – my body still filled with a dreadful poison, not the hurt expected of a death wound. I had the wit about me to bite my tongue against it.

I had to think quickly; what was to be done, now?

That the Council thought me dead was to my advantage. That they were politicians and not fighting-men was to my advantage again. Still, a caution: I had been dead once and survived; this Council might be old and decrepit, it still had a bite that could kill. I did not expect to survive again. I let the conspiracy continue its wordy debate . . . The element of surprise was mine.

I had found my feet, was moving before I was discovered. I took to the ladder not to the sword. Not through any sense of trepidation: I would have killed those men without hesitation. Only the chamber was too dim to find a clear mark, too small to make a full-bodied blow with my sword. I would have been swinging senselessly against stone walls, and in the dark.

Escape was the better way.

Though there was blood spilled, and damage done. To gain the ladder I was forced through that huddle of old men. I must have caught one. Ancient bones are fragile; they break as easily as a winter's brittle ice.

I had cleared the trapdoor and lifted the ladder before their cries went up. No doubt, astonishment and their own fear cut their tongues – as I would have cut their throats – rooting them to the spot. When the first of their voices finally sounded the trapdoor was already closed upon them, and their cries went unheard.

My stone talisman was held tightly in my closed fist. I had, unwittingly, grasped it, as I pulled myself up off the floor of the chamber.

Chapter Twenty-Three

The Pain of Norda Elfwych

Instantly, my nose was filled again with a stench akin to that of a rotting corpse. I had expected – in all honesty I am not sure what – to be met by fighting-men at least, a single standing guard for certain; or else, the scurry of servants, members of the house taking to flight, raising the alarm. There was none of it. The lower chamber was deserted. I see it now. The business of the Council was a private affair not to be overheard. I was always a dead man from the very start. And I had been carefully watched into that hole. No one in that tower-house expected me to come out of it again. Not alive.

I made the wooden steps to the Great Hall and thought to find it likewise empty. Only, it was not. Not quite . . .

Lowly Crows cried out, gave me a reminder of her continued presence, safely sat upon her makeshift perch within the high ceiling. She stayed put, not yet ready to make a move.

There, in front of me, was the Old-man, still sitting at the head of his table. Though he was unattended by any guard or servant or Council – the earlier courtly display had been a mask solely for my benefit – a golem, a fetch, needs none. I would have taken him for a dead man if it was not obvious he was looking towards me. His eyes were still vacant and unfocused, but he made a slight, deliberate movement of his head at my approach.

The deception played upon me at our first meeting was a game still a-foot. I had been slow at seeing this ruse for what it was. However, the Council had, unwisely, disclosed the truth in its debate. I was certain of its origin now.

'Norda? Norda Elfwych, you will reveal yourself to me! Where are you hiding? I know it is you.'

The Old-man's head twitched. His eyes appeared to take me in more seriously; he was considering something. Then his jaw moved, his mouth fell open as if he was about to speak. A string of bloody spittle caught ungainly between his lips.

I waited.

'I am here . . . inside the closet,' he said. 'I mean . . . I . . .' His words trailed off. His head suddenly lolled awkwardly to one side and then nodded forwards. His arms, resting on the table, gave way and his body slumped sideways. It looked, for the world, as if someone had been holding him in his seat, and now they had let him go. He had been dropped like a babbie's toy; a mere puppet.

The Graynelord's lifeless body crumpled and slipped to the floor. Only now could I see the great wound at the back of his head, splitting his skull. For certain it had been his death blow.

Above my head, Lowly Crows shifted anxiously upon her perch, disturbed by the revelation.

'I am here, Rogrig,' said Norda Elfwych, stepping out from behind a curtain that disguised the door of a night-closet. As she did, the distant shadow-tongues returned, between us, calling out to us both.

And their weak cry was . . . *pity*. And their weak cry was . . . *sin*.

And their voices bled tears.

I hardly recognized her. She looked gaunt; her face was drawn, thin and frail. Her eyes were black and set deep within her skull. Her red hair was a skein of ugly tats. Worse than unkempt, bedraggled; it stood awkwardly off her head, as if it had been used for a rope, or her leash (which is as close to the truth as we need to go). She had been dressed – I fear this was not her own choice – in a long, shapeless shift. It was spattered with blood and a mixture of other stains, less identifiable . . . Her feet and legs were bare. There were ugly broken bruises, blue and yellow welts; there was dirt. She stood lopsided, keeping her weight on one foot; as if to avoid the pain of a deeper, internal wound.

At her throat there was a cruel, jagged cut, showing signs of deep infection, where her gold amulet had been forcibly torn off.

I understood her pain . . . Truly. Only now was not the moment for my sympathy or sorrow. Let the shadows wail! For the man must not show it. Forgive my stone heart. Think me cruel. But I had seen worse treatment of a Pledge . . . She would live and that was enough. There was much else to discover here; little time to do it in.

'What is this mischief?' I said. 'My Graynelord lies dead and it seems his Council are the architect and you their . . . their what? Their *principle*? I see the trick played here but I am at a loss to understand why it was done.'

Moving slowly, Norda Elfwych came and stood over the body of the Old-man. 'It was I . . . I, who killed him,' she said, without emotion or effect.

'You! You? But, how . . . why? You pledged yourself to him, to my grayne, for the security of your own kin. What sense is there in that?'

'I dropped a bowl upon his head,' she said. She was shaking her head as she spoke. Was it vacant disbelief; confusion; both? The distant shadow-tongues gave me no clue. She glanced towards a stone doorway, to the stone steps at the rear of the Great Hall that surely led up to the balustrade and the bed chambers.

Did I understand as much as I thought?

'Eh? You dropped a bowl – no, a bloody pissing pot – you hit him on the head with a bloody pissing pot?'

'I did not mean to do it,' she said. 'It was full . . . unsteady . . . It slipped from my hands. I did not know he was standing beneath the balustrade at that very moment. We had only just . . . there had been . . . we were about to . . .' She was searching for a way to explain her cruel ordeal. She left her words unfinished. I did not need them.

Old-man Wishard, Headman of the Wishards, Graynelord of all Graynelore, was dead. His death had been a silly – a petty – domestic accident: he had been killed by a pot of piss.

Killed, by a bloody pot of piss!

What, my friend? You think it an ignoble end for a fighting-man? Would you rather I lied, and gave you instead a wild, heroic invention? An iron pot will crack your head as well as any sword. Mind, it was a tale the Beggar Bards would long be telling, to raise a laugh and feed their empty bellies upon a cold winter's night. Aye, and at a Wishard's expense!

I almost laughed in spite of myself.

'The eldest of the Council came and set upon me then,' she said. For certain, the man I had named Stiff Brittle. 'And not alone. He may appear an aged crock, only do not let that image deceive you. He left me, again, in fear for my life . . . aye, and for that of all my kin. There was ever bad blood between us: Elfwych and Wishard. Whatever the circumstances of this death, whatever the intent, the outcome was certain to be the same: a terrible blight upon my house. These Wishards would take their revenge upon us, and we have already suffered so . . . Can *you* tell me that it would be otherwise?'

I stayed silent, for I could not.

'I have no doubt I would have been slain . . . Their anger for the death of their Graynelord was terrible . . . Only, something stayed their hand; there was a deeper expression revealed within their faces. Dread, it seemed. Aye . . . dread. Not for the loss they had suffered. Rather, these men were more concerned for themselves.'

I needed no explanation. It was clear enough to me. With the Old-man dead his brother would rightly step into his place. He, with his own house and entourage, his own Council, his own politicians. These were men who had gone soft: who had bought their favours from the Old-man with flattery and quick minds. Sly as foxes. Scribes, who could twist simple words into serpents . . . as deadly as needs be.

I could see it all. With this death they were instantly displaced. Their title, rank, protection, influence, and wealth were all gone. (Had they not said as much themselves in their close confidence?)

'And I was the weapon of their downfall,' said Norda Elfwych. She raised her hand as if to touch the inflamed wound at her throat, only to stop herself short.

'And?' I saw in her face there was yet more to this.

'I could not let it happen,' she said.

'What then – you did not wish to die?'

'Me? Look at me! See what your kin have already achieved. How much more could I suffer? My death! Ha! What little would that matter? No. This was not done for me. My love is for my family, my sisters, and my grayne – what few of them remain – as much as my hate is reserved for the Wishards.'

She suddenly stopped, and gave me a meaningful look. Perhaps she was wondering where my loyalties truly lay . . . (Perhaps I was too.)

'I told them what I am,' she said.

'Eh?'

'I . . . told . . . them . . . Rogrig . . .' She drew out her words. There was a new despair in her voice; a terrible guilt. She seemed to shrink visibly under its weight. 'I said I could disguise his death. I said I could revive him. Oh, and how easily, how very quickly those old men saw the advantage in it; took the bait I offered them and made the idea their own . . .

'The Council began to argue among itself then. Though, not over the right or the wrong of it, but over how best it could be achieved. Was The Graynelord to be stuffed like a trophy, or embalmed, or else tied up with ropes and strings and handled like a puppet? It both shocked and enthralled them to learn that I could at once conceal his death and animate him without such barbarism. For all intent, I was to bring him back to life as much alike his former self as ever he was: enough to fool all but the closest of his kin.' She bowed her head, the memory become too difficult to bear. Her voice, already slight and trembling, grew ever less distinct. 'How eager they were . . . Yet on another day my revelation would have earned me my death. For certain, they would have burned me for a wych and enjoyed my roasting as an entertainment. How duplicitous are the minds of men, eh Rogrig?'

Norda paused, looked directly at me, though still I made no answer.

'It was decided he should be kept apart from all but the most loyal members of his household: from the people who knew him too well. His common kin recognized him only at a distance – if at all – and could be the more easily fooled. What nobody misses nobody notices. They would believe whatever deception was put before them.'

Again she paused. Her sore eyes wandered despairingly, as if she might find an easier route, a way to avoid making her explanation. There was none.

'This was no simple enchantment, Rogrig. I let go of my living spirit, fetched it out before them and laid it down upon the Old-man's cold remains; that fetid corpse. I used my Glamour to lift him up, to give his body a semblance of life, and warmth, and to disguise his death. They dragged my body to the night-closet. They dropped it clumsily upon the stone floor, though I breathed still and knew myself to be there . . .

'And in this state I have remained, betwixt the two; the living body and the dead. The one in stiff confinement and mortal agony; the other, its flesh peeling, its very innards seeping, rotting away . . .'

She stopped there, and would say no more.

I looked down at the corpse of the Old-man. Released of its faerie Glamour it had quickly begun to decompose. Pools of stinking liquid ran freely across the stone floor, finding its way into cracks, congealing there. Turgid flesh lifted from his bones, split, burst open and spilled its contents.

I, like the babbie of my distant childhood, felt myself sickened by it – though I was a hardened man – and the bile rose in my throat. I swallowed firmly, held it down. I owed Norda Elfwych that much, if not my heartfelt sorrow.

Lowly Crows, who had stayed well apart from us all this time, no doubt carefully watching our performance unfold, suddenly ruffled her feathers, stretched her wings, and flew down from the ceiling, landing on my shoulder. Her arrival was enough to remind me of our true purpose in this tower. She did not need to speak. And yet I hesitated, still . . .

Norda had allowed herself to be degraded, abused, hurt beyond reason, worse . . . Even now she was steeling herself to take up again the fetid body of the Old-man; for the sake of her family, her grayne. Her wasted eyes betrayed her. Only, I was come here to steal her away, to stop her from that very purpose. Why?

Because I was embroiled upon a bloody, faerie tale!

She saw my intent, suddenly revealed. For inside my head the shadow-tongues were crying out to me. I knew she heard them too!

'I will not go with you, Rogrig,' she said. 'Nor with your pretty bird here . . . (Who I see just as clearly . . .) Would you, of all people, expect me to?'

On my shoulder, Lowly Crows began to beat her wings in exasperation.

'You will die then, just as certainly,' I said. 'Take a look at yourself! And we might not be discovered as yet, and this house still quiet, but I do not expect it to remain so.'

'But these men are *your* kin,' she said. 'Would you not rather be dead than a broken man?'

'When we first met . . . upon the fells, upon the killing fields . . . you already knew of this fey task we are about.

I am certain of it, Norda Elfwych. It was I who was the ignorant fighting man, hardly aware of himself; only half alive until that very moment . . . Yet here I am, all the same, and in earnest. Truthfully, I cannot say how this will turn out. I only know I must see it through to the very end . . .'

'Even if you have to kidnap me to do it? You are ever a true son of your grayne, then!' She attempted a laugh, only the shot of pain was too cruel. 'Oh Rogrig, if my Pledge is struck, you know what will happen. You have seen the broken walls of Staward Peel. Would you have me invite yet another open conflict upon my family? My sisters are mere babbies. My poorly brother is no leader of men. He hardly knows which way around to sit upon his warhorse. I fear my grayne will not survive it. I have made my bargain with the Council, and I would keep it . . . '

Norda began to shuffle awkwardly towards the fallen Graynelord, her crippled limbs, stiff with pain, finding the movement difficult.

'Listen to me, and let the dead be!' I said. I put myself between Norda and the remains of the Old-man. 'Surely, Norda, you must see there is no stepping back from this? There is no safe way out. I ask you to come with us freely, but I cannot lie. I would use main force – let the blatant deceit of this Council be exposed for what it is. *There* is the hope for your grayne!'

'Indeed. The Headmen of the ruling houses of Graynelore would not take kindly to it,' said Norda. There was little strength left in her voice.

'It will mean an utter debacle, an open war between *all* men!' added Lowly Crows. The agitated flapping of her wings throwing up loose feathers.

'Yes . . . And what better distraction could we ask for?' I said. 'If the graynes are fighting in earnest among themselves they are not going to be looking out for us. There will be *no* faerie hunt.'

'No? Our escape is as good as made then,' said Lowly Crows.

'Men will be too busy lopping off each other's heads to worry about *how* this deceit came about,' I said, warming to my cause. 'And if they come to that conclusion afterwards, well, it will be too late . . .'

'Ha . . .' The brief mark of a real smile upon Norda's face could not hide her deeper pain, and was quickly gone. 'Then I have only one more question for you, Rogrig. How do you intend us to escape? I am in no condition to outrun old men, let alone a grayne at arms . . . You gained this house with persuasion, the wit of your tongue . . . bribery. Now, most men here believe you foully poisoned and surely dead. You could not pass through its locked gates unchallenged. And, as you see, there is no fight left in me . . .' She lowered her head, stood before me, decrepit. Her point was proven without further debate, or description. 'Or perhaps, like your unusual companion here, we could all sprout wings and simply fly away?'

Lowly Crows was suddenly pecking at my shoulder.

Now there was a good idea.

Chapter Twenty-Four

As the Crow Flies

'It was a feeble woman's jest, Rogrig. I was not being serious. Do not make me do this thing.' I was holding on to Norda Elfwych. In truth, I was forcibly dragging her up the stone steps of the tower of Carraw Peel. That she was racked with pain was obvious. I could not help that. I saw no other way for us to gain our freedom.

I could tell you that I knew how I would get us out all along, or I could tell you that the idea came with Norda's gentle faerie slight. Either way, I was resigned to it, and Lowly Crows, eager to play her part.

Movement inside the tower was relatively easy. Though the house was far from empty, nobody expected to be attacked from the inside. The greater defences were on the outside; in the courtyard and along the outer defensive wall before the great doorway – where, no doubt, Wint-the-Snoop still kept a weathered eye – and in the armed men of the bastle-houses that stood at points all along the valley, within eye and ear of the peel tower. It required little thought. If we intended to escape with our lives, we needed another way out: a route that did not involve us going back the way we had come.

For the most, the servants of the house we came upon stood rigidly afraid at our approach. Those still with their wits about them quickly withdrew and without raising the alarm. They had no wish to choose sides. And I had not the stomach or the desire to dispatch them, and let them flee. Even the few men at arms recoiled – I was still a Wishard, after all – uncertain of my intent until I levelled my sword in their direction. There was death then, I will not deny it. One man took a cracking blow to his head and the point of my sword skewered his gut, though not before he had made a flailing run at us first. I left another man to bleed out – a member of the Old-man's Council – sprawled upon the stone stairs, the dagger's arse pinned to his back.

The tower of Carraw Peel was built to a common pattern and a simple construction. It was a square stone tower with a wooden stair from the ground floor to the Great Hall (which could be broken up in a storm) and then a stone spiral staircase all the way to the roof. There were chambers, mostly bed-robes on each floor, with The Graynelord's finest apartments at the very top.

We climbed ever upwards, wanting only the roof – where there was a platform below the parapet, wide enough for men to stand guard and keep a watch across the wide open valley in front of them. As it turned out, the Old-man, or perhaps his Council, had been a confident leader: when we came upon it, at last, the roof was deserted. There were no men keeping the watch this day.

Lowly Crows knew what she was about. She took flight, leapt from my shoulder the instant she saw the first hint of blue sky above her, and before we were fully through the trapdoor that opened onto the roof. She flew directly towards the sun and was quickly a tiny black scratch, difficult to find there.

Beside me Norda Elfwych began to pull herself free of my supporting arm. Though she was ever an unwilling accomplice, breathless at the climb and sickening with it, she was determined to stand her own ground. (Do not measure courage by strength of arms alone, my friend.) I let go my grasp, if a little reluctantly.

And then, after what seemed to be only the briefest pause, Lowly Crows was returning to us. The sky above the tower had been almost clear blue. Suddenly, a brooding, rolling storm cloud engulfed the rooftop of Carraw Peel, blocking out the sun. There was no sound yet; only a vast movement of air, as perhaps a thousand pairs of wings silently beat in perfect unison. Not a thunder cloud then, but birds: countless black birds. This was a great murder of crows.

Then, together, as a single body, they came clattering down upon the roof of the tower, each bird seeking its perch at the exact same moment, and landing perfectly. I will admit, the racket of raking claws upon the stone roof, the sudden shriek as, in unison, they each let go a terrible cry, had our hands upon our ears and a cold shiver running down my spine.

In the courtyard below us there was instant commotion. Armed men were running aimlessly about the walls, pointing at us with drawn swords, calling to their fortunes, to their fellows, to their Graynelord, but helpless to act. A pair of bowmen loosed a string of arrows towards us. It was a futile gesture. The best of their willows clattered harmlessly against the wall of the stone tower, a good body length below us; struck like feeble fell-flies trying to break the leather-hard skin of a seasoned hobby-horse. At my back there was a vacant iron bar bell, swinging aimlessly in the wind, waiting to be rung out. I took a hold of it, held it still. There would be no alarm raised.

Lowly Crows was once more resting on my shoulder.

'Just exactly how many birds are you?' I said.

'Exactly?' she replied, enigmatically. 'All of them. Shall we go?'

Norda Elfwych was beginning to make some dreadful noises of her own; pitiful wild shrieks that skewered the air, now that she was certain of what we were about.

'How far do you think you can take us?' I asked the crow. From the top of the tower the ground looked an awfully long way down. A man's body is a feeble package. Dropped bones break easily.

'Far enough, I think . . .' she said. Only she paused, and gave me her rook's eye. 'We can probably carry you out of this valley and across the banks of the River Winding. After that, we shall have to see . . .'

'Probably . . .' It was not a retort; I was musing to myself. 'All right then . . .'

The birds fell upon us, engulfed us. All at once, and in a single motion, rising from their rooftop perches. It felt not unlike the fierce smack of a frigid ocean wave. They picked at our clothes, tugged at our hair, tore at our skin, let go again only to search for a better grip and to take a firmer hold. It was a violent rescue. It was desperate. There was no part of my body that did not feel the hurt of their intrusion. Common instinct made me reach for my sword as if I were attacked. It took all of my wit to stay my arm.

I heard Norda's feeble crying, lost it again among the squeals of the birds. Briefly, I saw her raise her arms as if to protect her eyes and face from the onslaught. I saw the lines of fine cuts open up upon her skin where countless agitated claws – in all innocence – took a hold and left an accidental reminder.

I felt the same incisions upon my own skin. I tasted a sweet run of blood upon my lips.

Suddenly I was lifted up; my feet were over my head. My arms were pulled out before me, and my fingers taken up as if the birds were lifting up the branches of a young tree. I felt my body hauled across the stonework of the tower-house roof. Damaging both, I feared, pulling loose stones free, sending them clattering to the ground, far below me. Then there was the sudden emptiness of open air; the brutal slap of the wind.

I was carried. I was dropped. Then diving, tipple-tail . . . Down. And down. And down again.

Frantic wings were beating, thrashing the air into turmoil.

And all the while the urgent squeals, the involuntary cries of the birds resounded, drowned out all else, as they took the strain, and felt the agonising weight of my torpid body – that was doing its best to drag them all to the ground and a certain death.

I closed my eyes against it – I admit my cowardly failing – only to feel myself rising through the air again. The cries of the birds grew louder still, as they gained the measure of the flight and at last carried me upwards and onwards; far beyond the great tower of Carraw Peel and out across the valley.

I was flying.

I was flying! And the whole of my world was laid out before me.

For one glorious moment I could see all the way to the Great Sea; and to the rim of the distant mountains at our country's heart, with the black-headed mountain, Earthrise, at their centre. I could see green fells, and the white of snow, and the yellow of a shoreline. I was dazzled by a sun reflected in the broken, surprisingly watery, face of the Wycken Mire. How strangely beautiful it all was. No danger there now. All was safe. I saw scatters of black stone, little more than tiny pebbles; no doubt the tower-houses and the bastles of the graynes, picked out perfectly against the green earth, and here and there among the first of the winter snow. How I envied the birds for this; their private world view . . . And I began to understand a little more of our Lowly Crows.

Then, of a sudden, the flight was over. The rescue was done with. The birds brought me back to earth. Where I fell, the birds fell with me. I hit the ground hard and landed in an awkward manner. My head caught a glancing blow against rock. I was gashed and I was winded, and a little broken, no doubt. My breath was stolen away. It caught in painful snatches, a long while after.

The birds let go their grip of me. They scattered themselves across the green sunlit fells, appearing to cast a dark shadow there so great was their number.

My head hurt, and was still spinning from the flight. The world was turning about me, and in an odd fashion, though I was now firmly rooted to the ground. I realized I had closed my fists about a clump of meadow grass; as if, without an anchor, I was sure to fly away again. It was some time before my eyes settled and I was able to sit up; though not without giddiness.

I looked about for Norda Elfwych, mindful of the remains I might find there.

Only, it was another strange sight that stayed my eyes before I found her out. High upon that rising fell there was a lonely stand of trees and of a truly uncommon kind I could not name. The trees were tall and bare-branched and rubbed shoulders, groaning softly as they caught against each other in the wind. Much of their bark had been scraped away revealing bare wood. They stood like a great crowd of wild men; their naked arms held up high and wide, and they were waving. The trees were always waving . . .

There, at last, I saw Norda Elfwych.

She had landed a little way off and appeared to be crouched upon all fours. Her head was lolling forward, her skein of rats-tail hair, lank and matted and wet, trailed upon the ground there. I could still see one side of her battered face. She looked both ill and befuddled, but at least she was alive. (Can a man hate so much, and yet still find pity in his heart . . . more, a kindling of respect? I hope so.)

It was the odd behaviour of the crows that next drew my attention.

Where they had landed, they had become very quiet and very still. Only the odd wing moved, tweaked by its owner or the wind. It occurred to me then, what a great thing it was they had done for us: however many their number, they had carried the full weight of a grown man – aye, and a woman, too – for several miles across the sky. If the act had all but finished us, what had it meant for them? We were forever beholden.

How long it took I do not recall, but at last the birds began to move again. First one, and then another, roused itself and, not without a struggle, took to the air once more. Slowly, others followed . . . A few held themselves in flight, confident in their strength, but the most turned again for the Lonely Trees and resettled there among the branches. And as they did, the arms of the trees settled too, and became easy, even if the wind still blew. The birds had surely come home.

Only Lowly Crows came to me; she fluttered down beside me, obviously exhausted at the flight, and yet agitated and purposeful. I would have seen the woman then, only, the bird persisted. She regarded me thoughtfully and rook-eyed.

'We will rest here only a short while, and then we must leave you, Rogrig,' she said.

'We?'

'I think you will be safe here, if you are strong enough?'

I glanced towards Norda, before I answered. She had slumped forwards, and was struggling to hold her head off the ground with one supporting arm. There was a string of spew trailing from her mouth.

'Yes . . .' I said to Lowly Crows, though I knew it to be a weedling lie. 'Go, and do what you must.'

'There are rumours to be cast upon the wind . . . Have you not heard them, Rogrig? Your Graynelord is dead, his final rule a deceit, and the conspiracy of his Council is unmasked . . . The graynes must be told of this treachery, and a bird can more quickly spread the tale than a man's word of mouth alone. Eh?'

'Then, give your story wings . . .' I said, forcing a smile.

Lowly Crows spread her own wings as if in response. 'Say something often enough, spread a rumour wide enough, hear it repeated back, and it is amazing how easily – how quickly – it is believed.'

'And if it also happens to be the accepted truth?' I said.

'All the better for that, my friend . . . Just not essential!' She turned herself about, looking quietly between Norda and myself as if to satisfy herself of something.

'It will be easier for our greater company to travel unnoticed behind the shadows of a rising war,' she said. 'When the whole world is out upon a Riding, no one is going to notice a little extra dust upon the road . . . Eh?'

'Not even Faerie Dust,' I said. Our sudden burst of laughter was real.

To her word, the birds' respite was short enough.

Lowly Crows took off, still weary; she had to beat her wings hard to lift herself into the sky. She was quickly followed into the air by the last of her kin. The Lonely Trees emptied with a great flourish. And the fell rapidly cleared. I would have lost sight of her among the body of her fellows if I had not come to recognize the distinctive shape of her wings . . . and heard her voice, calling back to me. I watched the crows until they were quite distant.

Only, not all of the black shapes on the ground had roused themselves to flight. There were as many that had not moved at all, were done for. As she flew higher, Lowly Crow's bird-song grew distant and faint, until there was nothing at all.

Inside my head, as if in sympathy, the shadow-voices too drew silent. The only sounds were the waving branches of the Lonely Trees, groaning again, and the cuss of the wind as it caught the broken flight feathers of the black shapes left behind, forlorn, upon the fell.

I gave in then, to my sorely body, and I lay my head down upon the cool grass. I closed my eyes for just a moment's rest . . . for just a moment.

Chapter Twenty-Five

The Debateable Land

The Crows flew, and they told their story, they spread their tale upon the air. And the ears of all Graynelore slowly turned toward them, began to listen and to take heed.

The death of a Headman, more, the death of a Graynelord, was doubtless a tragedy. It was also a series of unique opportunities. For some graynes, it was the opportunity to take their main chance, and to assert themselves and their authority over others; to attempt to gain a ruling influence. For many lesser graynes, it was simply the opportunity to make mischief, while their more powerful neighbours were temporarily looking in someone else's direction. Witless cowards were suddenly brave adventurers when, for a few short breaths, traditional enemies, old adversaries, were off making war. What better time to steal your neighbour's stock, their coin, their wives and their chattels . . . or take your cold revenge?

It was almost like an extended holyday.

A brief respite from the constant repression of a stronger grayne meant you could do some repressing of your own. It was a time to settle old blood feuds, and get your own back.

A shift in status, a change in leadership, was bound to cause havoc all across Graynelore (especially if the deed was contested or foul play suspected – and it ever was). The effects were immediate. It left the world out of kilter. Its balance momentarily shifted, teetering on the brink of the abyss – requiring a swift redress.

For certain, the chaos, the unrest, would be short lived: a matter of days only, weeks at most, before a new order was imposed by the strongest arm. Always the strongest arm.

It was a perfect time for a strange gathering of faeries to go about their secret business. There would be no coordinated attempt to find them out, no general cry of 'Wych! Wych!'

It was also a dangerous time, for of a sudden every man was an enemy. There would be no safe houses now. Keep apart, to yourself, eyes fixed upon the ground. Do not look a man in the face for fear it offends him. Do not be seen unless you mean to be seen. Do not draw attention to yourself until the matter is settled.

All claims, no matter how trivial or outrageous, became valid claims; every issue, debateable – and Graynelore, the Debateable Land. All justice, absolute; rough and ready, rude and bloody . . .

A man might have wished for some sort of celestial collusion, to help us out. Perhaps some did. Even the weather began to understand the change in our circumstance. An already watery sun stopped shining. Moody bruised clouds hung low in the sky, draped the landscape, and left the greater part of Graynelore beneath a layered shroud of constant rain or early winter sleet. Fog rolled in across the fells and heavy mist clung to the bottom of the hillsides and would not let go again; like frightened women drawing their skirts tightly about them against the threat of a violation.

The greater trails became deserted, and constant travellers a curiosity. Men mostly stopped travelling, in case their movement was seen as a threat or an intrusion worthy of a fight. And a fight always meant a death. The few tavern keepers stopped asking questions of their guests. It was not healthy to be too inquisitive. Across all Graynelore, the Strongholds rang out their iron bells, called in their close kin, barred their doors, took away their ladders, broke up their wooden stairs, and waited – hopeful that the rising storm would soon pass off and leave them be.

I felt a shadow fall across me, blotting out what my waking eyes saw as the light of the sun, and its warmth.

'Notyet?' I called out, sleepily. Hers was the first name to come into my dozy mind.

I opened my eyes fully, and thought I saw the dark outline of two figures standing across me. One was a lopsided Norda Elfwych, still visibly carrying the pains of our endeavours. The other figure, a stranger to me, was most definitely that of a hardened man. He held something in his hand – like a sword. I reached for my own, tried to raise myself up, only to feel the weight of a wooden staff pressed hard against my chest, pinning me back to the ground.

'Rest easy, Big Man, do not fuss so. *I know you . . .*' The stranger spoke through gritted teeth, and with conviction.

'Eh?'

'We do not want any misunderstandings here,' he said, leaning more heavily upon his staff. Though I took the sudden extra weight, felt the stab of pain, without revealing my discomfort. 'Let me be clear. I know you both . . . and I know what you are.' His voice was strong and it was steady. The man knew what he was about.

'It is all right, Rogrig,' Norda's anxious voice intervened. 'This man is a friend.'

'A friend you say? Ha! I fear . . . we have no friends!' I said.

'Begging your pardon, you will still be wanting some supper though?' said the stranger. As he spoke he took away his staff and allowed me to sit up. I lifted my hand away from the hilt of my sword, let my arm rest. He had not pressed his advantage when he might well have done, was worthy of a second thought.

I guessed the hour at early evening. It seemed I had slept away the remains of the day. There was a newly made campfire close by. (It was the warmth of the fire I had mistaken for the sun.) As he stepped aside, the firelight fell upon the stranger . . .

He was grinning at me, and it was an inane grin, which displayed a row of broken teeth. On another occasion, it might have inspired me to hit him. I . . . did not. I recognized him – not the man, but the breed, the profession – he was a Beggar Bard, no less. They are all broadly alike in manner and custom. Whatever their age, old or young, they wear the same garb, carry the same broken relics, and speak with the same tongue. (And yet here was a curious thing: in all my life I had not once seen two together. At the same place perhaps, but never together. Never a pair! They are solitary creatures who appear to shun contact with their own kind.)

There was a makeshift spit set across the fire, with skewered meat roasting upon it; small birds it seemed . . . Crow . . .? I could not blame a man for taking advantage of an unexpected windfall. And I had not eaten in more than a day, let alone fresh meats. I was hungry.

Did we truly consume the flesh of our own rescuers? Of course we did! Forgive our savage ways, my friend. The birds would certainly have eaten our remains in their turn. I would have expected it. And if, at our backs, the Lonely Trees groaned just a little louder and complained just a little more as we fed, they surely understood.

Afterwards, I watched the Beggar Bard busy himself, gathering up the plucked feathers. It was done to stuff a makeshift pillow, to soften up his bed or the like. He offered a handful of feathers to Norda, which she readily took and tied together in three small bundles. One – the smallest – she gave to me (I still have it). The second she returned to the Lonely Trees, tying them carefully to a lowly branch. The last she pinned to her shift, not to prettify herself, but as a remembrance – a keepsake.

It was an unusual interlude, that time we spent with the Beggar Bard, waiting upon the return of Lowly Crows. Norda Elfwych and I felt content to stay where we were, and in his company, for a second night. We were both in need of some respite. Norda had been sorely wounded, nay, brutally abused in her captivity, and the Beggar Bard appeared to give her some relief, succour; even a little healing I could not afford her.

We talked very little in that encampment. Not even the Beggar Bard. Mind, he did give us his name and called himself Ringbald. I was aware of him habitually fingering the relic that hung about his neck. When he caught me watching him, he only clasped the thing more tightly, as if to disguise it in his hand. I resisted the temptation to handle my own relic; rescued from the Council, returned to its clasp, and now bound tightly to my wrist beneath my cloth. Though I could not see how it was possible for him to know it was hidden there, I fear I still flushed a little, as if my secret hoard was found out.

I look back at all the Beggar Bards now and think I do not see true men, nor even true fey, but creatures of a different breed entirely, perhaps.

In that time, Ringbald made no attempt to explain his first words to me; if I pondered them often enough. How could he *know* what we were? It was a simple fact he had placed between us three. It was a truth that bound us faithfully together.

Neither did he give us his Bard's tale. He only ever offered us up a simple rhyme . . . It was on the second evening. He bade us to come and sit close by him, next to the fire, and he recited a short poem:

You cannot have love without hate,
You cannot know joy without first knowing sorrow,
You cannot have wrong without right,
Nor the light of the day without the darkness of night.

'Your words are quite beautiful,' said Norda Elfwych, adding, somewhat perplexed, 'What do they mean?'

I shrugged. What sense a Beggar Bard?

Ringbald only looked between us and grinned; his inane grin displaying his broken teeth. He nodded his head ever so slightly, as if in affirmation, but without further explanation. Then he settled himself down among the grass with his head upon his pillow of crow's feathers and slept.

Chapter Twenty-Six

Night Sounds

I was awoken in that night, with a draft of cold air. Norda had fallen asleep at my side, and close too, as an animal might have done to keep itself warm. She was not there now . . . Something had disturbed her. She was standing some way off, her back turned, her face lifted towards a black sky and a thin moon.

Where to now, Norda Elfwych? I thought.

I stood up. I left the Beggar Bard sleeping by the fire, upon his pillow of crow feathers.

Had I really rescued Norda from a torment, or had I simply stolen her away? Replaced one bitter trial with the beginnings of another? When she realized I was awake and beside her, she spoke.

'Do we have to live in this way, Rogrig? I mean, in a world where men are forever clawing at each other's throats, seeking only their own advantage?' It was an unexpected conversation.

'You mean; could we not all make a simple agreement and live together in peace and harmony?' I said, deliberately trying to make light of her question. 'We could write ourselves some common laws, perhaps. Sign a treaty, make our covenant. Set some men above us, always above us: to be our government. Do then, only as we are bidden to do, grateful subjects . . . and, for ever more.'

'Well yes, something of that sort, Rogrig. Why ever not?' she asked, suddenly sullen, as if resentful of my slight. 'It sounds perfectly reasonable to me. Would it be *so* very difficult? It is better than hate. It is, surely, better than this . . .'

She turned towards me; held out her hands. They glistened, black, under the weak moonlight. I knew blood well enough . . . One of her private wounds was bleeding afresh.

'Listen,' I said. 'The Graynelore works, if in its own peculiar fashion.' I was attempting to justify myself. 'Each grayne looks out for its own. We none of us trust our neighbours. But then, we do not have to. That is the simple beauty of it. When we need something we each fight for it. When we are contented, we leave each other be. Our strength is our success, and our assurance. It may not be a peaceful existence. But there is no pretence. No false diplomacy. No bloody lies.'

'Only bloodshed.' Norda Elfwych closed her fists. She lifted them to her brow; and in doing so, left her own blood mark upon her face. 'Only killings . . . And an ever withered soul!'

'You know where you are with an enemy,' I said, roughly. 'There are no politicians, with their poisonous words; sticking their subtle knives into your back, twisting the blade.'

'No there are not!' she said, fighting back. 'But only because your neighbour is too busy sticking his dagger into your chest. Can you not see it, Rogrig?'

Our words, if spoken lightly, had suddenly become a fierce argument.

'The graynes have always survived,' I said.

'And for you, survival is enough for the man?'

'I did not say that!'

'Well, it is not enough for me,' she said, shaking her head. 'Ask any imprisoned old man that same question. It is what you *do* with life that matters. I will not measure the quality of my life in years alone. I wish to live!'

'Oh, I have lived!' I said. 'There is no doubt of it, Elfwych. I have lived!'

'Ah yes . . . And what then of civility, eh? What of that?' she asked.

'I did not take you for a fool, Norda Elfwych. Civility, ha! It is just another fine word! Show me a civilisation – show me just one – that was not built entirely upon the force of its arms, and the repression of another.'

'That is the reiver in you speaking,' she said.

'I am a reiver! At least, I am a reiver when I need to be,' I said. I truly wanted her to understand, if my voice grew harsh. 'And it has suited me well enough. I know where I stand.'

I reached for my sword and drew it out. Not to hurt her – only to explain myself.

'It suits you to kill, then?' she asked.

'I have seen you in the frae before now!' I said.

'And that makes it right? Oh, the pitiful, arrogance of men!' she said. 'I have never known a sword do anything yet, but cruel damage.'

'Can you protect yourself with your tongue alone?' I asked.

'You might be surprised, Rogrig.' She paused, though only to suppress some other distant memory she would rather not bring to mind. 'Can you undo the work your sword has done?'

'I know what to do with this sword,' I said, brandishing it between us, letting it sing through the air. 'If I want something—'

'Want?'

'Need then. If I *need* something, with this sword I can take it.'

'Oh you can take all right,' she said, scornfully. 'And would you take me, *reiver*?'

'Take, from an Elfwych! Can you take what is always so freely given away?' The insult was . . . unnecessary. My anger had suddenly the better of my argument. I was sorely sorry for it, only never expressed it.

'Oh please,' she said, in rebuke, 'put that bloody sword away before you damage yourself—'

'And if you did not want me for what I am, what would you have me be, Norda Elfwych?' I asked, plainly enough. And I sheathed my sword, if somewhat noisily.

'Only what you truly are, Rogrig Wishard . . .'

'And what is that?'

She turned her back against me, before she answered. 'Be at ease with yourself, Rogrig; do you not see it yet? The shape we each take on, whether it is a common form or fey, is neither our curse nor a thing to be despised. It is our greatest joy. For it belongs solely to us alone. We are each of us a single universe—'

'Indeed!' My slight was scornful.

'A universe no other, man or woman, can ever know for certain, can only catch the glimpse we choose to reveal to them. They will never walk upon its solid ground or see its distant shores.' Norda turned to face me, eye to eye. 'You have carried your name around with you for long enough,' she said. 'It is past the time for you to own up to it.'

'Ha! Names!' I returned. 'Upon Graynelore, it is our names that have forever kept us divided.'

'Why then did you come to find me out again, if not for this; if not to finally bring us together?'

'We are on the same road,' I said. 'We are at least travelling the same way. In the same direction—'

'Ah! Are we the same then? Is that truly what you think?'

'I see we are of a kind, you and I,' I said.

'Aye, of a kind . . .' she repeated the words slowly, letting them hang upon the air between us. 'Only, you are my heart's ache – and its worst! Just as surely as I am yours! A Wishard and an Elfwych . . . I fear there is never a meeting place for us two. And it seems to me, if we are moving in the same direction, you are always trying to run away. While I am running home . . .'

I might have left Norda to herself. Only I determined not to. I had explained so very little to her and so very badly, and yet I had expected so very much more from her. Most of what she understood, even now, was of her own volition. It was always easier for this man to take, always so much harder for him to give back in his turn.

I stayed at her side, and I talked to Norda Elfwych again. I fear I have never been more voluble. I gave up the whole of my tale thus far, and more . . . without omission. What was said will always rest quietly between us. It requires no further report. What matters is this:

Even after we had talked ourselves out and grown tired, that singular night was not yet done with. There was still something more to come.

The unspoken voices, the shadow-tongues began again their ethereal wailing . . .

'Can you not hear them, Rogrig?' asked Norda.

'Eh?' I tried not to.

'Listen. Someone is calling to us. That is what first woke me this night. Not these bleeding wounds.' She spoke, emphatically. 'I was not certain of it at first. I am now. Someone is calling to us, once more. And this time we must find an answer for them.'

'Fuck – yes!' I had been a fool. I had forgotten my task.

I thought first of Wily Cockatrice, and then of the annoying youth, and the foolish, but beautiful pair of coquettes, who loved each other so dearly . . . They were all in hiding still, no doubt, somewhere in the wilderness. At our last parting we had all but let each other go – in our conscious minds that is – only now it seemed we were searching again, seeking each other out. Had they come to sense our successful escape? Or was it more simply explained? Had Lowly Crows' spreading rumour reached their ears?

Norda Elfwych was standing before the wind. She was trying to return their call, not out loud, but silently, with another inner-voice; her own shadow-tongue.

'Help me to reach them, Rogrig,' she demanded.

'I am,' I said, and I stood beside her. 'I am trying at least—'

'No, I mean . . .'

Rogrig, the man, let the wind blow upon his face, and felt the first kiss of rain upon his skin. Only I am not certain it was a man who made that call into the shade, and who, of a sudden, felt himself a greater part of all things. I knew the growing grass beneath my feet. I knew the river running. I knew the cold stone face of the distant mountain. I knew the ocean depths I could never see, and the starlit sky behind that scowling mask of rain cloud.

And in my turn, I listened to the call of the earth. It was easier this time. I tried to understand its meaning . . . I wanted to understand.

Deep in the shadows, somewhere, someone was laughing brightly. Someone was crying. Someone was hurt – no, being hurt. There was a great joy. There was a worse pain to come. There was sorrow.

And then there were horses coming at the gallop.

From all parts – the Graynelore was roused. The Great Riding had begun. It would be short lived, but it would be fast and it would be furious and it would be deadly. And it would leave no man untouched, unsullied.

A clear call inside my head:

Rogrig, please help us . . . Please help us . . .

'Eh?'

And then I was become myself again.

The work of that night took its toll upon us. We were both utterly exhausted by it, suddenly in need of sleep, and the blanket of forgetfulness that comes with sleep. It could not be fought off. It came upon us so quickly and so deeply that our slumber passed without either dream or night-torment.

When I came awake again it was fully morning. And though I was well rested, I was not yet fully restored. I was become aware, each faerie act, each uncommon display, had its cost; and the greater the deed, the heavier the cost. In that black hole in Wycken the payment had been taken in life and destruction. I would repair, given the time, but I would be warned; this was no easy endeavour we were embarked upon.

The unspoken voices lingered inside my head, incoherent murmurings . . . for ever more it seems. Then the real world intruded:

It was raining still. A fine mist gently brushed my face. I did not fuss. Indeed, I felt more myself for the touch of nature; only pulled my cloth closer about me to ward off the damp.

The Elfwych was nearby, unashamedly at her toilet. I stayed still a moment, watched her slyly (though without intent). Her dreadful injuries seemed to trouble her much less. She moved almost like her true self . . . Alas, only until she was assured there was no one looking on, and then this trick was revealed and she allowed her pain to show and crumpled a little.

There was no improvement in her. It was only a brave face.

As I sat up I realized there was a greater movement about our encampment. There were two figures standing close to the fire. And surely, there were birds again, roosting in the Lonely Trees?

Lowly Crows had returned to us. It was the woman in black who stood next to Ringbald. They were deep in conversation.

Did I feel some small resentment that she had not woken me at once upon her return, and had chosen instead a Beggar Bard's company and his confidence? I quickly let the thought pass (if I was intrigued by it). Lowly Crows never did anything lightly, or without just cause. I had no call upon her. And her business was her own.

Anyway, upon the instant their discussions came to an end and, before I could intervene, they drew apart, both nodding in assent as if an agreement was made between them. I could see that Ringbald was already fully dressed and ready for travel. He did not tarry, and took himself out of our company without further words. He only raised a hand behind him at the very last moment, waved a final farewell to us, as he disappeared over the brow of the hill.

With Ringbald's departure, Lowly Crows transformed once more; the woman broke apart, and in her place, upon the air, was a rising tumult of birds. The most flew to her kin among the branches of the Lonely Trees. Except for one – that Wycken crow. She flew to me and came easily to rest upon my shoulder.

'It is begun, Rogrig,' she said. 'We have stoked the fires, and fed men's desires. They are enraged; eager and ready to stake their claims with their blood. And now, our greater company are calling to us again . . . in want of our swift return.'

I felt I had known as much. The crow's confirmation only hastened our departure. We broke our camp within the hour.

Part Five

The Great Riding

Chapter Twenty-Seven

The Gibbet Tree

Without hobbs, we were forced to travel a-foot. We went lightly, and warily. Norda Elfwych always hobbling, her body stiffened with pain still. To her credit, she did not complain. If I offered her an arm for support she only made light of it and offered me her own in return. I shook my head at her. But made no further noise about it; let her be.

Lowly Crows, ever the bird in flight now, kept a constant vigil over our heads. She came to rest on my shoulder only when she had something important to report. Something that needed a better explanation than a whispered curse from a shadow-tongue . . .

Like, the sight of houses being raided. Like, foul murder being done. The fact that there were so few grazing beasts in the fields: there was only the odd hapless stray, standing forlorn; loan survivors, animals run carelessly off their pasture and unlooked for. There were only the scrawly druins, keeping themselves to the far horizons. They, the wiliest of creatures: the beggars of a wild and hardy breed. No bigger than the black-faced sheep, but sturdier than the hairy-cattle. Good summer meat and better winter fat. Excepting, they were impossible to catch for any but a true fell-stockman.

If there were any men about, they were about for a reason. And up to no good. They were better left to themselves, or run away from, unless you fancied your chances with your sword arm. There was already evidence of recent skirmishing. Here, the corpse of a slaughtered hobby-horse. And the remnants of a robber's haul strewn across the trail: deemed worthless, it had been abandoned. There, the body of a dead man crudely cut up; and sorely mistreated. All the right pieces, I dare say, only arranged in a most unusual, nay, distasteful fashion, even to my battle-hardened eye.

On a distant hillside I picked out the telltale signs of a revenge taken too far. There was smoke, rising – first plumes of white, then bruised black – and the orange glow of fire set against the sky. These were winter shielings I saw; a poor man's shelter; left to burn to the ground. Fuck your neighbour's wife if you have to, kill his eldest child, and steal the vitals from his babbie's mouth. But then, ask yourself this: if you take everything from a man today what will there be left worth stealing tomorrow? (Do you remember my warning, my friend?)

These were the first signs of it then: The Great Riding. All Graynelore was up in arms and upon the raider's trail, to the last willing man. It had all the makings of a dirty ruckus, an ugly scourging; a cruel and crude free-for-all. Lowly Crows had truly stirred us up a deadly storm: and us its cause. Us . . .

Where were we heading? For certain, our trail was less of a plan than it was a considered response. Finding the whereabouts of our broken company was not the difficulty. We knew where to look. They were all calling to us now.

The shadow-tongues, the unspoken voices, were become a great host.

Come to us . . . Find us . . .

Come to us . . . Find us . . .

They said. If not always the words, the sentiment: expressed in waves of turbulent sound. The cadence, the rhythm; rather like distant, but frantic birdsong. Like a crying wind, or murmured rumours; the howl of a storm or the rustle of dry bracken upon an open moorland. Yet, always with the same meaning:

Come to us . . . Find us . . .

Come to us . . . Find us . . .

We only had to seek them out . . .

And *there* was the problem.

They had deliberately drawn wide apart, were spread more thinly and across a far greater territory than I might have imagined. And at any moment I fully expected to be attacked upon the open trail. After all, to look at, we were a most agreeable target; only a single man alone, an ailing woman, and a flutter of crows.

Our principle tactic – our best defence – was to stay off the trade roads, and the obvious reiver trails. A circuitous route might be a greater labour and a far longer trial, but it was worthy of the effort if it kept our party alive. In particular, the Long Ridings of the ruling graynes were to be avoided at all costs. The Troll, the Bogart, the Wishard, and the Elfwych – aye, even the diminished Elfwych – and their eager blood-ties. Their numbers would be counted in hundreds, and beware any man who found himself crossing their path. There were few hot-blooded fighting-men among them who would have a care for whose head it was they were separating from its shoulders. *Any* man who as much as stood in their way was a declared enemy! Every traveller was become their fair game!

Paradoxically, there was an advantage to be gained by this. Of course, it hindered our progress, but if it kept us on our guard and always wary, it did the same for our own sworn enemies. It was much preferable to us finding ourselves the sole prey of The Great Riding.

Twice we came face to face with small bands of fighting-men: Short Ridings – three or four men, strong blood-ties, no doubt; the members of lesser graynes ready to take a chance upon a wayside ambush in search of easy spoil – who, on balance, decided we were not worth the cost of a fight. (A livid wound is a livid wound, however it is come by.) At the first meet, a stony eyed standoff was enough of a confrontation to satisfy both our parties. We each looked the other over warily or cockily (as was our want) and let our paths cross without incident. Not so much as a word exchanged. A mistaken greeting, even then, might have caused a deadly ruckus.

At the second meet, there was need of a slanging match. A rough tongue lashing! Which, it has to be said, we were *all* rather good at, and even enjoyed. And if it was only a light-hearted affair, with no lasting damage done to either side; better that than a death fight. We were caught out upon a lightly trodden path; a winding trail within a wooded grove. Lowly Crows gave us a warning, but there was little space for either of our parties to turn aside – gracefully. And neither they, nor we, would retire unchallenged. They came on; four men riding, two abreast. I could see they were poorly armed, with little more than long knives, and they already carried heavily loaded sacks. Their hobbs walked head down, labouring under the weight of their toil. I reckoned it was worth a bellowed oath to save the strength of my sword arm.

'Move yourself aside! You great pair of cack-handed fuckers!' I slung at the first pair, as we drew level.

I did not stand up to the argument, but stayed plainly open handed in their sight, kept my feet walking. If my instinct was still to make a fist of it and bring the beggars down.

'Pah!' The bigger lad looked down at me shrewdly. At once understood, by my gesture, I meant not to fight, only to argue . . . if he had a like mind. Fortunately, he saw the advantage, and took up my offer with a relish. He sucked on his nose; gobbed noisily at my feet. 'That's a big mouth on you, hard man. Mind, I can see you would both sooner shit yourselves and run, before you swung a piece of iron this way!'

'Aye, you reckon do you?' Norda Elfwych was suddenly animated. It seemed this was a game we all knew how to play. 'And you have, no doubt, pinned your own babbies to your table for fresh meat, long before now!'

'Well now, isn't *that* the ugliest face I've ever seen talking!' This was the smaller man of the leading pair. 'It's no better than a scrawly druin!'

'Better a druin's face than its withered hinnies!' cried Norda.

'Hark at the woman! I ken your breeches are so often slackened it's a fair wonder you bother to keep them tied up at all.'

'Fuck you!'

'Yes, please! If that's your best offer?'

'Dagger's arse!'

'Aye; and a wych's curse!'

'Ha! I'll have all your fucking jollies in a bottle!' Norda was making unusual faces at the last man in their line.

'I'm fair leaking myself! See? See? I'm fair leaking myself!' The man loosened his breeches, leaned over the side of his hobb, and aimed a piss at her as he passed her by. Fortunately, he was well off his mark.

'Ma hinnies' puddle! If that's your best shot maybe you are in want of a woman's help to steady your aim?' Norda gestured crudely with her hand.

At that, the man appeared momentarily confused; uncertain if he had been encouraged to some lewd act, or foully blasphemed against. He decided upon the latter. 'And is that really the hard man's sister talking?' he bellowed. 'Or is it his brother perhaps?'

'Come back here and find out for yourself!' cried Norda.

'Right you are then!'

'There'll be nothing but a cuss of a foul wind ballooning them pants!'

'Aye, for sure . . . there's a cuss of foul wind . . . only I know where it's blowing.' This last retort came half-heartedly. Mind, our two companies were well past each other, and a good fifty paces apart, before we finally gave it up, and took ourselves a breath.

'Norda, I am no innocent man,' I said, wryly, 'but that is a black tongue you have!'

'Far better a blackened tongue, Rogrig, than sticks and stones and broken bones,' she returned. Her face was bright with the lark. 'Far better that.'

'Ha.'

It is fair to say, that slanging match raised both our spirits, if only for a short while. Soon after, we left the easily trodden paths, travelled instead to the lonely places: to the waterlogged fens and to the barren moorlands dressed only with bracken and stone and wild gorse. When every man is an enemy, and every welcoming house but a trap, then every marked trail becomes a warning and a danger to be avoided.

Upon a time, we came again to that river's mouth, where our gathered fey company had once encamped. And for a good while more, we travelled north. We followed the coastline of the eastern sea border, with its cruelly exposed headlands, where there was no shelter and we were constantly beaten by the winds coming off the Great Sea; the brutal squalling tumults of air that had cut the face of the cliff-rock into devilish unnatural shapes. We went ever further, turned at last inland again, treading always upon unbroken ground, where there were no paths to follow; which might well have been our undoing, if Lowly Crows had not been constantly flying over our heads making sure of our way; if the shadow-voices had not continued to call, drawing us ever onward.

And so it was that in following this interminable, devious route we avoided any real trouble. And, here and there, in this hide-hole or that, along the way, we at last renewed our acquaintance with our greater company. First found was Dogsbeard. And then Wily Cockatrice who, in wanton celebration, lit her pipe and filled the air with an extravagant trail of green and purple smoke. Next found, was the elder-man: who was so excited at our discovery, he came at us out of cover, and all of a sudden, from among a string of elder trees. I had never seen him so animated. It took a skirling cry from Lowly Crows to stay my hand upon my sword, or else I might have turned upon him in mistake. Fortunately, in the event, we were well met.

Norda Elfwych was always received kindly and respect-fully into our growing company. There was an open show of friendship, if given a little solemnly, not to say with relief at the success of our adventure. Certainly, there was never any hint of faerie slight. Only a sympathetic eye for her diminished state; her cruel injuries that so obviously tormented her still.

Intriguingly, with each addition to our company my understanding of the shadow-tongue became a little clearer. It was more obviously defined – if not particularly easier to comprehend. That is to say, I could almost make out who it was who was sending which message, or making which noise; if I could not often translate the meanings. You see, we did not speak with one voice, not often in the same tongue even, or so it seemed. We each of us had a very individual way of calling; a coarse signature that belonged to us alone.

And among the shadow-tongues, there were the *others* . . . who made the ethereal noises; sounds as raw as the wind, as delicate as falling rain upon fallen autumn leaves. These were the voices that belonged neither to any living man *nor* to any fey creature; voices that might have always been there, calling across the ages, asking not for understanding but only to be remembered and heard.

At last there were only two of our company missing: Fortuna and Sunfast, the lithe coquettes; those closest of companions, who I had also known briefly for a pair of unifauns, and my lovers . . . They were not so far away now. Their voices were both distinct and strong, if disparate, it seemed, which only served to confuse me. Why were they not calling out together, when they were always together?

Inside my head, their calls sounded like a beautiful, untamed music. It reminded me of the tunes Notyet had played upon her wooden whistle in my childhood days. And we were so close to them . . . so very close to finding them. Surely it was enough for us to use our eyes and search them out?

And then, finally, there was the first of the pair before us – Fortuna – if stiffly crouched; cleverly hidden among the undergrowth some paces off the beaten track. She appeared timid, unwilling to break her cover and stand up, unwilling to show herself, even to us, though our approach was open and welcoming.

If her behaviour was, as yet, beyond my understanding, it left me uncomfortably wary, as if I should be on my guard against some greater unseen danger.

The faces of my close company had begun to turn sour. There was a look of consternation upon the faces of both the elder-man and Dogsbeard; elsewhere it was a bitter grief. What did Wily Cockatrice *see*? I felt sure she knew something more of the truth in this.

Above me, upon the air, the crows were in frantic disarray. Lowly Crows was calling pitifully. Suddenly swooping and wheeling, trying to draw my attention toward a stand of three oak trees a little way off the path.

Inside my head the unspoken-voices, the shadow-tongues, were changing their tunes. The sweet music was become fractious, distorted, and oddly disturbing.

Then it broke apart, splintered, like the shattering of a fragile glass.

Then, sudden, sharp discords; painful, resonant notes struck my inner ears. Physically hurt.

I was not the only one to feel it. Beside me Norda Elfwych twisted her face for the pain of it. Wily Cockatrice turned hers away that none of our company should see her mournful expression; or the sting of tears in her eye.

Can music cry, weep with despair? Can it mimic the lucent stars falling out of the sky? It touched my heart, my soul too perhaps.

Then it stopped.

Most violently stopped . . .

It was I who came alone upon the second of the pair, among the stand of oak trees. I would not have wished any other to see her in that way.

I found her semi-naked body hanging limply by its broken neck from a branch of the furthest oak tree; now become a make shift gibbet. Sunfast had been hung, stretched, for a common wych; left only the dignity of her torn shift. Her blood and loose shit ran down her bare legs, dripped from her toes, still warm. She was not long dead. Her death had obviously been tortuous, cruel, and prolonged. Her executioners unpractised with the rope and the knot . . .

If this had been the last of the tragedy it would have been enough. Only we were ever upon Graynelore! Wily Cockatrice had realized much more of it than I. She was stood upon the field, bent over, as if to a child, her arms gently enfolding Fortuna's distraught, cowering form. It was a hopeless gesture.

Fortuna would not be roused from her hiding place among the bracken. An utter wretch, she could not be pacified or consoled. The cowards who had brutally hung the one might well have hung them both together. These two had been the truest of fey creatures. They were not to be separated in life. Nor in death, either.

Fortuna died within that hour, though there was not a mark of violence upon her body. Her only symptoms: her despairing grief.

That pair's foul destruction seemed wholly a crime. I had only ever seen love and sweet innocence upon their faces. They had harmed no man. Graynelore was ever a most brutal world. And this time it had surely broken the bounds . . .

I looked about me then; in my fury I would have killed any stranger I set my eyes upon, guilty or no. It was perhaps fortunate there was no sign of anyone. As for the perpetrators: they were either too well hid, or had long since made good their escape upon our approach.

My companions stood by in dispassionate silence, content to be my witnesses. I set fire to that stand of three oak trees, would see no living accomplice remain. I burned them all to the ground and the swinging corpse with them. I left the second body in the place where it had fallen, still. I burned the bracken and the gorse, and laid waste to much of the hillside. The earth, at least, would remember these deaths and carry the scars of their passing.

Chapter Twenty-Eight

Rogrig the Wishard

Graynelore does not shy away at the mention of a death. To a reiver it is a plain matter; and a common enough necessity. Neither is death long mourned, nor often regretted, if there is not a vengeance to be taken.

Living men still breathe; life is celebrated, in the moment. And that was always enough. There is little sense in planning for a lifetime when men are hungry, angry, thirsty, enamoured *now* . . . A single good memory has worth; an unfulfilled dream has none. A day lived is better than a lifetime in waiting.

Our company were unwilling to move on until the hillside fires had fully burned themselves out, until the thin slivers of windborne smoke stopped rising from the blackened earth, and the ash had grown quite cold.

The ancient crone sat upon a lonely rock, drawing thickly upon a cold dry pipe, watching the last of it subside.

These deaths were a burden of a different kind.

It was to the practicality of a basic sum that we now had to give our full attention. We had set ourselves upon a task. It was a weight we had, thus far, failed to carry. We were after the making of a Faerie Ring: A Ring of Eight. Our greater number had been in want of only one – and that one was Norda Elfwych, whose freedom had been gained at such a terrible cost . . . to the crows . . . to the wych herself . . . And yet here we were again, still in want of numbers! Only now the shortfall had doubled, and become two.

I felt it was a hopeless task. Already angered, I could not help my rising fury.

'We were never meant for this, I think! What fucking use, our so-called *fey* talents? Eh?' If I could not use the edge of my sword to break open fresh heads, I could use my foul tongue, instead, to bruise a few egos. Mine own included. 'If I were a true *Wishard* . . . Aye, if I *were* . . . why could I not simply wish for our deliverance? I cannot wish death away! I cannot wish new life! What is it then that we know for certain? I see only passing shadows here! Aye! And bloody fools set upon an impossible adventure.'

'We know what we are,' said Wily Cockatrice, not unkindly. 'And I know there is more to this angry young man before me than meets the common eye.'

I would not have her consolatory words.

'Do you, now? Only, not *your* eye, eh? What is it that you really *see*, I wonder?' I said. 'You sit there no better than a blind old woman!'

Visibly affronted, Wily Cockatrice shuffled herself about, resettled herself, uncomfortably, upon her rock. 'I see it is well past time for you to take a greater hand in this, Rogrig Wishard!' This was the second time I had been brought to task.

'And *I* see guesses!' I said. 'Only guesses! Or is it our conceit? Perhaps we are only ordinary men and women, after all. Like any other.' I had the argument by the throat.

I would not let it go. 'Or are we an abomination . . . a foul deviance, rightly destroyed?'

'Not so!' she cried. Wily Cockatrice was suddenly up on her feet, standing high upon the rock. And I was pacing rings around its base. Lowly Crows was crouched uneasily upon my shoulder. She dug in her claws, used her wings to counter my frantic movement, determined to hang on.

'We chose the story that suited us best, is all,' I said. 'We called it fact, because we wanted it to be so . . .'

'And where does that leave us, Rogrig?' asked Wily Cockatrice.

'Stranded!' I said, throwing my arms into the air, for want of iron to swing, or a target to aim for. 'Stranded!'

'What then *is* our course?' asked Lowly Crows, her wings flapping wildly, finding herself almost thrown to the ground. 'Now that Graynelore is up in arms! Are we all to become good fighting-men and then dead heroes?'

'Fuck that! There are no heroes – alive or dead! And it seems to me, it is only *my* sword you ever see swinging, while others stand a-feared, shivering in their own shit!' I was being sorely unfair, said it all the same.

'Is there some sense here, at last?' Wily Cockatrice picked out only what she wanted to hear from my extravagant rant. 'Sometimes there are better ways of winning a fight than through the wielding of a war sword. Eh, Rogrig? We have not found the answer yet, only we are still searching . . .'

'I am a reiver,' I said, truculently. 'That is what I do!'

'Rogrig?' Norda Elfwych, who, with the elder-man and Dogsbeard, had watched my performance in silence, came and stood in front of me, as if to calm my mood. I would not look at her, and continued to pace wildly. I only included her inside my circle.

Rogrig?

This time it was the shadow-tongue that beckoned to me.

Rogrig?

'Fine . . . fine! What shall it be then? What would you all have me do? Will I make you all a fucking wish? Let me first close my eyes.' I turned myself about, flailing my arms, blindly. Set Lowly Crows temporarily upon the air. I played out the role of the blundering oaf; the foolish babbie I felt I had become. My tone was mocking. 'Is he here yet? Is he come? The lumbering Tom Troll I have wished for you – the bloody great rollicking gigant – is he come, strolling across the hill?'

I opened my eyes as if to take a look. There were several heads turned expectantly towards the brow of the hill. Settling herself, Lowly Crows raised her head and followed their gaze, crook-eyed.

The hillside stood empty.

'Nothing to see, then?' I said, flippantly. It was my turn to make faerie slight. 'Is there, no one there at all? Nah, I thought not – I rather thought not.'

Lowly Crows decided she had finally had enough of my petulant anger. She shit on my shoulder, took off to the sky.

Chapter Twenty-Nine

The Gigant

We were walking again; and at a measured pace. A forced march, Norda might have said. To what purpose? Maybe we simply wanted to put some distance between ourselves and that cursed spot where Sunfast and Fortuna had been so brutally slaughtered.

There was little talk between us. And I still continued in a bad humour: was caught a moody, brooding man among a most sullen crowd. I thought my anger was all for the death of the unifauns. Just for them. Only it was not . . . and hard to explain, my friend. It was for all those things in life you cannot have, and for all the things you have but do not want. The impositions and the expectations . . . The joys become burdens. Does that make any sense? I was a man yet – dissatisfied and uncertain. My anger was for me. It was for all of us. And it was for another . . .

I tried to let it go. I tried.

It seemed I had taken our lead; or else I had been given it without demand: no one among my company willing to make an argument.

'Where are we going?' asked Wily Cockatrice, a little cautiously.

'Does it matter?' I returned, truculently. 'Life is our journey. It takes us all to the same destination in the end, regardless of where we *think* we are travelling.'

'And is that morbid thought meant to comfort us, Rogrig?'

'No. It is meant to hurry you along.'

'Ah . . .' She let the matter drop.

Though I should have answered her more fully, and said that I chose my path with little thought, and simply put one foot in front of the next. Only later, upon reflection, I felt there was, perhaps, some inclination that turned me ever towards the north, and to the heart of Graynelore. Not because I thought it gave us the certainty of a destination, but because there was a kind of comfort in seeing the distant outline of Earthrise, the black-headed mountain always on our horizon (and there was a subtle encouragement from the unspoken voices). So much so, that whenever the ground turned us away from it, my hidden instinct was to quickly turn us back toward it again.

'Oh, for a simple foolish tune, played lightly upon a wooden whistle!' My words were hardly more than a muffled grumble. I had not meant to share them.

'What is it, Rogrig?' asked Norda Elfwych.

I twisted my face. I shook my head and badly dismissed Norda's honest enquiry.

Eventually, I was persuaded by my companions to stop so that we might all take a short rest. We had come upon a place where a few ruined blocks of stone stood up off the ground – almost as if they had been set there for just that purpose. I took myself apart, I said, to fetch us back some fresh meat – we were sorely in need of vitals – only in truth it was so that I could spend some time in my own company, with my own thoughts. Inside my head the unspoken voices had withdrawn, and sounded little more than whispered silence. I thought again of my . . . Notyet. I could not feed my wanting soul. Nor could I, even fill our wanting bellies . . .

Upon another day, the reiver might have looked about for the signs of wood-smoke from a campfire, better still, a stone chimney, then broken the house apart and stolen our repast. Only we were too far out upon the wilderness; there was nothing here of that sort. I returned with only the poorest part of a scavenged carcass; the hind end of a withered, scrawly druin, hardly worth its old meat.

We stayed that night where we were, and slept upon the ground. The few rough courses of broken stonework our only shelter within a scattered ruin. And only solemn clouds and an icy piddling rain for a roof.

In the early morning, we none of us woke the better for it. And Norda Elfwych, the worst of us; if in my selfish mood I chose not to see her fragility. We were *all* stiff and sore, and in want of a clean stream to bathe our soiled skin.

Do I wallow in self pity, my friend? Then I suppose I have reported our condition well enough!

Though I was in want of a clear destination – beyond the lure of the black-headed mountain – I would have had us quickly moving, and on our way again. 'We are best kept travelling, if we are not to find ourselves caught out,' I said. 'Graynelore is ever restless now . . . We have remade the best part of our company and, thus far, avoided the greater part of the rising conflict, but the danger is always there.'

It was Wily Cockatrice who held me back then. 'Wait, Rogrig. Let us stay here for just a little while longer. I see there is someone coming . . .'

'*See*?'

'There. Just off there.' She was pointing with the chewed end of her cold pipe.

The piddling rain had let up. There was a trail of mist drifting across the fell in that place. In the sky a chink of yellow sun had broken through the constant cloud. Among the ruin, where there was a gap in the broken wall, a man now stood. The effect was to surround him with a halo of pale yellow light.

He was a tall man.

He was a very tall man. The tallest I had ever seen.

I could bear no arguments.

'I did not seek to bring us to this forsaken spot!' I said. 'He has found us out, is all. I have not fetched him up. I have not wished him into existence! Do not blame me for this . . . this apparition!'

The big man, a stranger still, was obviously distressed and in a state of some confusion.

'I . . . I do not know how this came about. I thought there were voices . . . Someone was calling out to me, begging me to answer them.' He tried to use the ruined wall for a support. His massive hands grasped clumsily. He did not have the true measure of his own strength. He only pushed the wall over, set it moving instead. Stones tumbled erratically, their momentum scattering them further afield than they had any right to go. 'I only walked a few steps away from my own door and yet I was, of a sudden, out upon a great fell!' The face of the big man was stricken with fright. There was no deliberate lie there. 'I could not find my way back. Though, I tried. I did try. I was lost. Forever it seemed. Wandering . . . The voice was still calling out to me . . .' Cautiously, he held out his hand, first towards me, and then towards Norda, as if he would touch us but did not quite dare, as if he wanted to make certain we were real and not merely conjured phantoms. 'Am I dreaming? Is this a night-torment? Will I awake? Or am I already a dead man?'

Still I persisted, ignored his questions. 'This is not of my doing,' I said, adamantly. 'Yes, yes, it is obvious – he is of our kind. We were not aware of him, is all.'

'If you say so, Rogrig,' said Norda Elfwych. 'We are here . . . this gigant of a man is here, all the same!'

'Gigant?' said the big man, as if the idea had truly not occurred to him. 'My name is Licentious,' he added, as if in the way of an explanation.

I might have turned on Norda then and made a real argument of it. Only she was smiling . . . Not for me, I hasten. There was a look of compassion on her face. Even in her obvious fragile state, her concern was for the stricken man. She took to him as if she had been expecting him.

I might have scowled.

'Gigant?' the big man repeated, still toying with the idea. 'But my size is nothing,' he said, defensively. 'I have always been a little tall.'

'A *little* tall!'

'Is a tall man not *always* a gigant by default, then?' asked Norda, not unkindly.

'Eh?'

'By virtue of their . . . *height*?'

'Are all ordinary men, fey?' he returned.

'No. Of course not!' she said.

'Of course not . . .' He shook his great head, as if to shake loose his befuddlement.

'And you cannot wish us up another, Rogrig?' asked Lowly Crows, aside. She was become the woman again. 'It would be . . . most useful.' She offered her arm to the reeling gigant, without waiting upon my answer.

'No. I cannot,' I said, unheard. I might have scowled again. I was still disputing the facts of it, and yet . . . as I stood there, dispassionately, and watched my companions give succour to that big man, I also realized I was telling the absolute truth.

If, in my anger, I had – after all – unwittingly, fetched him up, I could not simply wish up another.

How did I know? How, indeed . . . You tell me, my friend. The act had taken something away from me. Something I had no way of measuring. Again there had been a cost, as there was always a price to pay when a fey creature used its . . . talents. I was aware of it, if I did not understand it; certainly could not describe it. And I was also aware that, what had been taken away would at last return to me again, given the time to recover, as was the way of faerie.

As was the way of faerie . . .

Did I believe it yet?

The gigant was not the only man sorely troubled, and a-feared.

Yet again, I would have had us all quickly on our way.

Yet again, it was the ancient crone who stood across the welcoming path and beckoned us to stay a while longer.

Chapter Thirty

The Illicit Agreement

'This is all very well and good. But we still have a problem,' said Wily Cockatrice. 'A Ring of Eight . . . A Ring . . . of Eight . . . Our numbers still do not add up.' The ancient crone was walking her fingers playfully through the air, as a young babbie might have done. 'I hesitate to say this, only I will say it all the same . . . There is *one* other path we could choose to take, if *some* among us were but willing to step upon it.' She gave Norda, and then I, a very odd, calculating look. It was an expression I could not interpret. 'A Ring . . . of Eight . . .' she repeated, slowly.

We all knew the detail. It was clear enough. It needed no debate.

'I can see no fresh path?' I said, curious of her meaning.

Wily Cockatrice ignored my comment, to ask an unusual question of her own. 'Among our gathered company, we are both young and old, yet is our age of any consequence to us?'

'No. I suppose not,' I said. 'We are all equally weary of this trail. Yet we all still have our beating hearts!' I shifted uncomfortably, uncertain of where this conversation was leading us. 'I do not see your point?'

'Well, Rogrig, for the sake of our argument, would you think that an infant might suffice to finally complete our gathering?'

'Look around you,' I said, suddenly perplexed. 'With respect, I see only old age and foolish youth. I see only us seven! There is no infant here! Nor is there any expectant mother about to whelp a fey pup!'

Wily Cockatrice's odd expression did not change at my outburst, unless it intensified. She looked again, directly at me, and then directly at Norda Elfwych.

Of all things, I felt myself redden, as if in embarrassment; something I had not done since a babbie, caught by my mother with a hand inside the wrong purse.

I had been slow to catch on, but I saw her meaning at last, and I saw the implication of it . . . So too did my greater company; the gigant, and the elder-man, and Dogsbeard. Even my Lowly Crows . . . They were, all of them, suddenly shy of Norda and I, casting their eyes upon the ground, unwilling to face us.

Had we been brought to this? I wanted another way. I wanted the shadows to tell me what to do. Inside my head a host of vague ghost-voices murmured together. Each voice added a single extra note to their song, and yet it was always a perfect harmony, even as a new voice joined in and made it perfect again. But their murmuring song was only an echo from a far distant past. It gave me no answers I was willing to take. I tried to listen, instead, to a new voice among them. But it was a weak, hollow note; a desperate cry from the gigant added to the general noise. The only true sound was coming from another place entirely. And it was not fey at all, but the distant clatter of hooves: horses coming at a gallop. Gaining ground and upon all sides. If the faerie in me sensed the approach, so too did the instincts of the man.

I let it go, for the matter in hand.

'I have no such desire for this woman!' I said, flatly, turning physically upon Wily Cockatrice. 'If this is your true meaning? She . . . She is an Elfwych! My constant enemy! She . . . We . . . We are allied to this task before us. Nothing more!'

Wily Cockatrice stood her ground, refusing to listen to my protestation. While Norda Elfwych looked blankly on, both outwardly and inwardly silent; unwilling, as yet, to partake of the argument.

'What? I think the man protests just a little too loudly!' said the crone. 'Upon Graynelore! Am I to believe this fighting man has – how might I put this? – never used his *sword* upon a Riding to his own advantage?' She paused. 'Do the cocks not crow, then?'

'Eh? But this is ludicrous, distasteful – both! And why lay this upon me . . . upon us?' I turned to Norda. 'I mean you no discourtesy, only . . . you have seen enough pain, and your strength fails. You are little better than a weedling. I would not dishonour—'

'What then?' exclaimed Wily Cockatrice, cutting through my words. 'I *see* . . . I see no other likely match. The bird does not lie down with the man. Or would you leave such an arduous, unwelcoming, task to this youth here, or perhaps, to this old man? I fear the one has not yet acquired what the other has already lost.'

Both Wood-shanks and Dogsbeard took a deliberate step away from us, ignoring the crone's slight, neither of them wanting to be drawn into the debate. Licentious too, turned aside, would not look upon us. He only rubbed his great hand upon his worried head, as if to soothe away his discomfort. (Certainly, he was not named for the man!)

'And am I to have no say in this matter?' said Norda Elfwych, suddenly indignant. Though her voice was a thin trail of words, and she was, obviously, already at something of a loss. 'Are we simple cattle then? Am I to be mounted like a common fell beast? I have done with whoring for the will of men!'

'I do understand this is something of an unusual request,' said Wily Cockatrice, almost contrite. 'But am I to take it that neither of you is willing? Is that it? Is the idea so abhorrent? Do you both refuse?'

We gave her no answer (unless it was a look of disdain).

'What have we here?' It was Lowly Crows who now chose to speak. 'Surely, this is not a matter of virtue? This does not require your love . . . not even a blood-tie. Rather, it is something quite different. Indeed, it is a great deal more: a fey match. No common thing! And, I fear, it is a question of our very survival.'

'What then . . . a means to an end?' I asked, angrily. 'Is there no *other* way?'

'There is always another way, Rogrig,' said Lowly Crows. 'We have waited, patiently, this long . . . we could always wait a little longer. Does time not take care of everything in the end? Another of our kind *might* just find us out . . .'

The implication was clear enough.

I took a brief moment to study the big man. It was I who had brought the gigant to us. Wished him to that very spot! And done it badly! Even now, he was party to our company only because of that piece of . . . of whimsy . . . that bound him to it. I could see it still, in the faerie-touched man. He might yet remain among us of his own accord. The shadow voices, that faerie cord that tied us all together, hung thickly about us now, but . . . (Aye! And was this faerie tale ever hanging by a, *but* . . .)

'Time? Time moves on, is all,' I said at last. 'Men must take care of themselves.' I fear I was being tricked into losing my own argument. All Graynelore was up in arms. We had been truly fortunate, but could not avoid trouble forever. It was only a question of who would find us out first.

Out of the shade, I heard again the clatter of distant hooves.

'We are so close now,' added Wily Cockatrice. 'And we are none of us immortal beasts! Surely we must, at least, try. Or it may all yet come to nothing.'

'Life and death, Rogrig . . . it is a matter of life and death,' said Lowly Crows. 'The man goes to war so very easily. How often do you steal the very fruit we are after gathering? Is this such a ponderous task; is it so difficult? What do you say?'

'I say—' I stopped myself. There were so many reasons, and yet so few. I wanted to find a better way of explaining myself, when there was none. The image of Notyet came briefly to my mind. I only shut it out. (How often I shut it out!) What more could be said?

Norda Elfwych inclined her head towards me. She regarded me, briefly, through narrowed – almost closed – eyes. She did not speak. There was only her shadow-tongue. It spoke quietly to me, said only this:

I, truly, do not want you, Wishard . . .

And I do not want you, Elfwych . . . I returned.

At least we both agreed upon something.

There was no more to it. There was no note of ascent. Norda Elfwych stood up and quietly walked out of our company.

I followed after her.

*

Even now I recall the event to mind reluctantly, and recount it publicly when I would remain silent, only because I fear I must – for want of the truth of my tale and not some poor confection.

We . . . came upon each other, not as lovers, rather as adversaries or, at best, participants. The place was a deeply shaded vale, chosen so that we might not fully reveal ourselves. She turned me over or I turned her. It matters not which. We brought each other down. The one, pursuer; the other pursued. We fell together, hitting the ground hard enough to bruise our skins. Fingers grasped, then – pawed awkwardly at breeches. I felt myself clumsily manhandled. She lifted her loose skirt, set her cloth aside. She drew herself down upon me and I encouraged it. Only like an animal covering another animal. The best ewe put to the ram. A physical act committed, not desired. Neither stolen but taken all the same. Demanded and given in turn without affection or lust. There was no pleasure taken in that rut.

Perhaps our indifference shocked us both?

We each drew apart as quickly as we had mounted, took up our iron weapons as if we might kill each other, still strangers and enemies.

'And if . . . if it should not . . . take?' I hardly dared look upon her. She was become so sorely effete. I stared upon the ground, stumbled over the question I would not have asked.

'*Take?* Spare yourself your blushes, Wishard,' she said, without effect. 'We are fey; a fey match. It already takes . . . Would you know him, would you know *our* son? Would you feel the babbie's heart?'

I started. 'How strange the ways of faerie,' I said.

'How *cruel*,' she said.

The cold air felt only colder for her answer.

We held ourselves where we stood a good while, neither of us willing to console the other, or be the first to turn away.

When, finally, we parted, returned separately to our greater company, it was without another word or comfort. I truly wish it were otherwise. And at this poor ending did I feel *nothing* for this Elfwych, nothing at all? If I did not, I should have done. If only the man's guilt – I was already trying to bury the memory of what had taken place between us.

Chapter Thirty-One

The Quickening

Something within our company changed from the moment we all came together again. We each of us felt it. A kind of drawing together . . . It was a physical thing. A sense of near completion? Perhaps that, perhaps more . . . It was a quickening. A quickening: of thought, of mind, and of body too. And as the beating heart of the unborn infant grew ever stronger within Norda's swelling belly, as is the way of faerie, we all sensed the wonder of it. (I needed no reminder of the man's guilt . . . that ever brought Notyet to mind.) We also sensed the overwhelming danger. And we understood that the world outside of ourselves was closing in around us because of it. Graynelore was aware of us, and what we had become, and would surely come to destroy us all if it could.

The air was alive. My skin pricked with the frisson of it. Inside my head the shadow-tongues were speaking. Altogether, all at once, in the same moment and yet each one was as clear as if it had spoken alone. More: I suddenly knew what they were trying to tell me, whatever the language, ancient or newly made.

And behind us, rising above the fell, standing far above the horizon, its foothills lost behind a screen of standing mists, was the black-headed mountain: Earthrise. She was calling to us with her own voice: a series of deep, sonorous, and majestic notes. And the ghost-voices, the ageless ones, come out of time, were calling back to her, answering the great mountain in their turn. And if these voices were all inside my head, they were also out there . . . in the real world.

And what of us, who were, at long last – but for the want of a timely birth – become the Eight? In that moment we were the smallest of men, the most insignificant of creatures . . . And we each understood in our own way, our state of being was at best an ephemeral, a wholly transient thing . . .

We were already beginning to move together. None of us were leading, none of us were led. We all knew the path to take, though there was no mark upon the ground. And the voices, our own included, whether real or imaginary, shadow-tongue or ghost, beckoned, coaxed us to it. There was no need to ask where we were heading.

Slowly at first, subtly, then more sharply, the ground under our feet began to rise. No longer the gently rolling turns of the southern fells; instead, the hard, unrelenting, rocky ground that would eventually become the mass of the great black-headed mountains themselves.

Mind, the earth itself was not beyond giving us its own surprise. The unforgiving ground, weathered smooth and grey, became, in places, a sudden vast carpet of black dust. It was impossible to decide what the dust was made of: fine grains of blackened sand, or a loathsome grimy soil, or shards of glass? Or was it some other natural or unnatural material beyond our knowledge? My nose caught the hint of a sharp, bittersweet scent; enough only to tantalize, not define. In all, if anything, it reminded me of a funeral pyre.

Our feet quickly disappeared into it, were swallowed up as we moved. Lowly Crows, who had all this time remained our human companion, transformed herself into the bird and sprang into the air to avoid it. Yet, strangely, the wind, which was beginning to blow strongly, and a turbulent beast, could not seem to lift the dust into the air; as if it was too heavy to shift, or else some other unknown force was holding it in place.

Stranger still was the way the ghost-voices changed their songs as we walked across the dust. Not complaining, rather, they were welcoming us; pleased by our presence there.

In front of me, the gigant lost his footing and stumbled in the dust. He lifted his massive hand to his head, as if he could use it to dampen the noises he could not yet comprehend.

'We are walking in the tracks of the fey,' I said, wanting him to understand. 'This ancient dust is their remnant. They are only trying to guide us. Listen to them. Their voices, echoing down through the long years . . . Can you not hear them?'

'What?'

'Their songs . . . the songs they are singing?'

Licentious only shook his troubled head. He ran his hand through the black dust, scooped it up and held it to his ear that it might help him to hear more clearly.

'Faerie Dust,' I said, trying to convince him; still trying to convince myself, perhaps. 'You know . . . it is the dust of faeries.'

'Remember the Beggar Bard's Tale,' said Wily Cockatrice. She was breathing heavily, finding it a struggle to walk against the shifting dust. 'It fell during the great war . . . at the death of the wizards. When their last battle was at its height, and their doom was at hand, the sky darkened and became full . . .' The old crone stood up a moment, drew in several deep gasping breaths before she was refreshed enough to continue. 'The day disappeared beneath a blanket of night. And then the dust fell. It fell until it covered the whole earth, until there was nothing left to fall and the sky became quite clear again . . .'

It had always been just a story, just a part of an ancient story . . .

Briefly, I slipped my hand inside my cloth and touched the stone talisman that was still bound to my wrist by its leather thong.

In the next few steps, we had walked clear of the black dust . . . Eventually, we crossed over the brow of the rising hill. There, we came upon a shallow dip in the ground. I could see well beyond: it was the beginnings of a great plain. An undulating plateau, rising gently, tilted to the north east, stretching away into the far distance until it touched the foot of the mountains proper. However, between the shallow and the open plain the land was draped with broken trails of ground mist. In places it ran clear and the ground between appeared hard and barren. Elsewhere the mist stood up high, caught between the branches and the trunks of a broad scattering of trees; their grey, vague twisted shapes could so easily have been mistaken for fully grown men mounted upon their hobbs. It was an oddly foreboding landscape.

We had come upon the fringes of The Withering, then.

Around us, close too, the air had grown suddenly incredibly chill, as if the earth had cupped its hands about that shallow spot to hold it there. I was walking upon a stretch of rough grass, not green in colour, but caught stark white where a snap night frost still lingered. The ground there lay ever shaded, in the lea of the hill, where the cool winter sun of the day could bring no warmth.

That was not all of it.

Above us, Lowly Crows wheeled across the sky, and, closely chased by her worried kin, she cried her distress at the sight laid out before her.

This was not only a winter scene, it was a killing field.

There was ice. The grass stood up stiff and white. Only there were dead men too: dead men held within its rigid grasp. Like grotesques, oddly posed, obscenely caught where they had fallen at the moment of their death. Their faces were still deeply lined in pain. Many of them were holding up their arms as if to defend themselves against the final onslaught. Still open mouthed as they gasped their last breath, or else made their death cries. The truth easily read within their frozen eyes. And not one or two or ten men, even. But dead men by the dozens, butchered together with their hobbs. A frozen army . . .

'And is this – abhorrence – also an ancient faerie deed?' The gigant looked between us, one to the next.

I shook my head slowly. 'No,' I said. 'I can see these deaths are newly made; to be measured only by the hours.' I looked about cautiously, the instincts of the common man, the reiver, rising to the fore. Perhaps there was danger yet about this place, if only I could find it out.

'How do you know this, Rogrig?' asked a wary Norda Elfwych. For a moment her hand strayed toward her belly, as if to shield the innocent ears of the unborn infant.

'There are Wishards lying dead here,' I said. 'And more than a few faces I recognize well enough . . .'

Among them, two at least must be named, if I would shed them no tears: Cloggie-Unthank, and Fibra; who were the

Old-man's younger brothers and would-be possessors of his sorely disputed title. They had been slaughtered, yet their raiment and baggage remained un-pillaged. A spilled sack lay upon the frozen earth between their bodies. Among its scattered contents was a mass of fine embroidered cloth, I knew I had seen before – upon the backs of the Old-man's Council. These were, no doubt, the brother's gathered spoils; souvenirs of their own campaign, now abandoned.

I had no desire to dig deeper – for the many tragedies of the scene were clear enough. And I knew one more thing then, and for certain, there was not long left to us now. Whatever path we were set upon, where ever it was leading us, we were almost there.

We passed quickly on; as quickly as our continued feeble disposition would allow us. Among the constant noises inside my head, there was still the clatter of approaching hooves . . . come louder now, and insistent. They would not be turned aside. The rising tide of war; The Great Riding, could not be avoided forever.

Chapter Thirty-Two

The Battle of the Withering

It is not in a reiver's instincts to avoid a fight. Indeed, the reverse is true. It is perhaps no surprise then, that in trying to forever avoid the rising threat of The Great Riding, we ultimately came full on into the frae.

And if, inside my head, I heard the tempest approaching, my eyes looking out upon the real world did not see it coming. The vagary of The Withering, the constant motion of its trailing mists, the mournful wraith-like apparitions that stood in the place of the trees, revealed no secrets. Even the birds in flight, could not see all men in this circumstance: come before us and behind, here and there, and there again; the weeping sores of a gathering war. The crows, now a baffled, worried crowd of beating wings, turned recklessly upon the air. Several warnings came together in an utter confusion; piercing cries, frantic hollers above the first clash and clatter of iron, each one demanding a first response. But if the birds could not call a warning for every threat, the man upon the ground could not answer every call. We might quickly have found ourselves overwhelmed upon the field.

I thought I heard a distant thunder . . . What we had seen captured within that frozen hollow was not the end of it by far, only a temporary respite. Fighting-men were suddenly come again from within The Withering . . .

Would we have become our true selves then, would we have smitten our foes with faerie magic? Ha! And found ourselves become ever more diminished; ever further away from our full strength? Perhaps even beyond its recall, when our greater task, the making of a Ring of Eight, was as yet undone. No, my friend, save our strength. I sensed there was an end coming, a final conflict, but this was not it.

About me, my company stood in sudden disarray.

'What do we do now, Rogrig? What do we do now?' The question fell from every tongue it seemed, beseeching. And every eye was upon me, old and young.

'Fuck,' I said.

I returned their look, saw within their eyes, knew with good reason I was not among a company of good fighting-men. The ancient crone and the elder-man: too old by far. Dogsbeard: too young and too afraid. The gigant: still a baffled man, who would only wish himself awake from a living night-torment. And Norda . . . the Elfwych: a failing nursemaid to an unborn infant, and soon upon a battle she alone must fight.

'Shit,' I said.

By the fortunes, we were not met with a main force, but with a series of rabbles. I could see these were disparate groups of fighting-men. Scattered bands of an already battle weary foe . . . if they were, as yet, unwilling to retreat from the field, still with strength enough to make a mischief and to break themselves a few heads. Each one bore the looks and colours of a different grayne, both great and small. I recognized their breed if not their faces. Better still: there was much cross-fighting betwixt and between. It was clear to me; they were not seeking out a common enemy. They were not come only after us but after each other. Any man's bones might reasonably be broken, any man's blood spilled!

Again the birds cried out their warnings.

It was far better for Rogrig Wishard to stand up for himself, and alone, to stay squarely the man and make a defence of his sword arm. If the faerie was diminished and floundering, the reiver could still make a fight. (Did I truly think on it? *Abandonment* . . . Did I? My friend, cowardice is ever a valid tactic, and only smart survival!)

Again the general plea: 'Rogrig, what must we do now?'

'Now? Escape!' I said. 'We must escape!' The words were upon my tongue before the notion.

To be embroiled within the action but not to be a party to the fight, or rather, not to be *seen* to be a party to the fight, required both a faerie's Glamour and their transient nature – that we might best deceive men's eyes – but it also required the reiver. I remembered another day, and a foolish faerie jig, made upon a Winter Festival. 'If we cannot fight them, then we will use our wits to avoid our enemy,' I said. 'And we will use our feet to remove ourselves from their company.'

'Eh?' Wily Cockatrice looked sorely puzzled.

'We will dance for them!' I said.

'*Dance*?'

'Aye! We will give them a faerie's dance, as we once danced before! Come, follow after me and do likewise . . .' I gathered up the old crone's cautiously proffered hand in mine and began my swirling jig. She took hold of the elder-man. And he, in his turn, made Norda and Dogsbeard his twisting tail, with the reeling gigant ever in pursuit.

In truth, I was not to see the better side of my companions this day. They could not fight, nor could they hardly run away with much conviction.

I tried to guide them through the stitches and knots of the shadows thrown by the mass of fighting-men as they wielded their swords and found their targets. Between sword tips and charging hobbs and falling men cut bloodily asunder. We were never our enemy's match. I used my sword only when it could not be avoided; either to parry a blow, or to lop off a nodding head or a leading sword arm. And if the remainder of my company – Lowly Crows apart – stood sorely frightened, danced rigidly upon the spot, while blood was being let, I bit my tongue in want of a better moment to chastise them for it.

How many times our lives were saved that day, how many times again . . . By the strength of my arm; aye, and by the guile of our shifting faerie's dance . . . Though as often, and more likely, by the simple distraction of our assailants by our common foe come suddenly upon us from out of The Withering.

In the heat of a battle you only know a man is your enemy when he is facing you down or running away. There was no good purpose in open flight. It only encouraged a deadly pursuit. Turning away from one approaching flank only brought you up against another, and at closer quarters. To go about unnoticed upon a killing field, to escape unseen, is a clever art for any man, common or fey.

I saw trailing strings of men flailing their swords – others, alone come out of the mist-bound trees, and randomly spread. Others again, in tightly gathered hordes. And come both a-foot and riding upon their hobbs. Yet there was a hesitation there; they were unwilling to stray too far away from the protection of the gathered mists (as if they themselves were cautious of another – greater – enemy).

'Stand firm I say!' I cried aloud. 'Move inside the fleeting shadows. Do not present yourself a target, yet do not be caught in avoidance. Stay alive!'

'This is a strange dance!' returned the Elfwych, and not alone.

The worst of it came from the Bogarts, who were small, stolid fighting-men, with little humour and as little brain, and who did not care for subtle tactics or battle plans. Their fighting style was no better than a basic rush: a hack and a slash. Mind, what their technique lacked in finesse it made up for in brutal reliability. If their axes found their target you were crippled at the least; though more likely you were broken apart and stone dead.

'Step aside! And hold! Step aside again!' I hollered, bullying my company into startled flight. A shrouded mist was our covering mantle the one moment, the stone man the next. This, a simple trick: for a reiver will forever attack the moving man first. He is your threat. While the stone man, frozen in fright (a pretence as good as any faerie masquerade) describes a passive weedling, or a coward, who can be returned to. His dispatch enjoyed for wanton pleasure, when the real fighting, the true danger, is expelled.

It was a risky measure. It worked all the same.

And so we danced upon The Withering, and so we jigged, and so we bettered them all in the end. Step by step by step.

At last we were come clear of those foul trees, and were well out upon an open plain. The fighting was gone behind: and not a mark upon us to regret, beyond the passing souvenir.

We were well pleased with ourselves. Only . . . had the mice escaped the cats a little too easily?

At our backs now, enough open ground that even the sound of the frae did not easily carry to us. In front of us, a rising plateau, and beyond, a wall of mountains, skirted by another curtain of hanging mist. Only this one stood up innocent and white, and seemed as soft as any summer cloud.

I thought.

Chapter Thirty-Three

A Cry Among the Mists

They emerged from the mist like ghosts, great lumbering figures, as if they were carrying the weight of their own deaths upon their backs.

Like ghosts . . . but not ghosts. Rather, these were men . . . These too were fighting-men. This was surely the main force of The Great Riding.

Lowly Crows squealed a shrill warning. High upon the air, she wheeled and countered frantically. Wheeled and countered. Below her, we stood out upon the plateau; a lonely company. It was too late for us to run for cover, or to try another subtle escape.

I began to see them clearly as they emerged from out of the mist, riding steadily towards us across the open ground. They were a great crowd, gathered purposefully, all of them mounted upon their hobbs.

At their head rode a man I knew well enough. Wolfrid Wishard, my elder-cousin. These men were my own close kin. At his side, rode his son, Edbur-the-Widdle. The whelp was sitting upon *my* Dandelion.

We could only stand our ground and temper their approach. To have made any other move would have been to beg a chase and a quick slaughter.

If Wolfrid would only talk to me we were all alive a little longer yet.

I stepped out from among our company, to openly make myself obvious to him. It was a courtesy only: I fear, he knew me there already, as I knew him.

The Great Riding came on, in truth, it was an impressive sight; perhaps as many as four hundred horses strong. They advanced until they were tight around us, stood up only when the noses of their hobbs were in our faces. I might have smiled at the tactic. A close crowd meant your adversaries had no room to swing their swords. Was Wolfrid shy of me, even yet? Had he thought he was come upon a faerie host?

His first words were addressed to the sky. 'The clouds are black and treacherous today, cousin,' he said. Wolfrid was looking up toward the murder of crows whose number seemed to have grown miraculously.

'I fear it is not such a good day to be abroad,' I returned.

'Indeed, we are both of us a long way from our home . . .'

At Wolfrid's side, Edbur snorted loudly, pulled at the reign of his hobb needlessly. Dandy twitched her ears, as if for the discomfort of it.

'What is it that we have come to, Rogrig?' said Wolfrid. He let his eyes slide across my company, man for man, as if in speculation. He had approached us, certain that our meagre party posed a threat to him; enough to require wary handling, and a subtle appraisal. Already I felt the mood had changed. He saw only ordinary men now.

'Will you have the truth, cousin?' I said. I would hold the man up a while yet.

'The truth?' said Wolfrid, with a growing smile. Again, Edbur snorted at his father's side. 'Is it only the truth you would offer me, then?'

I shrugged. It was my turn to cast my eye upon my cousins; the reiver and his whelp before their great army. I understood them well enough. Upon Graynelore, where most men were liars, there was little of value in any truth. Upon a killing field, it was hardly enough to make a bargain. I knew my words were never going to be enough to turn the argument this day. Wolfrid was already set upon his path. I gave him my story anyway. Why ever not? I told him my faerie tale, as you know it, my friend.

At the end, Wolfrid sat back upon his hobb, rested his hand upon the hilt of his sword. Not yet as a threat, he took comfort in what he knew best, while he considered my tale. He and I were always the same. At last he sighed, and shook his head in obvious disbelief.

'If the Old-man's Council were capable of one deceit, then they were certainly capable of another . . .' I said pre-emptively, though with little real hope of persuasion.

'What would you have us believe, Rogrig?' he said. 'Eh? That a wych took up the Old-man's dead body, and at the beckon of a twisted Council gave it new life! That you, no doubt a wholly innocent man, were only saving her from her peril, her torment . . . and then what . . .? You simply took to the air and flew away!' He paused. He could not hide the growing anger, the exasperation in his voice. Wolfrid was not a good diplomat. He was far better at using force to get his own way, than he was his tongue.

'Is it the faerie tale, or rather, is it the human tale I should believe? A foolish man so besotted, so enamoured, of a woman he would certainly kill his own Graynelord.

Do murder in his own household. He takes off with her, abandons all. He outlaws himself and her, both.'

At my side, Norda Elfwych was trying to push herself forward, trying to make herself known to him. 'But there is truth in this! And true witness!' she said. 'I for one—'

Wolfrid only raised his hand against her, dismissively, pointing to her belly, already swollen with child, as is the way of faerie. 'Ah yes . . . there it is again: the truth . . . And now, here before us are your true witnesses, Rogrig . . . a foul Elfwych and an unborn bastard!'

Norda drew her arms about herself, as if to shield the unborn infant from the taint; to protect the new life there, growing steadily inside of her. Wolfrid continued:

'Well, it seems there was more than one murder done that day. So many of our cousins greeted only with a sword . . . If only the dead might speak as eloquently as the living. Eh?' Again, he cast his gaze across our small company.

I felt a sudden quickening. We were almost upon the moment. This was not the time or the place for us to reveal ourselves: too hard the fight. Nor was it the time to die. More: I had no desire to take up arms against my closest kin. Here was Wolfrid, the Headman of my own house, together with the best part of my own family. And all come to make their stand against us; to make that spot another killing field.

Yet what was left to be said? Sadly, I could not answer him right for answering him wrong. It was a double-edged sword he offered me. Either way I knew there was death here. Sometimes it was easier to kill than it was *not* to kill. Certainly, it was far simpler than a reasoned argument. There was no escaping it. Wolfrid was here to pick a fight.

I knew the game. Wolfrid was not come on a faerie hunt, nor was he here simply to take revenge for his Graynelord's death (faithful though he had been). Cloggie-Unthank and Fibra lay already dead within an ice-bound hollow. It might have been at Wolfrid's own hand. It might have been at the hand of another. Matter-less. With every death, great or small, the balance of power shifted. With the death of the Old-man's siblings that balance had tilted, remarkably, in Wolfrid's favour. He had only to take it up. Wield it (before some other wanting man came and took it from him in his stead).

The Great Riding was the simplest of politics. More so, it required *no* considered thought. The graynes would continue to wield their swords at each other, until one of them came out on top.

I, Rogrig Wishard, did not stand in Wolfrid's way. No. I have said it before now; Graynelore is ever in need of its symbols of power. How often its leaders use that particular staff to lean upon. And how convenient it was for Wolfrid: that we should appear before him now. He had proved his loyalty to his Graynelord. He had proved his arm against his rivals. He had only to prove the power of his justice, the quality of his judgement . . . And we the example to behold!

Better a slaughter for a Graynelord's murder, than for the whimsy of a faerie tale. But there would be a slaughter either way.

'Well, Rogrig . . . Will you show me an open hand?' Wolfrid asked.

He was leaning across his hobb, facing me eye to eye. His look was asking questions. I knew him well enough. He wanted to understand why more men should die this day. He wanted to understand why old friends had become enemies. He wanted me to give him a reason to turn his hobb about and ride his men off the field, alive still and unharmed. He wanted a greater truth that made sense to him and gave him deliverance.

'Well, on the one hand, we always have our swords. On the other—' I gestured towards The Withering, where among the mists and shadows men fought yet, and further, to the distant shallow, to the place where we both knew bodies lay dead and frozen upon the ground.

Wolfrid simply shrugged.

I tried again. 'On the other, *other* hand—'

Wolfrid quickly interrupted me. 'Exactly, how many hands do you have to reveal here, cousin?'

'Only as many as I need to make my play . . .' I faltered there, my feeble jest unheeded.

I had nothing more to say to him.

The moment was come.

All about us, eager fighting-men, patient until now, stiffened in their saddles, steadied their mounts in readiness. Their breath came suddenly hard and fast.

And the air was become suddenly pungent. It stung my nose. I knew that sign well enough. Close beside me, at Wolfrid's side, Edbur-the-Widdle had pissed himself.

Beneath him, Dandy snorted disdainfully. Through her leather mask her eyes sharpened upon me, knew me there. Among all, the snitch would be made to pay for his youthful folly . . . aye and for Dandy's dishonouring. And I knew she would see to this in my stead, if, in the event, I could not.

Hands resting upon hilts drew swords and would come to blows.

Only *I* did not want this. Truly, *I did not want this.* Still I hesitated.

Lowly Crows did not.

As I look back upon that scene now, I feel as if I stood by and watched as she made her attack; akin to one transfixed by it. Perhaps I was. Perhaps I did.

The man, Wolfrid, upon his fine grey hobby-horse, silhouetted against a wretched sky, his hand raised within a fisted iron-bound glove. The mob of crows crying murder, suddenly plummeting, falling down upon him . . . Choosing him for their first victim, and relentless with it. One upon the next upon the next, throwing their collective weight against him, using their beaks and their practised claws. Each blow compounded the last, left a cut or a hefty bruise. And Lowly Crows' dreadful, screech; a foul, demonic sound to every ear there, human and faerie . . .

Him, striking the air blindly with his sword: finding contact with the birds only because their number was so great his weapon could not be avoided. The bodies of headless, wingless, birds began to fall like some kind of obscene rain.

While impotent men – the majority and seemingly stupefied – stood about, rigidly fixed and unmoving.

Still, Lowly Crows attacked. Again and again and again, until blood-red ribbons of flailed skin hung from Wolfrid's distorted face and from the poor grey hobb's exposed flanks.

It was the man who fell dead first; well before the horse.

Only then the greater field came back to life, openly clashed, and brought their iron to bear upon the frae.

I would not have had it so.

If I was a Wishard – more than a man with a name – if I could, truly wish . . . I wished then.

How quickly a world can turn, and turn about again.

The sky, suddenly tormented, broke open upon the instant. The standing mists, now lying dormant at the foot of the mountains, sprang up, a mass of flailing tails and rope-like spirals; rent the air to the very heart of a glowering storm. Came back to ground again, not only driving rain, but a raging torrent; a rising wall of churning waters. Without a warning it took up both friend and foe alike. Its cruel edge divided riders from their horses, and swept them away. It ran them off their feet and turned them into the ground. It drove them apart with such a vicious fury there was not the briefest inch of time for men to see their fate, or understand its root. There was not a reiver among our horde canny enough to parry the blows of that storm.

Not even, I, its maker.

Though I might have closed my eyes against it, and wished that I could . . .

Indeed. And found myself at a loss, sterile and unable. The cost of the deed not yet fully paid out.

As was the way of faerie . . .

Nevertheless, I would wish again. I would . . .

Part Six

The Faerie Ring

Chapter Thirty-Four

A Ring of Eight

When I opened my eyes again the storm had passed and the waters receded. The sky, though worried still, was at least passively at rest.

I was stood out upon the plateau – become another killing field.

There had been a most terrible act of violence. There had been a small act of mercy. Both, it seemed, committed by my own fey hand. All about, the Long Riding of Wolfrid-the-Wishard, The Great Riding, lay in utter devastation.

Yet I was not standing alone. There was my company – a ring of solitary figures. They were untouched by the storm I had wished for, protected by the shield I had wished for. Speechless, bewildered by the event: mercifully unharmed.

The immensity of the act took up all of my wits, stole the strength from my body, and for a long while after. Again, that part of me that was fey was left utterly spent.

So, I continued to stand there, sorely diminished, the weedling man, waiting upon the return of my full senses, content in the knowledge that my company stood there with me. Inside my head there were no voices, no songs, or meaningless drawl. The shadow-tongues were speechless. There was only silence. Utter silence. For there was nothing left to say; nothing needed to be said.

When I next heard a sound, it was real – the cry of a babbie.

It was the cry of a newborn infant, in sore need of first succour, and giving full vent to its lungs. Amidst all, Norda Elfwych had born her child. There had been more than one battle fought this day, and hers surely the greater for her victory.

I tried to bring myself fully awake and seek the pair out; only to find myself suddenly reeling giddily and light-headed; suddenly on my knees, floundering upon all fours, for want of the character to hold myself upright.

Norda Elfwych sat apart. How very small she seemed, how fragile; crouched upon the ground, her arms tightly wrapped about herself. And so insignificant the tiny thing she cradled there; I could see no more of it than a bundle of rags. Again I heard the babbie's plaintive cry. And did my stone heart at last go out to them? Indeed . . . they cast a shadow there that gives me trouble still.

Wily Cockatrice came and stood resolutely before me.

'She is best left, Rogrig, best left . . . And you . . . you must look to yourself, and take a hold of the man, for we must get on,' said the ancient crone. Her voice was gentle, cautious almost, but resigned.

We must get on . . .

We must get on . . .

I slowly nodded my head, content to let her speak; soothed by her words, as much as if it was I who was the infant again, and held still within its mother's nurturing arms.

'Our company of Eight is . . . at its best,' she said, before briefly casting her eyes toward the distant peak of Earthrise. The black-headed mountain, stood up, as if entirely alone, between a break in the weathered, storm-damaged cloud that draped the sky. 'We are all here, all together at last. And alive – and that is enough for the purpose of our task.'

'What – then, you mean it could be done here?' I said. 'Completed; finished – right here! In the middle of a bloody battlefield! In the middle of nowhere?'

In my eyeline I could see Licentious, the lumbering gigant. He was stood among a patch of the black dust; a dazed, a worried man. As I watched him, he bent to the ground and picked up a handful. He let it spill slowly through his open fingers, almost mesmerized. It danced lightly upon the wind as it fell back to the earth. Where it had been upon his skin it left the faintest stain of red.

I struggled to my feet.

'Wily Cockatrice is right,' said Lowly Crows. The bird was once more become the woman, and already standing purposefully close to the ancient crone. 'It is worth a try, at least. If it is ever to be done, then this is as good a place as any.'

'It is not as if we are going to be disturbed again,' said the elder-man, who now came and stood at my side.

I let my eyes stray across that killing field, picking over the bodies of the men, the women, the horses, and the doomed youth – the dead.

Though, I could see, not all of the men who lay there were become corpses yet. Standing a good way off across the field were a few dozen men a-foot, and their remaining horses. All grey, all solemn, and unmoving: the small mass of common survivors. If they saw us at all it was clear they did not know what to make of us or the event that had befallen them this day. Certainly they would not try to come at us again. They refused even to move themselves to the aid of their own stranded living-dead: the broken horses that still twitched or shied; the broken men that cried out loud where they lay badly injured, seeking only an easy end.

Now, and in future times, my kin would leave this stricken field ever untouched. And many years later it remained un-plundered; a sacred faerie ground, and a Wishard's graveyard.

I would have looked no more upon it, except there was a sight to behold: out of the distant grey column of men and horses, there was a slight movement, after all. First, men gathered together in a close huddle, then men standing deliberately apart. One man walked cautiously forward, leading his hobby-horse. After only a dozen steps or so, and hardly clear of his companions, the man stopped again. He used a hand upon its rump to encourage the hobb to continue before him, only for it to kick back at him, and come on at its own pace. Then he turned away and walked back into the column of grey. There was no real telling who that man might have been; if, for a fancy, I truly would have liked it to have been Edbur-the-Widdle, alive still (for I had no more stomach or desire for further killing or revenge). Perhaps it was.

Dandy walked on across that field of dying men. For certain now I knew it was her. Still dressed in her leather mask, the point of her iron horn gleamed, caught for a moment in the light of a breaking sun. She kept coming, stepped over the dead, plodded through the random scatterings of black dust, until she was close enough to find me out. And then, with only the slightest snort and a twitch of an ear in recognition, she set her teeth about a patch of green meadow grass that stood proud of the dust and began to chew upon it, contentedly.

*

There was to be no faerie dance, no sweet chanting; no songs. There was to be no gathering circle, no holding of hands, no magic . . . not even a binding Ring.

Where he stood, the gigant fell down upon his knees and bowed his great head.

Norda Elfwych remained sat upon the earth, embracing her raggedy baby . . . her son . . . *my* son . . . In silence, she rocked herself gently back and forth, as if she meant it for a lullaby.

The elder-man stood up proudly. He spread his arms wide in a mimic of his own tree.

Lowly Crows transformed into the bird and settled herself upon her favourite spot; that is, riding high upon the air.

Dogsbeard, in the way of a child, simply lay down upon the ground and looked up at the sky.

Wily Cockatrice lit her battered wooden pipe, closed her old eyes, and sucked deeply upon it, until a great plume of grey and blue and green smoke issued from her mouth and her nose, and the unruly flame singed her wiry hair.

So, my companions stood about, or else sat, or lay down flat upon the ground. They took wing upon the air, or they knelt down in prayer.

And I . . . what did I, Rogrig Wishard, do?

For an instant, my mind was struck with the memory of the prancing unifauns, Sunfast and Fortuna, in all their fragile beauty. Then:

I made a wish. That is all. Nothing more . . .

I made one last wish.

Even in my weakened state, it was enough it seems.

How very quietly the world changed.

Had I expected the unspoken voices, the shadow-tongues, and a crying wind; the calling out of a thousand lost names? Was our History to come to our aid; were the long dead to return, and was a great pageant to be played out?

No. Not now. There was none of it. Now there was – only us. Each of us exactly as we were; plainly described. We shared our thoughts equally between us, unbridled now. I knew them all and they knew me:

The shift, among her murder of crows; the childish elf; the wyrm; the dryad; the wych with her newborn babbie; the gangling gigant, and I – the wishmaker. As one, together:

The Ring of Eight . . .

The silence came first: compelling, utter and intense, and as real as if it had taken a solid form. All voices were made mute; both the common and the fey. Bird chatter, feet pacing across stony ground, restless hooves, and the moans of dying men; the rattling chatter of a distant stream, and the sighing breath of the wind . . . all manner of noise stopped then, and yet the world continued on a while: a silent mime.

Until, only the briefest moment later, we all became suddenly still. I was certain I was still drawing my breath, only there was no outward sign of it, no movement. We were frozen, locked in a space between times. Betwixt was, and now, and will be. Even in the sky, the billowing clouds and the flapping wings of the crows were caught and held stiffly, as if they had been captured within a painted picture, unruffled by the wind. And yet it was real. The world about us, and everything in it, had simply stopped, and stood utterly still.

Then it began. The dust, the black dust rising: lifting off the ground. It was not windblown, not taken up by a warm eddy, not shifted by a human hand, but rising of its own volition. Nor was it moving in trailing wisps, or in patches, but in its entirety. It rose ever skyward, and from visible horizon to visible horizon; as far as could be seen in any direction. All across the fells and the hillsides, both far distant and near too, it rose up. Great black walls rising . . . stretching out into the sky. Most spectacularly of all it lifted from the very head of the black-mountain. So complete was the effect, it appeared to render Earthrise a lowlier mount than its nearest neighbour upon the skyline.

I felt the Faerie Dust moving over my skin; between my fingers, and upon my arms, and upon my face, and in my hair, and in my eyes, tingling – no – stinging me, raising welts and drawing irritating scratches. It left my exposed skin damp, not with sweat, but with blood. Yet the pain and the irritation did not matter to me, was almost welcome; like the pain of a foul tooth as it is cut from your mouth.

And then there was noise, after all. First, slight pinpricks of sound, in a rising pitch. It gained in intensity, becoming a fierce ringing hiss; enough to match the movement of the spiralling banks of black dust, as it swallowed up the sky and stole away the sun. What little warmth, what little winter daylight there had been went with it. All Graynelore within my sight became a grey, a sombre, shadow-land.

And my thoughts? . . . And the thoughts of the shadow-tongues inside my head; the Ring of Eight calling out together?

This is all of our making . . . This is all our own . . . This is ours . . .

If I had had the wit to wish again, I would have wished for this . . . next:

Suddenly the black dust turned upon the sky, and not black any more, but a swell of bright glowing colours that dispelled the gloom. There were greens and gold, purples and reds, yellows and silver and blues: only their names alone cannot help define them. Endlessly changing hues so intensely rich I realized I was a witness to their creation for the very first time. And these were not the colours of a dead blackened earth, not merely random threads woven from a scattering of dust:

There, stretched out before us and all across the heavens was the Faerie Isle – The Living Isle . . .

This was what we had wanted all along. This was our one – our sole desire. And it was the answer to a foolish man's simple wish.

If a lifetime can pass in but a single instant (which it can), then a single instant can last for an eternity.

Only there were no more wishes to be had . . . The truth was revealed.

The instant was, at once, completely undone. What we knew we had seen we had not seen. What we knew to be true was not true. Our belief, unbearably, cruelly replaced by a singular disbelief:

There was no miracle to behold.

There was no Faerie Isle, after all.

Upon the moment there were broken strands of black dust coming down out of the sky, falling toward the earth. Though it was a thin scattering reached the ground, without substance, that did not even cast a shade. The most of it dissipated upon the air, as if it were taken up by some great, unseen hand, to be carried away and beyond the knowledge of all men.

The image of the Faerie Isle that had stood, briefly, out upon the sky was disappeared. It was gone as if it had never been there. And with it went all my senses; and my sensibility.

Chapter Thirty-Five

When the Dust Finally Settled

Had I been lost inside another dream, another night-torment? I recognized the first feelings returning to my inert body. It was not a sense of joy, or excitement, rather, an intense human frailty, together with a deep note of pain; something in the way of strength ebbing away. As if I had been bodily holding the Faerie Isle in the sky, and being unable to hold it any longer, I had at last failed and let it fall.

Around me my greater company were also coming to themselves. We were no longer conjoined: the Ring of Eight was taken apart. My thoughts were my own. The shadow-tongues were silent.

At my side, Licentious, the gigant was standing scratching his heavy head. Confused, or defeated? Norda Elfwych – cradling her raggedy baby – was quietly weeping, and would not be consoled.

It was then I realized, impossibly, the sun was warm upon my back. I looked up into the sky, almost afraid of what I might see there. The sky was clear . . . not only of clouds. It was empty.

It was quite empty.

There was no Isle.

I had seen its formation. I had seen its disintegration. Its creation . . . its destruction . . . Seeing is . . . not always believing. I wanted it to be there; needed it to be there. Wished for it . . . Only there were no more wishes to be had.

We had done nothing. We had achieved only this . . . and there was nothing to see for it.

The Ring was broken. And the world about us stood utterly unchanged.

I was not the only one perplexed.

'Did it not work then, Rogrig?' asked Licentious, befuddled. 'Only I truly thought it did.'

'And I . . .' I said, 'and I.'

The gigant began to nod his head, only to shake it instead.

'I do not understand any of this . . .' said Norda Elfwych, between her tears. 'What sense?'

I could only shrug. I looked toward Lowly Crows, who had come to ground the woman in black, and toward Wily Cockatrice. They were standing together, a little distant from us, and in a preoccupied manner. They were looking toward the east, as if they were searching for the still waters of the Great Sea; though it was far beyond the horizon and out of view. There was the beginning of a smile upon each of their faces, and a tear with it, a joyful tear . . . a sparkle in their eye.

'I see nothing,' I said, truculently. 'We have failed so miserably! What is it that you see that raises such a smile, such jollity?'

Wily Cockatrice turned to me, distractedly, almost as if she had not realized anyone else was standing there. 'Rogrig! Rogrig – But we have not failed at all.' She was still smiling.

'Eh?'

Her answer drew the attention of our whole company, who shifted about, or turned their ears, or took a step closer to hear her out.

'The truth of it is; we cannot restore the Isle . . .'

'Cannot, could not, will not,' added Lowly Crows.

There was an immediate uproar. Raised voices, both real and from the shadow-tongues inside my head, and with them some raised fists too! And a sudden throng massed about the crow and the ancient crone demanding an explanation. Oddly enough, the pair only chortled and laughed the more, while Wily Cockatrice took up her smoking pipe and sucked and blew and sucked.

'Wait! Please . . . My dear friends, listen to me. I will not play you any longer. It is a simple truth. We cannot restore the Faerie Isle because it is *still* there.'

'What?'

'You cannot repair what is not broken. You cannot bring back what has never been lost. It is still out there, just where it has always been; circling our world upon the Great Sea. Only, unnoticed by men . . .'

'Unnoticed?' I fumed. 'Then what – for fuck's sake! – have we been trying to do all this while?' Forgive my foul tongue. I was in fear of losing the plot of my own tale. And a man can only take so much faerie slight. I did, at least, restrain my arm and save my hand from the hilt of my sword.

'The Faerie Isle is unseen because the world has lost the ability to see it. Not because it was destroyed by foolish wizards in an ancient war. Not because it has ceased to exist. The wizards destroyed only themselves, but the rest of the world chose to close its eyes anyway, and stopped seeing; believed the ending they were given.'

'But the stories of the Beggar Bards . . . They all say . . .'

'Beggar Bard, stories!' Wily Cockatrice spat the words out as if they were sucked poison. Then, more softly, 'If only men would truly listen to what they are being told. I know what the stories, *say* . . . Rogrig. But you only have to believe that the Isle is there to know that the Isle is there. You do not need a cartful of Faerie Dust to make it appear. You do not *need* to see it at all . . . Only, see it if you must, Rogrig! See it if you must!'

'And then, what of the black dust . . .? Are we only foolish children making castles in the air?' I asked, feeling no less of a fool, for the question.

'A mark,' said Lowly Crows. 'It was a beacon, a signal.'

'And the purpose of the Faerie Ring,' I asked, 'if not to raise the Living Isle?'

'First, to set the signal,' said Wily Cockatrice, 'so that they would come to us when we were ready for them. And second, so that we might—'

'What?' I interrupted her, fiercely. 'Wait! Wait! Wait! They? They, who? *Who* would come to us? Tell me! *Who*?'

Wily Cockatrice eyed me coldly for a moment. She put her pipe to her mouth and drew upon it angrily, made a great show of the smoke. Then, she shook her head.

'Ah . . . I have said it before. You must not always look toward great age to find great wisdom, Rogrig,' she said, matter-of-factly, before pointing the end of her pipe firmly at Lowly Crows.

'Why, it is the Beggar Bards, of course,' said Lowly Crows. 'The Beggar Bards . . .' She turned her head and gave me the rook's eye.

Chapter Thirty-Six

The Eye of the World

Mountains *can* be climbed. Questions can be answered and the most difficult of puzzles can be solved. The greatest deeds are not always the most spectacular to behold.

We were to make one last, earth-bound, journey together. I carefully set Norda Elfwych and her raggedy babbie upon Dandy. The hobb took the imposition most graciously, and bore the load without annoyance. And while Wily Cockatrice, Dogsbeard, Licentious, and Wood-shanks came after us a-foot, Lowly Crows chose my shoulder for her perch. If Earthrise was not such a fearsome challenge in its newly diminished state, it was still a hard-fought climb all the same. Remarkable then, that there was no disquiet at the task or the toll it took upon a company already failing by measures. Indeed there was not a single complaint before we achieved its summit. You see, this time we were not a company journeying alone. The Beggar Bards came after us. Aye, to that very same spot . . .

The Beggar Bards: all of them; each and every one, perhaps two hundred or more in number, though they were not easily counted. They arrived always alone, without a companion, and all came in their own time, just as they expected to. That is, the never-time that belongs to a Beggar Bard's tale, and is not easily reckoned or reconciled by common men.

They too struggled up that mountain, came upon it from all sides. Found a way. Some, possibly many, travelled in sight of each other. It did not spur them on to a greater effort. It did not shy them away from their task. They simply came on, regardless, and from every corner of the Graynelore (it has so many). They arrived: a-foot, and sitting upon horse and cart, and riding upon their hobbs – until the rising ground beneath them forbad it, and forced them to scramble, often down upon their hands and knees. They climbed steep scarps and came across rock-strewn scree slopes that shifted dangerously beneath them with every step.

The youngest of them appeared to be little more than babbies. The eldest, among many, was much older even than Wily Cockatrice, the ancient crone.

And when at last they found themselves upon the summit of the mountain they each did a most simple thing. (After first taking a short respite, either to catch their breath, or to bite upon a piece of bread, or to suck upon a pipe, or to scratch away a needy itch, or to wipe away a lathered brow . . . Or else to take a moment to contemplate the world now revealed around and about them: from the unknown wastelands in the North, to the Marches in the South, and to the unending shorelines of the Great Sea.)

And what they each did was this:

They put their hands inside their cloth and took out a small piece of broken stone – that often flashed with gold, glittered temptingly in the sun – and they laid it down upon the ground. Each stone was left upon exactly the right spot, and met perfectly with the last one placed there; edge for edge, line for line, without a mistake or need of correction. And so the tablet of stone grew and the patterns upon its ancient time-worn face were slowly revealed.

I felt it was a most sacred deed.

In all of this, the Beggar Bards did not purposefully look to seek us out there. Their tales were all told . . . When eyes met, a few lent a cautious greeting; a nod and a sly wink; a discreet bow. Though they did not ask anything of us eight. And we did nothing more than wait there for them all to come. No one of them was needed any more than any other; no one of them could have been done without. If there was never a time when two Beggar Bards came face to face upon that mountain top.

By chance I recognized Ringbald when he came and left his own precious relic. He stayed no longer than any did. I showed him my hand in friendship and he showed me his in turn, only to turn away, as each and every one of them turned away, and immediately began his struggle back down the mountainside. At that moment, from off my shoulder, Lowly Crows launched herself into the air, and come to Ringbald's side; she transformed herself once more into the woman in black. In this way, and in private conversation, she accompanied him a little way along his downward path, only to return once more to me . . .

And so the thing was done.

I have seen many things in my life. I have known no greater wonder than this.

When all of the Beggar Bards had come and gone again, there, laid out before us on the ground, was a stone tablet. Upon it, there was a map. There were markings made for all things living, as well as for all things naturally dead. Around the edge there were words cut into the stone, in a language and of a description beyond any of our knowledge. Everything was there. Nothing was missed out. The Great Wizard had truly known his world in all its subtle complexity, in all its simplicity too. This was the true Eye Stone. And upon it was shown a Graynelore complete in every form, excepting . . .

Excepting, there *was* a gap in the face of the tablet.

A single shard of stone was still missing.

There was, as yet, no Faerie Isle.

I did not make a great fuss of it. I knew the part I had to play. I put my hand inside my cloth and laid it upon a strap of leather bound to my wrist. I unwound it and drew out my precious talisman. I took off its clasp, threw away the leather thong, and laid the fragment of stone carefully in its rightful position.

And so, the Faerie Isle was at last revealed to us . . . without a wish, if not without a Wishard. And where it was marked upon the stone tablet, there it was in truth for our fey eyes to behold – standing out upon the distant sea. We had only to look for it with the right eye, and in the right circumstance, and toward the right spot to find it there.

'How very small it is . . .' said Norda Elfwych. 'How very small and insubstantial . . .' She raised her arms, lifted up her raggedy babbie, as if to let it see.

'How miraculous . . .' I said.

An island, floating upon the sea, passing slowly across the horizon . . . Never still, nor ever wanting to be still. And where it moved upon the Great Sea it moved again upon the face of the stone tablet: the one, a perfect model of the other.

As I looked upon it, and between the faces of my company, I realized there were expressions of concern.

'What is it?' I asked Norda Elfwych.

'Well . . . if the Faerie Isle is indeed found again . . . does that mean that all the creatures of fey are to return into the world?'

In truth I did not know. 'I have never given it any thought,' I said, carelessly, 'I suppose so.'

'And are all faeries, *good*?' Norda winced slightly at the use of the word as if it was indicative, but not quite appropriate. (Good and bad are so close together, and yet so far apart in faerie as to be less than satisfactory terms of measurement, if not, quite hopeless.)

'Are all men, good?' I replied.

'I fear, hardly any at all,' she said, quite dispirited.

'There is your answer then,' I said.

'I thought so,' she said, and nothing more on the matter. Though the memory of that short conversation was, in after times, often to come back to me, if not in this tale.

Wily Cockatrice had rather more immediate concerns.

'Ah, but then . . . how are we to get there . . . across the Great Sea?' she asked, at the same time, sucking furiously upon her pipe. 'A wyrm cannot fly home, nor will she take to the water and swim . . .'

'How indeed?' said Lowly Crows. 'Unless, of course, you will make us another wish, Rogrig, and give us a ship and a crew to man her?'

I paused . . . did not reply to her at once.

I was standing at the very top of Earthrise, the black-headed mountain, upon the threshold of a dream. My back was turned firmly against my past. Before me was the Faerie Isle. I was about to find my true home at last.

I had only one, regret.

Notyet.

Her name rested upon my tongue, where it stayed, unspoken. The time for wishes was past, for now.

I shook my head, gave Lowly Crows her answer.

'No?' she said, adding, not unkindly, 'then, I suppose, it will be down to me, again.' With that, the woman was once more transformed. The sky above Earthrise drew in, and became deep black again. Not with dust, nor yet with cloud, but with a great host of birds, come out of every part of the world, and in a number far beyond our counting. Of course, if we were to wait for as long as it took them all to appear, then my tale, which is fast approaching its desired end, would become far longer than it might, so I will say only this: appear they all did.

And if there had been a man watching us at a distance, he might have thought he saw a great storm of birds. He might then have imagined there was a dragon in the sky, and a wych, and an elf, and a host of other fey creatures. And among them, strangest of all, he might have seen a man riding upon a unicorn. And it might have seemed to him that, together, they rose up into the sky upon a tide of black wings. And that they appeared to come down again upon a far distant Isle that stood out upon the Great Sea. Only the moment they did, the Isle was suddenly no more and the sea was just the sea, after all. And the sun was shining, and its light ran between the distant waves, and then broke apart, into a thousand points of perfect gold . . .

Chapter Thirty-Seven

The Faerie Isle

At the end, would you have come with me to the Faerie Isle, my friend, would you have followed me there and seen it for yourself? In truth, there is very little of a tale in peace and beauty and tranquillity. And the place is not so very different from the lands you have already known.

What I remember best of it is that very first view. Sat upon an enormous shelf of rock, rising out of a broad green pasture, was a pair of magnificent wyrms, lazing together in the sun, their shining scales of purple and red and silver, their great tails endlessly twisting about and about them. There too the living forests, where the dryads and the woodland nymphs stood out to greet us. There too the kelpies frolicking in their blue-green pools. And the trolls, and the bogarts, and the dwarves, seated at the entrance to their dwarven holes, just as the Beggar Bard tales had so often described them. And more, much more, and many: only, these were, truly, as of nothing. For most fabulous of all, out upon their golden pastures was a great host of creatures, moving together in the way of a herd. These were the unifauns; the gentle, the beautiful unifauns . . .

And there, upon that wondrous Isle, we eight were to stay a while; and regain ourselves. We were to learn, and to remember what we had once been, become what we truly were, and be forewarned of what might, in later times befall us . . .

I stood before the mirrored pool and saw, at last, my own true fey image reflected there.

Though, we were not, all of us, to remain there forever.

You see, my friend, there is a bitter with the sweet; a final sadness yet to sully the picture and to stain our hearts a little redder still. For if I was to know the joy and the beauty of a growing child; I was also to know the sorrow of a dying mother. Though each deserved better, of both men and the world . . . I cannot, no, I will not describe Norda's final moment (though you would beseech me) for that belongs to her alone. The measure of her frailty was too great to be undone. She was never meant for old bones.

Know only this: the man's stone heart did, finally, break, and give her up a tear . . .

At the end, Norda called to me from out of the shade, and in her fading shadow-tongue gave me her final farewell:

You cannot have love without hate,
You cannot know joy without first knowing sorrow,
You cannot have wrong without right,
Nor the light of the day without the darkness of night
. . .

I understood.

Epilogue

Rogrig the Confessor

It was in the fullness of a summer's day when I found myself, at last, before the door of a familiar house. I had been a very long time absent.

I was sat upon Dandy. Lowly Crows was perched upon my shoulder. Licentious, the gigant, ambled idly a-foot, at my side. He carried a young boy upon his back, who giggled lightly for the lark. The child was elfin. Though I knew him for a Wishard; a Wishard out of an Elfwych . . . My son, whose name was Sarrow. We had been travelling at our ease; I had given Dandy her head, let her decide upon the path we should take. She had, of course, chosen to take herself home.

There were some new faces among the men, the women, and the babbies who stood out upon the fields, and upon the roadsides, and at their open doors, watching us as we strode past. There was the odd stretch of burnt ground, where, perhaps, a shieling had once stood, or where the mark of an old scourging had not yet quite healed. But little of matter had changed thereabouts.

The bastle-house that had once been my childhood home looked strongly built still. Its walls were solid and unbroken. It stood out under the sun. Someone was at a wind-eye keeping a close watch at our approach. Though, the few men who stood in our path as we came on turned their heads and shied away from us. They were either feigning indifference, or ignorance of who we were. Men, such as us, who were obviously faerie-touched, were never likely to be well received here.

When Dandy stood up in front of the door, I knew why she had brought us here.

'Old Emma's Notyet!' I cried out. 'Notyet Wishard! I am Rogrig Wishard, also of the Three Dells and born of Dingly Dell. You know me well enough!'

There was a brief moment's silence. The face within the wind-eye stepped away into the darkness of the house. Then the door of the house was made ajar.

'Yes. I know you, Rogrig Wishard.' she said, from out of the dark, and without appearing. 'And you can piss off! Go back to wherever it was you came from!'

At my shoulder, Lowly Crows beat her wings furiously, as if to ward off her foul tongue. Licentious turned his head, lifted his great hands in mimic of a shield, and eyed me cautiously. Only to realize I was smiling.

'Are you certain about this?' he asked.

'Yes,' I said.

I dismounted, took the child from the gigant's back and sat him upon Dandy for safekeeping. Then, with my two companions for support, I stepped into the house, regardless of the welcome.

This was not going to be an easy meet.

*

'Will you sit down, will you sit?' I said. Notyet was pacing furiously across the earth floor before me. I could see her face was red with anger, and already wet with tears. 'Please . . . There is so much to tell you. I must explain it—'

'Must you?' she said, keeping up her pace. They were only words, and yet she used them with such venom I could not mistake the rebuke. Nor could I make any answer other than to repeat myself.

'I must explain—'

'Rogrig! You stand before me as if we have never been apart.' She turned, stood up abruptly, and brought her face close to mine. 'You smile sweetly and beg me to sit down. For the fortunes! The seasons have turned over, and turned again! Where the hell have you been? And what manner of man have you become?'

Before I could answer her, she had moved away, was unravelling a bound cloth, and preparing to take up a rusting iron sword, two-handed.

'Listen, I – Many things have happened,' I said, feebly. 'Difficult to explain . . . I have done some stupid things . . . bloody stupid. I thought it was for the best, but . . .'

Already the sword was flailing dangerously. Though, I made no move to avoid it. She was unbalanced and aiming well off her mark.

'Only stupid!' she said. 'You have sent me no word in all this time. I had you for dead, among all the rest. Aye, and long dead!' Again the sword flailed. It slid across the wall and notched a wooden table. 'Not one single word for me! I can think of far better rebukes than stupid!'

Where to begin? I wanted to tell her everything. Only now the end of her sword had suddenly become her pointer to drive home her remarks. A wagging blade is not the easiest of confidants. Though I did try . . .

I let my tongue run quickly over the events of my tale, put emphasis where I might, left empty holes where I thought it prudent.

Notyet was sorely unimpressed. I was forced to step aside as her sword sang close to my ear.

The gigant, as well as he might – being, obviously, far too big for the room – had already backed himself away into a corner. While Lowly Crows had lifted herself off my shoulder and flown up into the ceiling, lest she would catch an accidental blow meant for me.

'Oh, yes? And what do you take me for, Rogrig? Are all the birds in the sky really the prettiest of little faeries? Are all the trees sweet wood nymphs and every wildcat a true wych's familiar?'

Can so many words say one thing, and yet mean so very different?

'Well, yes . . . I suppose some of them are,' I said. I admit my poor answers were not helping my cause.

Again the sword came down and drew sparks as it raked the stone hearth and scattered burning cinders from the fire.

'Ha! And I suppose Tom Troll here, really *is* a gigant?'

'I thought I was the one who was not so bright?' I said, letting my anger get the better of me. I had not meant to lose my temper with her. 'The clue is in his name . . . and the . . . the height thing!'

'And my name is, Licentious,' said the gigant, unhelpfully.

'This is what you would have me believe, Rogrig?' she said with a scowl, stabbing the end of her sword toward him.

'Yes,' I said.

'This!' The gigant, forced to retreat, backed clumsily against the wall, cracking stone.

'Yes.'

She lifted the sword again, as if to make it swing in my direction, only one-handed now; her wrist was not practised enough to take the leverage. The blade rang out loudly as it clattered to the floor. She let it lie there.

'Anything else?' she said. She folded her arms, glaring. Dared me to speak again . . .

It was too late for swaggering bluster or half-truths. I asked Licentious and Lowly Crows to leave us, before I continued. They, for all their bravery, could not escape that house quickly enough.

I began my tale again, with the worst of it – well, the worst of it, as I figured she would see it – spoke plainly.

'I . . . I have lain with a faerie,' I said.

'What? What are you saying now?' she returned. 'Is this your true confession, then? At last . . . You have lain with a . . . you have what?'

'I think you heard . . .' I said. 'And I . . . I am not only the common man you think you see before you—'

'You? You are a dagger's arse, Rogrig! Is this the best you can offer me? You play me lazily, for a fool, and make fun? This is the Graynelore. I am not blind to it! I have seen men before now, rutting the common whores . . . taking their easy pleasures upon the Ridings . . . Only now you would have me dress it up in a . . . a babbie's tale! With faeries and all—'

'No. For the love of the fortunes, no! Listen. Please. What I am telling you is the truth. And *real*—!'

'Oh, just leave me alone. Will you? Go, and drown yourself! Take a great leap into ma hinnies' puddle! If your absence was not bad enough . . . you can only lie to me, still.'

I might have braced myself, in fear she was about to raise her skirts and rudely piddle upon me! She . . . did not.

'I know how it appears,' I said. 'I do know. But I do not lie. I mean what I am saying. I mean it, and I will tell you, Notyet . . . I have been so often scared. Aye . . . scared.'

I wanted to take a hold of her.

I wanted to bang her about the ear and knock the rotten truth into her.

If only, I could have made a wish . . . I stopped myself. Better the ordinary man, now, and *not* the fey Wishard.

I did nothing.

'Have your rant,' I said. 'Take up your sword. Break my head in with it, if you must. Surely, I deserve it. Only, believe me. This was not a weak man's passion. Rather, it was a necessity, not a wanton lust. It was she took from me, not I from her. There was no caress in her cold touch. It was a stranger's hand. If there was a desire, it was only the desire of a thief to steal.'

'Oh, I beg of your pardon,' she said. 'I misunderstood! It was obviously you who were wronged here, and not I! And perhaps it was ever *our* loins that brought us two together, never truly our hearts . . .'

I closed my eyes for a moment. I could not bear to see the look of pain upon her face.

'Now you twist my words,' I said. 'I did not intend this . . .'

'No? What did you intend, then? Why are you here? Am I to want you still – is that it? Am I to forgive you for your . . . *honesty*? Tell me Rogrig, what must I say to allay your fears?' Her eyes, soft with fresh tears, burned with fury.

'Say . . . Say only this: if a motherless child were ever brought to you, you would mother him and not blame him for his father's . . . weakness. For myself I ask for nothing. I will go, if you want me to go. I will not return here . . .'

'Ha! So, you have come here only to give me a task, then! Is this it? You would leave me with your faerie-child – your changeling, and steal away again. Rogrig, this is unbearable. What kind of a man are you?'

'I am . . . I am a . . .' How hard, and for how long had I been trying to answer *that* question? Could I not do it yet?

'Speak, will you. Speak,' she said. 'Say something, say anything to me, or else be damned for your silence! I swear to you, I will take up this sword again and I will cut you down with it.'

'I am a man who has made mistakes . . .' I said. Though truly, she did not want to hear my follies. I tried again. 'I am . . . a man who is in love . . .' I said, prising the words from my tongue.

'Aye?'

'With you, Notyet.'

'Then, you will say it, Rogrig Wishard.'

'Have I not already?' I said. 'You are my heart's meat. What more is there?'

'Say it, *properly* then . . .'

'I fear I have killed men with far less trouble!' I said.

'Say it!'

'I am . . . in love with you,' I said. 'I love you. Once, and for all . . .'

There was no hint of faerie slight.

THE END

Acknowledgements

With thanks and love to Hazel Moore (née Kerr). My mother. Who was the one who reminded me of my own Reiver heritage and started me down the path of discovery that was eventually to lead to *Graynelore*.